I0614610

# Treasured

## by

## Rose Thorgaard

*A Dark Mafia Romance, Book One*

This is a work of fiction. Names, characters, places, and incidents are either the product of the author's imagination or are used fictitiously, and any resemblance to actual persons living or dead, business establishments, events, or locales, is entirely coincidental.

**Treasured**

Cover Art by *Lisa Dawn MacDonald*

The Wild Rose Press, Inc.
PO Box 708
Adams Basin, NY 14410-0708
Visit us at www.thewildrosepress.com

Publishing History
First Edition, 2023
Trade Paperback ISBN 978-1-5092-4798-1
Digital ISBN 978-1-5092-4799-8

*A Dark Mafia Romance, Book One*
Published in the United States of America

I didn't know much about Livia Rossi aside from the candy-coated version via Michael. She was the apple of his eye, and it showed. Now that I thought about it, it was probably more of a weakness on his part. He had always been a formidable man, striking fear in the hardest of criminals, and yet, he was a teddy bear when it came to Livia. With him away, every single one of his rivals knew how to bring him to his knees. His little burden was now mine.

## Dedication

To everyone who encouraged me to tell the stories that kept me awake at night and dreaming during the day.

# Chapter One

*Dante*

"Dante? It's time."

Michael Rossi's voice rattled over the phone with a hint of wariness I was not used to. He was usually self-assured. He never worried about anything, but now he sounded anxious. I didn't even need to see his face.

I took a deep breath and reached up to scratch my beard. "All right, boss. I'll get on the next plane out." *Damn it.*

"Thank you. I was hoping it wouldn't come to this, but I can't take the risk, not while I'm here." Michael sighed heavily. He never felt bad about asking me to do anything, but the fact that he seemed sorry now told me everything I needed to know about this job—it was going to be a royal pain in the ass.

"I understand, Michael. I'll take care of everything. Don't worry."

Even though I was less than happy about this, he knew damn well that if he asked me to slit my own throat, I would. I felt the need to reassure him, though. This wasn't about offing someone who had stolen money or fucked his wife—not that Michael ever married. We had that in common. In our line of work, neither of us wanted to worry about a family. Unfortunately, the little burden that fell into his lap was now mine.

I had only just stepped out of my apartment when I got the call, and now my plans for the day were foiled. I stuffed the phone back in my pocket, turned on my heels, and went back inside to pack. Pacing through my bare apartment to the bedroom, I threw open my closet to pull out a suitcase. Hopefully, this wouldn't go on for too long, but I grabbed a second suitcase, just in case. I was halfway packed when Nero came in. The second he saw the suitcases on the bed, he started whining, tucking his tail between his legs. He inched closer and licked my hand.

"Don't worry, boy. You're coming, too. Put on your mean face."

I hated having to leave him behind, but there was no time to arrange for him to get on the flight with me on such short notice. One of my guys would have to send him after me. I didn't trust anyone to take care of my dog for however long I'd be gone, and I thought he could be helpful once we got there. Nero was a sleet gray Cane Corso. The biggest softie with me, but a mean motherfucker to anyone who so much as gave me the side-eye, though it was rare that anyone tried. I patted his head and went back to gathering my meager belongings.

Money hadn't been an issue for me for over fifteen years, but old habits die hard. I learned not to accumulate so much crap that I'd inevitably end up having to pack up when I had to move again. And it was a good thing because I didn't know how long I would be in California. Most of my apartment fit into the two suitcases, and I slammed them closed on the bed before I took out my phone again to book the plane ticket.

As soon as I got confirmation that I was due on a flight in three hours, I left the apartment to hail a cab. Of course, it had to be rush hour when the call came. Now I had to sit in traffic for God knew how long and hope I didn't miss the flight. Michael had never needed to whip my ass into shape, but he would somehow find a way to do it if I missed that flight. I owed him everything, so if I had to babysit his niece for a few weeks, then so be it. But I hated when I had to tail someone that was either unaware or unwilling.

I didn't know much about Livia Rossi aside from the candy-coated version via her uncle Michael. She was the apple of his eye, and it showed. Now that I thought about it, it was probably more of a weakness on his part. He had always been a formidable man, striking fear in the hardest of criminals, yet he was a teddy bear when it came to Livia. With him away, every single one of his rivals knew how to bring him to his knees. Maybe this would never have been necessary if he hadn't smothered her so much.

I stepped out onto the street to make eye contact with an approaching cab driver through the windshield. None of that waving or whistling like a madman. One look and he screeched on his brakes. I swung open the door and slid inside.

"JFK. Take Grand Central. I don't have all day," I ordered, bracing myself for the lurch forward as he took off.

I'd met Livia Rossi a few times when I made my regular drop-offs, but me and the rest of the guys were always under strict instructions never to speak to her unless absolutely necessary, and to always avert our eyes. It was ludicrous to me that Michael thought any of us would be stupid enough to try anything with her. The one time someone tried to chat her up, he left with broken ribs and found himself without a job in zero seconds flat. I didn't see why they drooled over her. Forbidden fruit, I supposed.

I hadn't gotten a good look at her since she left for California, until now. Michael had given me a photo of her to make sure I found the right person, and I looked down at it as the cab headed to the airport. Maybe I just wasn't seeing it. Brown hair, brown eyes, decent smile. Nice tits, but I had seen plenty of tits in my day, and I wasn't too impressed. In the photo, she stood in Times Square in a sundress and floppy hat, chuckling about some secret joke to herself. It was a candid shot, and the only thing I wondered was, who even took that photo if just breathing near her was a death sentence? She seemed much too cheery for my tastes. It must have been nice to be so unaware of the danger around every corner, but that was all about to change.

I couldn't imagine caring about anyone that much, and I didn't want to. It sounded like a horrible position to be in, especially being helpless to do anything to protect them. It was surprising how many mobsters even bothered with families, knowing their rivals had the perfect target to strike if they hated them enough. Things were different than they used to be. As Michael used to put it, they never fucked with families or kids in the good old days. It was apparent that everything was on the table now.

Not that Michael Rossi had chosen this responsibility. It was thrust on him when Livia's parents died, and I had to respect the guy for stepping up to take care of her. Honestly, I was shocked that he even let her go as far as California. Out of sight, out of mind.

After almost two hours of sitting in traffic, I finally

reached the airport. I'd have to run to get through the check-in process. I could strong-arm a lot of people, but airport security was always an annoying process, no matter who you were. I made a note to myself to save up for a private jet, chuckling to myself. I had everything I needed in New York and couldn't picture myself going anywhere else. Except maybe Italy, someday.

I had never been to the old country, always being too busy with Michael's demands. He didn't trust many people, but he trusted me. He trusted me even more than his replacement at the head of the family, which was saying a whole hell of a lot. I didn't make waves, but I knew where my loyalties lay. I never cared who wore the crown; I only cared who deserved the respect.

I plastered on my most fierce scowl as I sped through the airport, making sure that every man, woman, and child got out of my way on the way to the gate. I didn't relax my face until I sat firmly in my seat on the plane. Nothing came between me and a direct order from the boss. Well, the only boss that mattered.

The first hurdle was behind me, but the next would be significantly harder. I didn't care at all if she didn't want me watching after her. I just hoped that she wasn't going to be a spoiled brat about it. The last thing I wanted to do was chase after her drunk ass as she went from one frat party to the next. She could do what she liked, but somehow, I believed she'd be on her best behavior. I doubted she would have been dumb enough to misbehave, knowing that I would report everything I observed to her uncle. She cared what he thought of her. Maybe this wouldn't be as hard as I thought.

Once the plane took off, I relaxed in my seat and took out my phone to listen to some music to kill time. It was always the one thing that calmed me—either playing music or just listening. I tried to convince myself that I wasn't a little worried about this job, but I was. Guarding the only thing Michael Rossi cared about was nothing to take lightly. He didn't have to say it; if something happened to her under my watch, I would be dead without a second thought. If I wanted to go on breathing, I'd have to learn to care at least a little.

I dozed off for a few hours, and when I awoke to see palm trees out of the tiny plane window, I heaved an exasperated sigh to myself. I always hated California. I'd have to resign myself to shitty food, no shade, vegans everywhere, and the heat. Where would I get a decent steak in a place where people liked to eat grass for sustenance? Stuffing my phone back in my pocket, I then proceeded to right my seat and get myself ready for landing.

As soon as I stepped out of the airport, the humid air hit me with a slam. I scowled as if that would scare it away. It was well after ten o'clock, and I couldn't understand how it was so hot when the sun wasn't even out. I hailed a taxi and headed straight for the apartment that Michael had asked me to rent months ago, when all hell started breaking loose. It was originally just a precaution, but it was good thinking on his part. At least I had somewhere for me and Nero to stay.

****

I got up early the next morning to take care of my first two objectives for the day. Buy a car and pick up my dog. I had a car back home, but I didn't want to drive anything as conspicuous as mine while I was here. If anyone was here looking for Livia, the last thing I needed was for them to see a notorious mobster car trailing her wherever she went. Glower firmly snapped in place, I walked into the first dealership I came across and left in a plain silver sedan at a good price. It wasn't my style at all, but it would do for the time being.

I headed toward the airport as soon as I settled into the uncomfortable seat in my new car. It was time to pick up one of my two prized possessions—the other one being safely stowed away in the apartment. When I approached the pick-up desk, I gave them my no-nonsense voice so that they would get on with it and give me my dog. I watched the attendants rush to fulfill my request, and they eagerly handed him over. I could practically see the guy pissing himself as he brought the cage out, and I couldn't help but laugh a little.

When they brought him out, Nero wasn't even barking. Just a little warning growl, which immediately stopped once he saw me. "Good boy. Did they treat you well?"

The attendant rushed to assure me that he was fed and watered properly during the trip. I hastily threw him a hundred and left. Once Nero was acclimated to the apartment, it would be time to go meet Livia on campus.

I hadn't given much thought to how I would approach her. Michael had permitted me to go about things as I pleased, and I appreciated the fact that he trusted me enough to use my discretion with *his* most prized possession. But I wasn't under any impression that I could do as I liked with her. Mainly, he was giving me the choice of whether to tail her quietly or introduce myself and hope that she would cooperate with me. I had done my fair share of stalking in the past, but I thought maybe the straightforward route would be better this time, since I wasn't trying to kill or kidnap her. The second part was a remote possibility, but it wouldn't be necessary just yet.

From her picture, she didn't look like she had an ounce of fight in her, so I chose the latter. I left Nero with a sizeable bone to occupy him, then left to find the woman who would be my ward for the next few weeks. Hopefully, it would only be a few weeks.

As I drove, I noted the length of time it took to drive between her apartment complex and the college she went to. Michael had assured me that Livia told him everything about her extracurricular activities outside of school, but I somehow doubted that. What twenty-two-year-old woman went to school and came home every night with nothing in between? By the time I was twenty-two, I'd gotten into enough trouble for ten college-aged girls—and never spent one day in a classroom past the age of seventeen.

He took care of her rent and expenses, and I knew that because I was the proxy for sending out the checks. I found it hard to believe she spent her free time just doing schoolwork. Then again, I didn't know her from Eve.

Even though it wasn't part of my official duties, I also noted any Italian restaurants in the Glendale area, of which there were few. One that I drove past had a sign in the window that read *Vegan options available,* and I had to laugh. That pasta must have tasted like cardboard. It was definitely one place I wasn't going to try while I was here. Unfortunately for me, there wasn't a lack of bars in the area. Being in an unfamiliar place, under immense pressure from Michael, and drink everywhere as far as the eye could see. I didn't need the temptation. I forcefully turned my eyes to the road again when I saw the college campus come into view.

This place was bigger than I remembered from the map I had looked over on the plane. I wanted to be prepared, not being forced to ask a bunch of random students for directions. It would be extremely suspicious to walk in and start asking people about Livia's whereabouts. As I got out of the car to take a look around, I saw more than a few students who looked stoned out of their minds. Luckily, Michael told me she wasn't any social butterfly, which was good. It didn't bode well to have anyone else grilling them for information about her. These kids were so out of it they'd probably tell her life story to anyone who asked.

According to my notes, she was usually in the studio working on her art when she wasn't in classes. This was probably the only thing that intrigued me about her so far. I had to admit that I was curious to see her paintings. Michael pretty much thought anything that fell out of her was gold, but I wanted to see for myself.

As much as I could manage to stay out of sight, I approached the studio and took a quick peek in the window. There were a few other students there, but Livia stuck out immediately. She was the only one there that didn't have multicolored or bleached blonde hair. I could only see her profile as she sat on the stool, chewing on the end of her paintbrush. She stared into the canvas as if she were seeing something no one else could. I wanted to get a look at the canvas, but her look of complete absorption pulled me in, and I couldn't look away. It reminded me of myself when I used to play music. The spell was broken when she got up suddenly in a huff of exasperation. Creative block, I knew that feeling well.

I didn't want our first meeting to be like this—me

staring at her through a window like some kind of peeping Tom. She was completely unaware of my presence when she started gathering her stuff. I would need to drill some social awareness into her head. She couldn't just go around with her head in the clouds like that when she was being hunted by dangerous men like me. She was lucky that I was on her side.

Pacing back to the parking lot, I figured it was as good a time as any to officially meet Livia Rossi.

Chapter Two

*Livia*

When it happened, I was leaving the studio. I had been making myself busy working on my latest project for over five hours, and I was exhausted. When I was painting, I often lost track of time. I would get in the zone and completely forget where I was or for how long I had been there. Ever since I first got my hands on paint and a flat surface of any kind—it captivated me. My mom had been an artist herself, having her work exhibited in several galleries before she gave it up to be a homemaker. Being a good Italian housewife and chasing a kid around didn't leave much time for painting. I saw this as following my dream, as well as carrying on her legacy in whatever small way I could.

My mom was also a fan of oil paints. She tried to keep up with her art when I was really young, and I used to sit next to her and play with my toys while she worked, but I was always more entranced with what she was doing. Watching the way those random smears created a concise image always amazed me, and that was probably what set me on the path to becoming a painter like her.

I wasn't as close with my father, not that there wasn't love there. I just thought that he didn't understand me. My mother and I had always been two peas in a pod, and he was always working. He didn't have time for a family, and sometimes I wondered why he ever bothered with us at all.

Some of my mom's work still hung up in my bedroom back at my uncle's house. I hadn't brought them to California, though. I wanted a fresh start, and to forge my own identity apart from my life back in New York. Although I wished I had at least taken a few pictures of them for inspiration because right now, I felt completely blocked.

This piece was something I had been working on for days, trying to get it just right. I was almost there, but something just wasn't right, and I couldn't put my finger on it. It was only the grumbling of my stomach that brought me back to the here and now. I wasn't usually a morning person, and I had been eager to get to the studio, hence my skipping breakfast this morning. Like an alarm clock, my stomach urged me to take a break. I sighed to myself and went about cleaning my brushes and squaring away all of my supplies. It was always more difficult to pack the items back together when I was tired, and I eventually gave up and started piling things together haphazardly. That mess would be a problem for future me, I told myself with a chuckle.

I had several bags with my brushes and paint on one arm, and several rolls of canvas under the other. Luckily, I had my car here, so I wouldn't have to cart the supplies on the bus again. Sometimes, my friend Eric would borrow my car, and I made sure to pack lightly on those days. I hated having to take public transit, but I couldn't afford to say no to the only decent friend I had made in the last four years.

Eric Walsh was a photographer who I met only a week into my freshman year. I was trying desperately to blend in and agreed to attend a party after being handed an invite by a girl I had only spoken to once before. She seemed friendly enough. The party went smoothly while we were talking about art, but once they started talking about their personal lives and upbringing, that was when I realized that I had nothing meaningful in common with these people.

I found myself sitting outside the house on the stoop, and it was only the clicking of a shutter that alerted me to the presence of someone beside me. He was the dictionary definition of a typical Irish guy. Curly red hair, fair skin, and freckles. It seemed like he worked out to compensate for looks he saw as a shortcoming, but I had always thought he was handsome. Nevertheless, from the beginning, it was never like that with us. I had no interest in dating, and he never pushed me for more than friendship, which I was immensely grateful for.

I often played his muse, Eric taking photos of me while I worked. My favorite photo of his was one that didn't even show my face. It was in the studio here, and I was washing out my brushes when I heard the snap of his camera. I hadn't thought anything of it, but it amazed me when he showed it to me. The colors cascading from the brushes looked like a rainbow melting into the metal basin of the sink, manipulated by my hands. The light trickling in through the window sent a stream of sunlight through it, making the colors even more vibrant. It was a truly breathtaking photo. I had a copy of it on my dresser at home; I even made him sign it for posterity. I was sure he would be famous one day. While thinking about that photo, I smiled to myself. I finally finagled my way out of the front door and held the door open with my foot as I rushed out.

The humid air felt like a punch in the face as soon as I stepped out from under the awning in front of the studio. I still wasn't used to the lack of seasons in California. It was hot most of the time down here, and the damp air was something I still had yet to adjust to. I walked to the parking lot with my bundles, being careful not to bump anyone on the way.

The campus of my college was huge, and there were always a ton of students milling about at all times. They did night school here as well, so even at night, you would see people walking around with their easels, cameras, and other artsy paraphernalia. I chose to go here mostly because it was public, therefore more affordable for me. My uncle Michael paid the tuition, but I still didn't see the need to take advantage of his charity, which was how I saw it. I had been a burden on him for long enough, but he insisted anyway. I offered to get a job, but again, he refused. He didn't like the idea of me working when he insisted he had plenty of money. It wasn't that I doubted he had money, but it was how he got the money that bothered me.

The biggest reason was that this was about as far as I could get from New York without leaving the country. Uncle Michael would never have allowed me to leave the country for school, so L.A. county was the best I could do. As much as I loved him, I wanted to put as much space between me and that life as I could manage. I shook my head to rid myself of the lingering thoughts of New York and kept my focus on my balancing act.

When I got to my car, I quickly unlocked it and popped the trunk to load my supplies, before closing it and heading back up to the front. I only just brushed the door handle with my fingers when a heavy hand landed on my shoulder.

"Livia Rossi…"

I heard the deep gravelly voice coming from behind me, but I couldn't see the man who had an iron grip on my shoulder. He sounded like he smoked a pack a day. I froze in place, trying to decide whether to turn around or try to run. Who the hell did he think he was, putting his hands on me?

"Who are you? What do you want?" I grated at the stranger. All kinds of alarm bells went off in my head, and I failed to sound as self-assured as I wanted.

He eased up his hold, which surprised me. That would work to my advantage, I decided. I didn't know this man, and I wasn't about to wait around to see what he wanted. As soon as his fingers left my shoulder, I swung around and thrust my knee up into his groin, earning an earsplitting growl from him.

"Fuck, woman!"

The man curled over, falling onto his knees in front of me. In a panic, I used all the strength I had to shove him onto the ground before I threw open my car door and jumped inside.

My hands shook as I scrambled in my purse looking for my phone in case I had to call the police. I nervously peeked out the window to see the man still struggling to get back up to his knees. I only wanted to take a quick look, but something about him felt off to me. Black wavy hair pushed back from his face, olive skin, neatly trimmed beard…he looked slightly familiar, and that only scared me more. Aside from Eric, I didn't know anyone really, and definitely not anyone who looked like him. I kept my eyes glued to his huddled form as I continued digging around in my purse.

I felt the smooth screen of my phone and yanked it out, tossing half of the contents of my purse onto the passenger seat. I shakily unlocked it and prepared to dial 911 as I started the engine. Before I backed out, I risked another quick peek out of the window.

The man wasn't there anymore. My heart began to slam in my chest. Where had he gone? I pulled out a little too quickly, nearly hitting a parked car across from me, but I managed to pull out onto the main street, and I was off. My heart was still pounding when I got on the highway because for the entire drive, I was anxiously peeking out the rearview mirror trying to see if anyone was following.

I couldn't help but agonize about where I had seen that face before. I didn't recognize his voice, but even just from his accent saying those few words, I could tell he wasn't from here. He wasn't dressed like someone who went to art school at all. I only got a brief look as he was curled up on the pavement, but it looked like he was wearing suit pants. He was only missing the jacket.

I wanted to try to put this weird incident out of my mind, but I couldn't stop myself from wondering what that man wanted from me. But in this day and age, you don't mess around when a random guy grabs you. You just run. I felt like I was driving on autopilot because I somehow reached my apartment without even realizing it. It was almost like I blacked out for the entire journey. As I parked and turned off the car, I flipped down the visor mirror and tried to snap myself out of it.

*Okay, Liv. You're home. No one followed you. Relax.*

I tapped myself on the cheeks lightly to wake myself up a bit, then climbed out of the car and retrieved my art supplies before heading up to my apartment. As I walked in, I dropped everything at the door, feeling suddenly more tired than I had been in a long time. I barely made it to the couch before I passed out into a deep sleep. The stress must have knocked me out, because when I woke up, it was already half-past five.

In a panic, I jumped up and checked to see if I had missed any calls. It was Tuesday, and my uncle Michael always called on Tuesdays. I hoped I hadn't missed him, because I was becoming more certain that this strange man had something to do with him and my family. I was almost too scared to tell him, but I knew I had to. The more I thought about it, the more I put the pieces together. His olive skin and dark hair...He was Italian, and not from California.

I paced into the kitchen to get a drink, and as soon as I gulped down the entire glass, my phone rang. *Oh, thank God.* I slammed the glass a little too hard on the counter, but it didn't break. I ran back into the living room to grab the phone. "Hello!"

I heard the robotic voice go through the familiar spiel. "This caller from that prison, do you accept the call, blah blah blah." Since it was something I'd heard a million times before, I quickly answered, "Yes."

After a few seconds, the phone clicked, and my uncle's voice came on. "Sweetie, how are you?"

I smiled at his affectionate tone. "I'm doing okay...well, I'm not. But I am happy to hear from you."

There was no point in pretending everything was fine. He had learned to look for vocal cues over the past four years, so he always knew when I was hiding something. I didn't often hide things from him, but what twenty-two-year-old didn't have at least one or two secrets?

"What's going on?" he asked, concern in his voice.

I didn't know how to go about telling him this without him going into defensive mania. He had always been insanely protective of me, and suddenly I was relieved that he wasn't here to smother me even more. I blurted it out quickly and braced myself for his immediate anger. "Some guy grabbed me in the campus parking lot. He really freaked me out. And he knew my name, too."

He grunted, almost in dismissal. "What did he look like?"

*Seriously?*

"I didn't get a real good look after I kicked him in the balls and ran, Uncle Michael. He had black wavy hair. And he looked Italian."

I shrugged, forgetting that he couldn't see me. He sounded like he was thinking hard, but then he started laughing. I raised my eyebrows in surprise. I didn't know why he thought this was funny. "I would think you would sound a little more concerned when someone tried to assault your only niece. What gives?"

"Sweetie, that was Dante, my best guy," he answered casually. "I asked him to go out to the coast and check on you for me."

*Oh shit!* "Oh, no…"

He just kept barking with laughter until I heard a guard yell at him to keep it down. "Sorry, but that is fucking hilarious. He has his work cut out for him." His tone was teasing, but it only irritated me more.

*What am I, a baby?* "Why, though? I've been doing fine here. I don't need some random guy to check on me. I tell you everything, anyway."

"Precaution, okay? Just humor me," he stated casually, and I didn't miss the undertone of his demand. It said *no arguments.*

I already knew what this all meant, but obviously, he couldn't say more over the phone. All calls at federal prison were monitored, and any probing from me could only get him into more trouble. "Fine. But he better not get in my way."

He grunted. "Be nice to him, Livia. He has my authority to look after you as he sees fit."

*Ugh! Are you kidding me?* I refused to make a promise I couldn't keep, so I assured him I would try, and then our time was up. I dropped the phone on the coffee table and slumped back onto the couch with a huff.

I knew it was disrespectful to give him an attitude, but I didn't want to have a minder. And that's basically what he would be. I wanted to ask him what the sudden danger was, but I knew he wouldn't be able to say. This meant something bad was happening up in New York. I usually avoided all news that had anything to do with organized crime like the plague. The only part of my old life that I still held onto was my uncle, Michael Rossi.

He had raised me as his own since I was ten years old, and I really saw him more like my father. When my parents died, he stepped up in order to care for me, and he always made sure I didn't lack for anything. I thought that losing his brother had made him more afraid of having me running around in New York with no one to look after me. Of course, I was an adult, but he still saw me as the little girl I used to be—innocent and scared. In some ways, he wasn't even wrong, but I hated to be seen that way. I could hold my own.

Just ask *Dante* how his balls felt when I dropped him on the pavement.

I had been so scared to tell my uncle that I wanted to leave New York, but it surprised me when he gave me his full support. Even though it meant I wouldn't be able to visit him regularly, he insisted that I go. At first, I thought he was just trying to be supportive of my dream of becoming an artist, as he had always been from the first time I picked up a paintbrush. However, the more likely reason was that he wanted me as far away from the life as possible, especially because he couldn't protect me anymore.

He was arrested the day of my eighteenth birthday. He had planned to have a huge party for me with everyone we knew. It would mostly be his associates and their kids who were close in age to me, and some of his friends. Food from the best caterer in Manhattan, a band, and lots of booze. Not that he would allow me to drink, of course. The only sip of alcohol I had tasted until that point was wine, and usually just one glass with dinner. I had been so excited to celebrate adulthood in style, but unfortunately, the party never happened.

It was five in the morning when the feds started banging on the door, warrants in hand. I had always been afraid of this day, and my worst fear came true. They ushered him out in cuffs, wearing nothing but his robe, leaving me to be questioned and harassed by the agents who milled around the house, searching everything. I didn't know anything, but I knew better than to speak to the police by then. When they tried to grill me, I kept my mouth shut and insisted I was clueless, even though they didn't quite believe me.

My uncle had kept me fairly sheltered from the

lifestyle he lived. I had met many of his associates over the years, but he warned them not to get too friendly with me or tell me anything. When I was a kid, I used to think of his stoic, mute men as gargoyles. For the longest time, I didn't even know men could be any other way.

My uncle chased away any boys who sniffed around me for more than five seconds. It wasn't as if people didn't know who we were, so the few guys who approached me in the first place were only angling to get in good with my uncle. The last thing he wanted was for me to be used as a steppingstone, so I couldn't even blame him, thinking back on it. I did at the time, though. I was a dumb, sheltered girl who didn't understand the danger men could bring.

I silently mourned the loss of my freedom as I picked at the small hole on the arm of my couch. If I had known I was about to have some thug following me around and reporting everything back to my uncle, I would have sowed some more wild oats first. Not that I had ever really been a party girl. My life in California had been all about making something of myself in a place where no one knew about my family, and I could be judged by more than my last name.

I wasn't a part of that world anymore, but I had a really bad feeling that my past was about to bite me in the ass.

## Chapter Three

*Dante*

Jesus fucking Christ. Already I wanted to kill Michael for making me do this. Judging by the volatile response I got from his precious niece, she clearly didn't remember me. I almost didn't recognize her either, with the ridiculous way she was dressed. A baggy, paint-splattered shirt and ripped jeans with sneakers. That was definitely not the Livia I used to know. California was full of a bunch of hippies and pretentious wannabees. It seemed to me like she molded herself to fit in almost perfectly, but there was still something about her that screamed *I don't belong here.*

The second she laid her coffee-colored eyes on me, she went into full attack mode. My balls were aching even hours later when I finally let myself into my new apartment across the hall from her. It was good for her that I hadn't brought Nero with me. He would have torn her a new one, and that would not have been fun to explain to Michael.

I thought it was overkill for me to be that close, but I couldn't say no. He had no children of his own, and he coddled that girl like she was royalty ever since her parents died. I didn't think I had exchanged two words with her in her life, so it wasn't surprising that she didn't recognize my voice. It had been years since I'd seen her, and obviously, a lot had changed. When did she become such a vicious girl? Her sudden defensive nature had me taken aback because she always seemed so demure in the past. I was not looking forward to having to deal with her if this was the way she was going to behave.

I wasn't excited about this job in the first place, but I owed Michael my life. When shit started hitting the fan, I found myself on a plane to California before I could think twice. The boss tells you to do a job; you do a job. Even behind bars, Michael was formidable enough to exact his punishment if anyone disobeyed him. And everyone knew that when it came to his niece, there was nothing he wouldn't do to keep her safe.

I used to have some sympathy for her since she was an orphan, like me. Michael had taken me off the streets when I was twenty years old and given me a purpose. That was something we shared in common—he saved both of us. But right now, with sore balls, I didn't feel any sympathy for her. I cursed myself for my inability to break a promise, because I wanted to get my dog and get the fuck out of here. *If I could just have a drink. No.*

I knew I was getting too heated and needed to calm down fast. I hadn't picked up the thing in years, but it was the only thing I could do to avoid going across the hall to tell Livia to go to hell. The second of my two prized possessions was in the bedroom, and I unlocked the violin case with shaking hands. I didn't think I'd still be any good, but as I began tuning it, muscle memory kicked in. Once I decided on a calming song to play, I slid the bow along the strings in one long stroke. The sudden rush of nostalgia overwhelmed me as the soothing notes reverberated off of the walls of the small apartment. I only screwed up a few times in the beginning, but then I got the hang of it and played the song through to the end.

With my blood pressure getting back to normal, I put the violin away and went to the kitchen to ice my aching balls. Nero sat at my feet, whining. "What, Nero?" I asked as if he could answer me. His eyes were the same color as mine, and I swore they gave me a judgmental look. "I'm calm. Go eat your food."

He ran off a little too eagerly toward the front door, and I peeled myself off the kitchen chair to follow him. I found him at the front door with his nose jammed under the crack, desperately sniffing at something. "Good boy. Doing my work for me already."

I stepped around him and looked through the peephole. Livia was standing outside her front door, talking on the phone. *Maybe her uncle. I wonder if he'll tell her I'm living across the hall.* I decided against going outside, even though I was tempted to guilt her for her hasty attack on my manhood.

It surprised me that Nero didn't bark at her. Usually, he went insane whenever someone came to my apartment back in New York. I hoped that "California chill" hadn't infected my dog already. Just then, I heard her say a name I recognized. Eric. Michael had told me about any people who were involved in her life. This way, I would know who was a threat and who wasn't. According to him, Livia only had one friend named Eric. A guy friend? I wondered how Michael had been okay with that when he had always chased men away from her in the past.

Immediately suspicious, I leaned closer to the door to hear anything else, but it was silent. I took a look out the peephole and she was already gone. She had something in her other hand while she was on the phone, and it seemed like she was about to go somewhere. It was after nine o'clock. Where would she be going at this time?

Nero kept whining at my feet, so I figured I'd kill two birds with one stone. After wrestling him into his harness, I took him downstairs to let him relieve himself while I took a look around for Livia. A quick glance past the parking lot said her car was still there.

A stone fountain with benches surrounding it sat neatly in front of the complex. It was nice enough, but apparently, my dog was utterly fascinated with the damn thing. He started dragging me in that direction, and I scolded him because I knew he'd try to piss on it. After I managed to get a hold of him, I realized what he had been chasing. I looked up through the fountain's sprays and saw chestnut hair, then a glimpse of Livia's profile. She was sitting on a bench on the other side of the fountain, looking down at something in her lap with her brows furrowed in deep concentration. I recognized that look.

The anger from earlier dissipated. I also hated being disturbed when I was focused on something. For some reason, I decided not to confront her now. She was safe enough, and I could easily keep an eye on her from afar. Tugging on Nero's leash, I started to back away before she spotted me.

Unfortunately, the stubborn beast decided to defy me, ripping the leash out of my hand, and he took off. "Fuck! Nero, you *stunad*!" I shouted, forgetting that I was attempting stealth. Usually, I was a pro at staying incognito, damn dog.

*Well, I guess I have no choice.*

I lurched forward to grab the leash and glanced up to see her shocked face staring back at me. We stood there, taking each other in for several long seconds before she finally spoke. "Oh, it's you."

She looked embarrassed. *Good. She should be.*

I tried to rein in the anger that slowly bubbled up again. I gave her a snarky grin and a wave. "Yes, it's me. I'm your new neighbor."

She recoiled. I wasn't happy about the situation either, but felt a little offended at her distaste for the concept of living across the hall from me. I raised my brows at her to elicit some kind of response. When she finally gazed up at me, I saw a flash of confusion cross her face. "Not across the hall?"

"Yeah. Michael said he wants me close by. Is that a problem?"

I gave her my stern voice, almost challenging her to take issue with it. She pursed her lips as she instinctively reached out to pet Nero. He didn't growl, he only leaned in for her to pet him, like a simp.

*What kind of guard dog are you?* I wanted to ask him, but he was too busy being doted on by the same girl who had treated me so rudely. I was almost jealous for a second. Almost.

"No. I kind of figured he would ask you to do something like that. I just…"

"What?" I asked, watching Nero lie down at Livia's feet in a pose of adoration.

She shook her head quickly. "Nothing. It's fine…but I am sorry that I kicked you. You just scared me." She saw my eyes drifting down to the notebook in her lap, and she quickly snapped it shut, setting an irritated gaze on me. "Don't you know how to approach people more nicely?"

"Look here,"—I took a step closer to her and met her annoyed stare—"I'm sorry I scared you. But I'm not happy about having to chase you around, either. So don't kill the messenger, Livia."

She scoffed. "So, you're going to follow me around everywhere now?"

"If I have to," I answered simply.

She tapped her fingers impatiently on the cover of her sketchbook. "And naturally, you'll also be reporting back to my uncle."

She wasn't asking, but I answered anyway. "Yes. Just doing my job. And I'd appreciate it if you would just cooperate and make both of our lives easier."

She sighed the most dramatic sigh I'd ever heard. "Can you at least tell me what's going on? What's the real reason for this? Clearly, you're not here just to 'check on me.' "

"Is that what he told you? Jesus, Michael." I couldn't help but laugh, which only made her angrier. I had to tell her something, this way at least maybe she would understand why this was all necessary. "Your uncle is coming up for parole soon, and there are some people who don't want him coming back. He's worried they might threaten you."

Her eyes widened and she quickly looked around to see if anyone was watching us, then lowered her voice. "And he thinks that they're going to come all the way to L.A. to hurt me?"

I gave her a noncommittal shrug. I thought this was all overkill, but an order was an order, and it wasn't like it was out of the realm of possibility. "Maybe. He wasn't willing to risk your safety. You're out here by yourself and he's in prison. So, he sent me to look out for you."

I tried to ease her concern because she looked terrified, and I was surprised to find myself *not* wanting to scare someone.

"He must really trust you then," she answered quietly.

"Yes, he does. So, are you going to cooperate or not?"

"Fine. Just don't treat me like a child. My uncle always does that, and it drives me crazy," she snapped as she got up from the bench. I didn't step away to let her out, but she pushed past me anyway.

"What were you drawing?" *What?* Why did I ask her that right now?

She halted, then turned to face me again with a nod toward the sprays of water. "Just the fountain."

"Can I see it?" She hesitated for a moment, but finally opened her notebook to show me. *Pretty nice.* "I like it."

She took the sketchbook away before I could examine it any further. "It's a rough sketch."

I had seen some of her mother's work in the past, and it was similar to Livia's, but there was a certain quality to it that was all her own. I had to admit that I was a little impressed. "No, I mean it. It's really good."

She raised a brow at me and changed tack. "Do you have any artistic talents?"

*Shit.* I assumed that the walls of these apartments were paper-thin, and now I knew that I was right. "Not really," I said smoothly, but something in her eye told me she knew I was bullshitting her.

With an eye roll, she huffed. "All right. I'm going upstairs now. This job is going to be very boring for you, so I apologize for that."

"Somehow I doubt that!" I stared after her as she stomped away from me like a child. She was teasing me, and she enjoyed every second of it, that sly smirk on her face. She was infuriating.

I waited an appropriate amount of time before going back upstairs. I doubted that she'd want to have another run-in tonight. When I got upstairs, I leaned into Livia's door for a moment to make sure she got inside safely and heard the faint sound of music. Satisfied with my job for the day, I dragged Nero away from her door and back home. *California will never be home.*

I started my surveillance the next morning, taking note of her schedule. She woke up around ten on weekdays to go to classes before going directly to the studio to paint. After a few days, and only a few brief conversations with her in the hallway where she gave me one-word answers to my questions, everything became fairly routine. She never seemed to do anything but go to school and work on her art. But now it was Friday, and she begrudgingly informed of her weekend plans during a not-so-accidental run-in in the hallway. I was still a little pissed at Nero for outing me before I was ready, but due to his sudden obsession with Livia, at least he always alerted me to her presence when we were at home.

She didn't look surprised when I opened my door to find her in the hallway lingering in front of my apartment, and she scowled at me. "I'm going out tomorrow, and I'd appreciate it if you make yourself scarce if you must follow me around. Eric doesn't know about all of this, and I don't want him to."

I leaned against the frame of my door and stared down at her. Her gaze shifted, but she stood rigidly in front of me. I couldn't tell if she was only pretending not to be intimidated, or if she really didn't care who I was or what I did for a living. A few moments passed before I said, "Don't you think that's unwise, considering your uncle's enemies could be out there looking for you? They might try to weasel information out of your friends. Sorry, friend," I corrected myself, bringing myself down to her level of hostility. I didn't understand why she was so nasty, and why I couldn't manage to let it slide without growing angrier myself.

"Since we don't even know who might be after me, I'm not sure that I'm even worried about it. It's probably all just my uncle being overprotective like always. It's not like his tactics have always worked in the past." She froze the minute those last words came out of her mouth. Clearly, she hadn't meant to let that slip.

Instant alarm bells went off inside my head. "What does that mean?"

"Nothing. I'm just saying, things happen. I don't want to drag my one friend into this so that he can decide being my friend isn't worth it, just like everyone else throughout my life. Just back off, Dante, okay?" Livia quickly punctuated her demand with a whip of her long hair as she turned away from me.

I wasn't going to let it go, but I conceded for the moment. I had to give it to her. She was determined, and I knew I wasn't getting anything else out of her just yet. *Let her think she won.* "Whatever you say, *principessa.*"

My little endearment earned me another mighty scowl, and I felt the corners of my lips turning up into a smirk. I didn't know what it was, but I got a lot of enjoyment out of pissing her off. The flash of anger in her eyes only amused me more, and I chuckled lightly as

I watched her stomp back into her apartment, slamming the door without another word.

Chapter Four

*Livia*

I was coming back from checking my mail when I again heard beautiful music coming from Dante's apartment. Over the past week of being professionally stalked, I had learned almost nothing about the man whom I was supposed to trust with my life. He didn't seem to care who I was, showing me the barest amount of respect when we spoke. He definitely didn't like to talk about himself, and yet he knew everything about me and my life. Well, everything worth knowing.

I found myself looking forward to hearing his music for two reasons. One, it meant he was occupied and wouldn't immediately come outside to ambush me with questions. And two, because he was actually quite talented. It was his only redeeming quality thus far. It seemed like he was ashamed of it, because this great hulking man had actually looked embarrassed when I tried to ask about his talent. When he evaded my question, I thought I saw a brief glint of pain in his hazel eyes. I hated that I was not only curious, but that I was still thinking about it the next day as I got ready for my outing with Eric. I really hoped that Dante didn't plan on making himself known. *He could hide in a bush for all I care.*

How could I have explained to Eric that my main

reason for being in California was to escape the drama of my Mafia family, and that a bunch of mobsters might come after me at any moment? He was a mild-mannered guy, and I couldn't imagine him not panicking when he realized who I really was. That part of my life was in the past. The person I was now, the person I showed others, was the real me. Not even Dante could ruin this for me.

I didn't venture onto the party scene often, but since this would be a chill night with Eric and some of his friends and not a wild frat party, I'd happily agreed to it. He'd been nagging me for ages to expand my horizons and meet new people, but I barely had the energy for just one friendship. Growing up the way I had, I didn't know how to maintain close friendships with multitudes of people. If I had as many friends as Eric, I'd have to spend the entire day texting them all, and then I'd have no time to study. I didn't know how he managed it.

It was mostly going to be an informal art show of sorts. Eric and his fellow photographer friends were going to display prints of their best work in the studio, and there would be snacks and drinks as well. I secretly thought that had been the real reason Eric wanted me there—he was a sucker for my cooking. Aside from painting, it was the only other talent I possessed. Not that it was a passion of mine, more like a necessity. My uncle was helpless in the kitchen, and unless we wanted to eat at Castellano's every night, I had to learn how to cook.

I prepared stuffed mushrooms along with some antipasto for everyone to snack on. Luckily none of Eric's friends were crunchy granola Californians, most of them also being from out of state, so I was confident that everything would go off without a hitch. When I pulled the mushrooms out of the oven, I left them to cool while I went to get dressed.

It was rare that I wasn't in my usual uniform of jeans and a T-shirt covered in paint, but since I wouldn't be painting tonight, I decided to dig through my closet for one of my old outfits. I had an expansive wardrobe because my uncle always insisted that I had the best clothes. It always seemed a waste to wear designer label dresses when I knew I was going to get dirty.

I almost welcomed the idea of taking a break from my constant work, since I was stuck anyway. The painting I had been working on was sitting lonely on its easel in the living room, unfinished. I had even started a new piece, but that too was left unfinished. As I slipped on my dress, a weird flash of nostalgia startled me, but I quickly brushed it off. A night out was exactly what I needed to distract me from my recent lack of progress, and the unsettling feeling that seemed to coincide with the arrival of the pain in the ass next door.

Which reminded me, I had to let him know when I would be leaving, so that he could tail behind me in his own car. After a week of this, I still wasn't used to it. Maybe I could slip out and avoid him, I thought hopefully. Even though I wasn't quite taking this threat seriously, I thought it would probably be a stupid move and decided against it, as tempting as it was.

Even if I had tried to escape the building without Dante, I knew Nero would sniff me out, the little rat. I had been slightly afraid of the dog at first, but he seemed taken with me, which annoyed Dante to no end. I made a big show of showering the dog with affection whenever I saw him, just to annoy him further. He seemed to think he had a mailman slayer on his hands, but Nero was nothing but a big softie. Honestly, I wished some of his nature would rub off on his owner, who ironically acted like more of a beast than a man.

Once I made up my face and slipped on my shoes, I stood before the mirror in my bedroom. I had to admit, I looked decent when I actually tried. I pinned my long waves back, leaving a few tendrils framing my face. I skimmed my hands down the sides of the deep purple body con dress, that I was surprised I still fit in. Satisfied with the result, I teetered on my heels back to the kitchen to pack up the food for the show.

Even though Dante couldn't see me, I still huffed in annoyance outside his apartment as I lifted my fist and knocked heavily on the door. I heard Nero's audible sniffing under the crack, which lightened my sour mood. A half-second later, the door swung open and I wondered if he'd been standing there all along.

Dante's eyes widened when he saw me, almost like he didn't recognize me. I immediately felt my face heat and addressed it before he could make another backhanded comment. "Yes, I own a few dresses. I'm not always a slob."

One corner of his mouth turned up. "Now, is that any way to greet me?"

"You were looking at me like I was an alien." I scoffed at him, irritated already. I turned back to my apartment to fetch the food.

Ignoring my comment, he stepped out of the apartment and sniffed the air. "What is that smell?"

"Are you going to insult my cooking, too?" I retorted as I shut the door behind me with the containers of food in my arms.

He laughed at me, seeming to be quite entertained by my frustration. "No. I was just surprised to know that you can cook. It smells delicious."

Not ready to let my defensive stance go, I had my comeback ready. "Because I'm such a sheltered *principessa*? I'll have you know, my uncle, whom you love so much, would have starved to death if it weren't for me."

He cocked his head. "Unlikely, seeing as he frequented my family's restaurant often." He took a step closer. "Or don't you remember?"

I tried to hold back my surprise. "You're a Castellano?"

He only nodded, but offered no more information when he reached out to take the food from me. It struck me then. That was why he seemed familiar to me, and yet I hadn't been able to place him. I remembered visits to Castellano's Italian Bistro with my uncle. He usually left me alone at the table in order to conduct his business in another room while I picked at my food and listened to the band playing in the background.

I felt a sudden wave of emotion when I recalled hearing about the original owners' deaths, but I wasn't sure how they were related to Dante. It was kept pretty quiet, no doubt due to my uncle's bribes to the media and police. It was almost like they never existed at all, as the restaurant was sold, and they kept the name. I snuck a peek at Dante, and I could tell he regretted bringing it up. He fell quiet and shut his apartment door, checking a few times to ensure it was locked before he gestured dramatically for me to lead the way. His sudden haughty attitude soon rid me of any warm feelings toward him. *Jerk.*

He trailed behind me to my car, carefully loading my stuff into the backseat. "You have an entire craft store back here. Don't you ever have any passengers?"

"No. Only food, art supplies, and sometimes Eric, but he sits in the front." I didn't have to explain anything to him. He was here to protect me, not to get to know me. "Mind your business and get your nosy ass out of my car."

"Ah, but technically, you are my business, *principessa.*" Dante took his sweet time pushing aside rolls of canvas and packs of brushes to make room for the containers.

"Stop calling me that!"

He laughed again, and I practically threw myself into the driver's seat to get away from him. He closed the back door and approached the driver's side window. "You need to lighten up, Livia."

His condescending tone had me squeezing the steering wheel, imagining it was his neck instead. "Somehow I don't think my uncle would enjoy knowing how goddamned rude you are to me." *Did I really just threaten to tell on him, like a five-year-old?*

"Michael happens to love my sense of humor. What he isn't a fan of is that damn filthy mouth of yours," he retorted, leaning into the driver's side window.

I clicked the button to roll up the window. He leaned back only to avoid the pane of glass smashing his face. Right before it shut completely, I got out my last comeback. "Fuck you."

Knowing I wouldn't be able to hear his response, he mouthed his infuriating pet name again before he stalked off toward his own car. I swore that if I rolled my eyes any harder, they would become stuck that way permanently, as my uncle had always jokingly threatened me when I was younger.

When I arrived at the studio, I squealed into the parking lot and scrambled out of the car, retrieving the food as quickly as possible. I just wanted to get inside before Dante reappeared to piss me off even more. Who the hell did he think he was, chastising my foul language? I was a grown woman. I guessed it really was a boring job to him, if the best he could do was report back to my uncle the number of times I swore. I didn't think I had such a dirty mouth, but my uncle never liked me using the Lord's name in vain. He wasn't religious, but he was raised in the Catholic church, and I supposed certain things would always feel taboo to him.

I shook my head furiously to try to rid myself of my worsening mood. I plastered on a smile and headed to the studio. I knew Dante was nearby, but he didn't make himself known. By now, I had become pretty good at being aware of when I was being watched. The tiny hairs on the back of my neck rose as if he were directly behind me, his heavy hand on my shoulder, breathing against my bare neck—only this time, it wasn't fear I felt.

I hated to admit that having him nearby made me feel slightly more secure, but I still didn't want everyone to know I had a bodyguard. This was California, not New York. People would think that I was some kind of obscure celebrity or something, and that was unneeded attention that I just didn't want.

Something thankfully interrupted my train of thought when the studio door opened and I saw Eric's face. "Liv! Finally. Get in here!" He stepped back to hold open the door for me, and I breezed inside, not allowing myself to peek behind me to see if Dante was back there, watching. I knew he was.

"I brought your favorite. Don't hog them all," I

scolded.

Eric just brushed me off and led me to where he displayed his work. Of course, I had seen all his photos; I was in half of them. I wanted to enjoy the party and forget about my situation with the brute outside.

But defying my logical side, I took a quick look over my shoulder. It took a moment to locate him because, with his dark hair and skin, he blended into the night. The lamp posts in the parking lot almost illuminated his eyes against the darkness. But he wasn't looking at me. His focus was on the display of photos in front of me. It was too dark to see the expression on his face, but I knew it would be suspicious to keep staring out of the window to study him. No one could know about this, and I certainly didn't want him to see me staring at him and get the wrong idea. *Pretend he isn't there.*

I turned back and found Eric's hopeful face, and his collection. The photo in the center was of me, but most of my face was absent from the picture. I hadn't seen this one before. It was a black and white shot he must have taken of me last week, the last time I worked on the piece that had me completely stumped. "Wow, I didn't even realize you were there that day. I was so in the zone!"

"I know! I even called out your name a few times, but you were completely gone. So, I took advantage of the opportunity." He jutted out his chin and beamed. "Good, huh?"

"Not to be super vain or anything, but it's amazing. The way the light catches here." I pointed to the ray of sunlight illuminating a strip of my hair. "I wouldn't think it would look so breathtaking in black and white."

"Believe it or not, it was less vibrant in color. It took something away from it, somehow," Eric explained. "I think I might enter it in a contest or something. With your permission, of course."

"Permission granted. I'll finally be famous...for something positive this time." I muttered that last part to myself. Eric was so captivated by his own work, he didn't seem to hear me.

One of his friends approached me with a cup of beer. "If it isn't the muse! I feel like I've seen you more in print than in person," he said as he handed me a drink. "I'm Chad. You're Livia, right?"

I didn't drink much but accepted the drink happily. Maybe that way I'd get a little more comfortable with all the attention on me. I quickly slurped it down. "Yeah. I don't get out much."

"What do you do?"

"I'm a painter," I answered. "Mostly oils on canvas."

He nodded and turned to survey the room. "You didn't bring any of your work. Why not?"

Eric lightly slapped my back just as I was struggling for an answer, bringing me another drink. "Because she's bashful. But I assure you, her work is amazing. She's a damn perfectionist."

Chad chuckled and gestured to the crowded studio. "Aren't we all?"

"Not compared to Livia. No one sees her work until the last brushstroke is done, except for me, of course." He gave a haughty smile to Chad, who took an almost imperceptible step back.

"Oh. I didn't realize..." He darted his eyes between us like he had just made some connection he hadn't seen before.

*Oh, he thinks we're together!*

I waited awkwardly, hoping for Eric to correct him, but he stayed silent. "No, no. It's not like that. He's my best friend," I responded before things got any more awkward. I could have sworn I saw a flash of some emotion cross Eric's face in my peripheral vision, but it was gone as soon as I turned to investigate.

After Chad wandered off, just as mystified as I was, I chugged my beer and immediately got a refill. I hadn't drank this much in years, and it was already going to my head. Eric ushered me around, introducing me to the rest of his friends and showing me their work, but the energy between us was suddenly tense. He and I had always been comfortable with friendly affection in the past, but now he was pointedly keeping his hands off of me.

I made some excuse about leaving something in my car just to have a reason to get away. I swung open the door and rounded the corner so that no one could see me from the large windows out front. Leaning against the side of the building, I downed the rest of my beer and chucked the cup in the trash. I really hoped that wasn't disappointment I saw on Eric's face.

I had no interest in a relationship of any kind, and the last thing I needed was to lose the only friend I had because he wanted more. I wasn't capable of giving anyone more, no matter how much I might have wanted to. Eric was good-looking, intelligent, and amazingly artistic. But there was just nothing there. Not for him, or anyone else. I unclipped my hair, starting to feel like I was getting a headache from the pins in my hair. As I was shaking out my waves, I saw his boots enter my vision.

"You shouldn't be drinking if you're planning on driving home," Dante chided me with a strained look on his face.

"It was a few beers. I'm totally fine. I thought you were going to make yourself scarce. What if someone comes out and sees me with you?"

I felt myself instantly growing more annoyed at his proximity. Students were walking around everywhere, and someone was bound to notice this giant of a man in front of me. He stuck out like a sore thumb, and it had nothing to do with what he was wearing. He just didn't look like he belonged, and I was sure it was as obvious to everyone else as it was to me.

He shrugged noncommittally. "I was just humoring you. My job is to keep you safe. Hanging out in a parking lot all night makes that kind of difficult, especially if someone roofies your drink and drags you away."

I had to force myself not to react to his comment. "Whatever." I turned away from him and strode back toward the studio.

"Good mushrooms, by the way!" he shouted back.

*Ugh.* That was why he had been hanging around in the back of my car for so long. Didn't he know how to feed himself? I didn't respond, knowing he was aching to get a rise out of me. I went inside and didn't spare him another glance for the rest of the night.

## Chapter Five

*Dante*

I felt like I'd seen the back of Livia more than I'd ever seen her face. I didn't know what it was about her that made me want to pull on her pigtails and push her into the sand. The compliment I threw out at the end was because I knew I was acting like a grade-A asshole. She seemed to get more pissed at me when I complimented her than when I was straight up insulting her. After thirty-five years on this planet, I still didn't understand women.

I kept a close eye on her for the rest of the night, barely bothering to stay hidden for her comfort. The way she was dressed, with all those men hanging all over her, was a recipe for disaster. Even though she didn't look back at me, I knew she was trying to piss me off when she repeatedly accepted drinks from the bros that had basically formed a circle jerk around her.

*A little celebrity now, aren't you?*

It was reckless of her to allow that boy to take so many photos of her to plaster all over the walls. Any one of her uncle's enemies would know her face if they walked by the studio's huge windows and saw them. Even I couldn't take my eyes off of them. There was something about that one photo that held my attention, though. Eric had captured something that wasn't tangible. It was that same something that had me star-struck that first day I found Livia.

The picture only featured half of her face, from the cupid's bow just under her lean nose, her plump lips that she had been gnawing on, and her dainty chin. Her dark waves framed her face. The stream of light coming in from the window lit an almost blinding band across her neck and hair. I remembered that outfit, too. Eric must have taken that photo the day I was there, watching her through the window. It was as if the memory had been printed onto that image directly from my brain.

There was something about the pure artistic concentration that was so easily read, even without seeing her eyes that made the photo breathtaking. I had to force myself to look away several times, remembering that I was supposed to be here watching out for threats. I had never been able to be distracted this easily on a job before, and I found it pretty disturbing. *It's just a good photo, you've seen it, now get your damn head on straight.*

What was more disturbing was the sheer amount of drink that this petite woman was guzzling right in front of me, as if she were saying *fuck you* with every sip. I had counted at least five beers in the past hour, and she didn't take a break to drink any water, either. *Amateur.* She was going to have a hell of a hangover in the morning.

When I finally saw her stumbling outside with Eric practically holding her up, I decided the jig was up and made my approach. As I got closer, I made eye contact with Eric first. His eyes went wide immediately, and I felt myself smirking. Now that was the kind of reaction I usually got from people. I had almost forgotten how it felt, spending the past week with Livia giving me nothing but dirty looks and snark.

"Can I help you?"

The Irishman looked ready to piss himself when I stepped into the light coming from the front door of the studio. He squared his shoulders like he was ready to fight.

I couldn't help but smile at the notion. "I'm Dante, Livia's…friend. I'll take her from here."

She seemed to sober up just a little from hearing my voice, and she lifted her head to look up at me, registering my presence in front of her. "I told you to stay out of my way."

"You know this guy?" Eric hoisted her up farther, fixing a protective gaze on her that had me willing myself not to laugh. He couldn't protect her from a plastic bag. Lucky for him, there was no danger of that here.

Livia sighed. "He's a family friend. Yes, I know him."

I reached forward again, quickly getting tired of this conversation. "I don't need to explain myself to you. I've known Livia for years. Who are you?"

I knew who he was, of course, but I took the opportunity to intimidate him. He made it too easy as he stood there, anxiously trying to stand tall with his shoulders back, while also holding Livia up—it was comical.

I saw the flash of fear in his eyes, especially after his stare trailed from my face to the tattoos peeking out from the neckline of my shirt. He deepened his voice in a feeble attempt to ward me off. "I'm Eric, her best friend. And she has never mentioned any family or family friends. Where did you even come from?"

"None of your business. I'll take her from here."

"No, you won't. Eric hasn't had anything to drink. He can drive me home," Livia protested.

I didn't sign up to be questioned at every god-damned turn. Technically, I hadn't signed up for any of this, but I tried to settle myself and remember that Michael needed me to take care of her. Using a fraction of my strength, I peeled the Irishman's arm from around Livia's waist, then scooped her up into my arms. "I don't have time for this. You're going home. Now."

She tried to fight me for a moment, wiggling and pounding at my chest. I let her get her frustration out as I walked her back toward my car, leaving a bewildered red-haired man, watching us in complete shock. Once I had her safely buckled in the passenger's seat and slid into the driver's side, I started the car and began driving toward home.

I thought it was strange that she wasn't bickering at me or telling me to fuck off. I assumed she had passed out, but when I glanced over at her, her eyes were open and focused on the dashboard. "Are you going to tell my uncle about tonight?"

She looked so vulnerable and contrite I almost wanted to lie to her. "I have to."

"I wouldn't have drunk that much if you hadn't been such a jackass. I'm sure you're not going to tell him that part," she argued with that snarky tone she seemed to have perfected into a science.

I couldn't help but grip the steering wheel tighter to quell my anger. "First of all, I'm not here to be your friend. Second, drinking like that to make someone mad is just plain stupid. You're only hurting yourself."

"I'm not stupid. I was annoyed. Forgive me for wanting to let loose for one god-damned night."

I gripped the wheel harder. "Filthy fucking mouth. I should put a bar of soap in there, *principessa*."

"You're a hypocrite!" Her wide eyes fixed on me. "I bet you're just pissed you couldn't join in. Maybe I would have asked you if you knew how to act like a normal person, instead of being this giant walking, talking refrigerator."

"I've been to better parties. Cheap beer will give you a shitty hangover." I managed to calm myself a little, counting back from ten with a few deep breaths. "You said you weren't going to be difficult."

"I lied," she stated simply, and turned to stare out the window without another word.

After a silent car ride, I pulled into the apartment complex, where Livia immediately jumped out and stomped away from me. Again. This time, I wasn't going to be so nice and let her stalk off. I was fucking sick and tired of looking at the back of her head. When I climbed out of the car and slammed the door, Livia froze. "Come back here and talk to me."

"Why should I?" She gave me her now famous scowl and sass, which only served to boil my blood further.

"Because you can't do stupid shit like that. You can't hold your drink. Look at you, you're wobbling right now!" I reached her in just a few strides in case she was about to fall.

She snorted at me like the brat she was. "What do you know about me, anyway? Did my uncle give you a handy dandy dossier on me?"

"He did, actually."

47

She probably hadn't expected me to admit it, but what did I have to be ashamed of? I wasn't stalking her for fun. This was my job, and probably the most annoying one I'd ever had.

"Why did you speak to Eric like that? He's done nothing to you," she said, changing the subject with an eye roll.

*Roll your eyes at me one more time, little girl.*

I approached her slowly when she continued to stumble again. It was like trying to sneak up on a terrified animal. For every step forward I took, she took a step back. "He was pissing me off, acting all protective like I was some kind of pervert. Protecting you is my job."

"I thought you liked coming across like a scary predator."

I felt my fists clench. "I like coming across as someone not to be fucked with. And you seem to love doing just that." I took another step closer until she was just a hair's width away from me, her face meeting my chest. I leaned down to whisper in her ear, and the second my breath hit her skin, she shivered. Somehow, I doubted it was from fear. "You know one thing that wasn't in your dossier? It didn't state anywhere that you were a little brat. Go figure."

Livia tilted her head back to show me her eyes, and they were filled with nothing but pure unadulterated determination. "I'm not afraid of you, Dante, so don't try to intimidate me."

I had to give it to her, not many people could take a stare down from me like she could. "I'm not trying to intimidate you. I'm trying to keep you safe. We're going up to your place and you're going to drink some water and take some painkillers so you don't feel like the dead tomorrow."

I gave her the sternest tone I could, hoping that she wouldn't argue with me again. But who was I kidding? She always argued.

"I feel like the dead already," she slurred and promptly fell into my arms.

It was a good thing she was such a petite woman. I looped my arm around her waist and hoisted her over my shoulder. There weren't too many people outside, but I did get a few odd looks as I walked into the building with an unconscious Livia thrown over my shoulder like a sack of rice. She wasn't completely out of it, because I kept hearing her soft whimpers as her head lolled around on my back.

When I got upstairs finally, I reached into my back pocket with my free hand to retrieve the duplicate key to her apartment that I had made in case of an emergency. After unlocking the door, I paced straight into her bedroom to gently lay her down on her bed. I clicked on her bedside lamp and left her there to get a glass of water and some painkillers.

When I came back with the water, it surprised me to see her sitting up in bed. "Did you carry me in here?"

I wanted to be angry with her for being insolent, but she looked so vulnerable, huddled in her bed with her knees scrunched up to her chest. I knew what it was like to be drunk and miserable. Being yelled at would only make it worse. "Yes."

She was quiet for a moment. "Okay."

I handed her the water and said something that rarely ever came out of my mouth. "Livia, drink. Please." Her eyes widened slightly, and she reached for the glass, taking a few slow sips. "Good. Here, take these. You'll feel better after you get some sleep."

She took the pills from me and quickly swallowed them. "Why are you suddenly being nice to me?"

"Because you need it." Not really an explanation, but it was as good as I was going to give her at the moment. "Lay down."

She kicked off her heels and crawled under the blankets, not bothering to take off her dress. I was sure she would have undressed if I hadn't been there, so I let it be. After a few minutes of sitting there quietly, I heard her even breathing, and assumed she was asleep. I got up to leave, but felt her hand clasp around my wrist. "Dante?"

I wasn't used to people randomly putting their hands on me, but for some reason, I didn't pull my hand away. "Yes?"

"Every girl my age drinks," she said in a tired voice, her eyes half closed. "Why did it bother you so much?"

I took a deep breath and glanced down at her. "I'm an alcoholic. It's a slippery slope, especially for people like us, who grew up dealing with the shit we did. Don't use alcohol as a way to cope with your feelings, Livia." I didn't know why I said it. Maybe because she was near unconscious, or maybe because she was finally being a little more amicable.

"Why would you care?"

"Your uncle has already lost everything and everyone he loved. But he still has you, and it's my job to keep it that way. Go to sleep now."

I walked away without looking back. I shocked myself when I opened up to her, and a little part of me was afraid of what I'd see if I glanced back at her. Why did I care, indeed?

\*\*\*\*

I thought the way things went down the night before embarrassed Livia, because she didn't leave her apartment once for the rest of the next day. I knew I should have probably taken the time to check on her, but I couldn't help but feel all wound up over my hasty confession to a drunken Livia. Why had I told her that? I didn't want her to pity me. What if she asked more questions about the road that led to my alcoholism? I wasn't ready to talk to anyone about that. I would never be ready to relive that night again.

Feeling any kind of extreme emotion used to lead to me reaching for a bottle to kill it as quickly as possible. Now, I did the only thing I could. I pulled out my violin and began to play. When my phone rang the moment I started to calm down, I cursed. I put the violin back down and reached into my pocket for my phone and looked down at the screen, answering it with a sigh. "Yes, I accept the call." I waited a few moments before I heard Michael's voice. "Hey."

He didn't waste any time. "How is everything with Livia?"

I tried to think of how to put it without insulting his niece directly to him, which I was sure he wouldn't appreciate. "She's okay."

Michael laughed. "Don't lie to me. Just give it to me straight."

"Okay, but remember, you asked for it. She's a pain in the ass." I braced myself for Michael's yelling, but it never came.

He chuckled into the phone. "Now that I believe. What did she do?"

"She got pissy with me yesterday about having to be

51

followed, so she got drunk just to spite me. I had to carry her home." I honestly wanted to forget the entire night, but I promised Michael full disclosure, and I never went back on a promise. Especially not to him.

"I'll talk to her. I'm sure that wasn't easy for you to see. Is she all right?"

But then I did hear yelling. It wasn't coming from Michael's end of things, but from the hallway outside my place. "Fuck! Hold on. I heard something in the hallway."

I dropped the phone as I heard Michael's concerned voice asking me what was going on, then rushed to the front door and threw it open.

Livia stood in her doorway; all the blood drained from her face. She didn't seem to take notice of me standing there, her eyes glued to the floor. I followed her gaze slowly to the dead rat on her welcome mat. Goddamn it.

## Chapter Six

*Livia*

I barely had time to register what I saw before Nero charged forward, barking furiously at the dead rat at my feet. I didn't look up at Dante, but saw he was alarmed by the increase of nervous energy in the hallway.

"Are you okay?" The concern in his voice was evident.

I couldn't force words out, and just continued to stare at the doormat. Eventually I found my voice but had to shout over Nero's barking. "Y-yeah. It just scared me, that's all."

Dante came toward me, gently tapping the rodent with his foot. I supposed to make sure it was dead. With a tone of finality, "We need to get you out of here."

"What are you talking about? It's just a coincidence." I wasn't sure if I was trying to convince him or myself more.

He shook his head as if I were the one being ridiculous. "So, you think a rat came all the way up to the third floor, just to give up and die on your doorstep?"

"Yes! Either that or a cat killed it and brought it up here. I'm sure one of my neighbors has a cat."

He ignored me to yell at his dog. "Nero! Quiet! I need to fucking think here." I was surprised when Nero immediately quieted down, but he stayed at my side, licking my hand for comfort. "I think this is a thinly veiled threat," he said. "We can't ignore it."

I crossed my arms over my chest, unable to believe what he was suggesting. Even if it had been a threat, did he expect me to abandon school to run away like a coward? "I think you're overreacting."

"Am I, *principessa*? I'm not the one who shrieked the building down just now." He conveniently didn't look at my face, or he would see me scowling at him again. Suddenly, he snapped into action. "Shit, Michael!" He ran back into his apartment, leaving me alone with Nero. A minute later, he returned with the phone to his ear. "Here, you talk some sense into her."

He handed me the phone, which I hesitantly brought up to my ear—only to hear my uncle's frantic voice. "Livia, sweetie, I think you should err on the side of caution here. Dante told me what happened."

"Uncle Michael, I really think it was just a coincidence. Besides, I graduate in a month; I can't leave!" I looked up to find Dante carefully watching me. "Where would I go?"

"Home," Uncle Michael said simply. "Look… I might be getting out of here soon. I don't want to miss out on any more of your life. We can be a family again, sweetie."

I felt my blood run cold at the idea of returning to New York. Attempting to cover the sudden fear that overcame me, I glanced up again to see Dante's furrowed brows. "I-I can't come back yet. I won't. Please…"

"You're in danger there, and Dante tells me you're not cooperating with him. There's only so much I can take, Livia. I'm not a young man anymore." He didn't often lose his temper with me, but I could tell he was almost there. "Don't make this more difficult than it has to be."

I wasn't going to back down. If I had to face everything again, I at least wanted to do it with my finished degree. I just wanted to live my life on my own terms for once. Surely, he had to understand that. Yet here he was, asking me to come back and be a part of it all again.

He left me no choice but to appeal to his deep-seated desire to keep me away from the lifestyle he was so accustomed to. "I have to finish school. I want to make a life for myself, apart from all this. Don't you want that for me?"

I heard the guard inform my uncle that time was up, and he groaned in frustration. "Yes, I do. I have to go, but this discussion is not over. Stop arguing with Dante and do what he says. I love you."

"I love you, too…" I hung up the phone and handed it back to Dante.

He grabbed my wrist without another word and pulled me into his apartment. "Wait here while I go dispose of the roadkill." He shooed Nero in my direction. "Go with Livia."

After he practically pushed me down on the couch, the dog settled down beside me, laying his head on my lap. I was still so shocked from the chaos of the past ten minutes, I stared straight ahead, trying to process my uncle's request. More like a demand. Go back to New York? The idea filled me with such dread that I started to formulate a plan in my head in case they tried to force me to go back. I wouldn't do it.

It was only when my eyes focused on the violin in front of me that I realized where I was. Dante *did* play. I knew it. While taking in the rest of the apartment, I noticed there wasn't much to see. It didn't look like he had settled in at all. There were no homey touches or décor, just the basic furniture and necessities. The only thing that stood out was the musical instrument in front of me. Imagining him playing the violin made him seem a little more human. Although, I could hardly picture this tattooed, gruff man creating the awe-inspiring music I heard coming from his apartment on an almost daily basis.

I stood up from the couch to get a closer look at it. The spruce it was carved from looked smooth but worn from use. I reached out to rub the body of it, and my fingers glided up to the strings. I was tempted to pluck them, just to hear the calming vibration coming from the instrument.

"Don't touch it."

Dante's voice, coming from behind me, made me jump out of my skin. I could almost feel the heat coming off his body, even though he wasn't touching me.

"I wasn't going to break it. I'm not a child, you know," I responded in an offended tone, withdrawing my hand from his precious possession.

Dante scoffed. "Could've fooled me, the way you talked to your uncle. Why don't you want to go back to New York?"

I could play that game, too. Ignoring his question, I turned to face him. "I've heard you playing it before. You're good. Why did you lie when I asked about it?"

His eyes widened when the compliment left my lips. I surprised myself too. It came out before I could stop myself. He quickly gained his composure, and the expressionless mask went back up. "It's private. Why don't you want to go back?" he asked again.

I slumped back onto the couch. "It's private."

Dante rolled his eyes. "See? Insolence. It must have been a nightmare raising you."

"Only with you, because you're a bully."

His mood suddenly changed, and his face broke out in a conspiratorial smile. It took me aback, because for a moment he almost looked like any normal man. He really did have a nice smile, with straight white teeth and full lips. I had to look away as a little heat rushed up to my cheeks. *What is going on here?*

"I have an idea. Let's make a trade," he suggested in a soft voice that sounded almost unnatural coming from him.

"What kind of trade?"

"You tell me why you don't want to go back, and I'll play a song for you." Dante grabbed his violin, handling it like it was a newborn baby. He seemed so confident that I would agree, settling beside me on the couch as he began tuning the violin.

I surveyed him suspiciously. I knew I wasn't going to tell him the reason, but I wanted to hear him play in person, rather than muffled through his front door. I squared my shoulders and met his gaze. "You have to go first."

He let out a breath of defeat. "Stubborn girl. Fine. What do you want to hear?"

I thought about it for a moment, considering giving him something really complicated just to see him mess up, but I knew what I wanted to hear. "The song you were playing that first night you moved in. It was nice..." I probably shouldn't have admitted I remembered, but it was too late. My eyes shot up to meet his, but he didn't seem to notice my embarrassment.

He only nodded, then brought the violin to position and began to play. The melodious song seemed to fill the entire apartment. Sitting so close next to him, I could almost feel the vibrations of the strings on my skin, giving me instant goosebumps. It was so calming that I started to feel myself physically relaxing, leaning back against the couch and closing my eyes. When the tempo picked up, I opened my eyes to take a peek at the confounding man who was playing the most beautiful music for me.

He was deep in concentration, his eyes closed as if the music were calming him as much as it was me. His features softened, and somehow, he looked years younger. It was then that I realized I didn't even know how old he was.

There was so little I knew about this man who made it his business to know everything about me. What had he been through? What drove him to drink? I found myself thinking about his confession the night before. I spent the entire day thinking about it. I was pretty sure the only reason he divulged the information was because he was hoping I wouldn't remember it, but I did.

The questions kept swirling in my mind. Why was he a bodyguard working for the Mafia when he could easily have been a concert violinist? I should have made him promise to tell me something about him in return. I shook my head to rid myself of the thought. I wasn't telling him anything, but it startled me that I had even considered it for a moment. Opening up was the most dangerous thing I could do, because every time I did, I was unceremoniously abandoned. Why did I care what Dante thought of me? And why did I find myself becoming more and more intrigued by him?

I didn't realize the song had finished until his face appeared in front of me. "Where did you go?" he asked, surveying me closely.

"I was lost in the zone. That was beautiful..." I said, and snapped out of my reverie.

Dante looked almost shy to hear my uncharacteristic praise, but he instantly schooled his face to go back to his usual stoic expression. "Thank you...Your turn."

*Damn it.* I should have used the time to think of a fake reason. I stayed silent for a few moments, as if I were ruminating about how to begin. I was half hoping that Dante would get impatient and give up, but he kept his intense stare on me and waited. There was a hint of something in his eyes that I couldn't figure out. If I hadn't known better, I would have thought he actually cared. *No, don't be silly.*

"Well...I mean, can you blame me? My uncle said it himself. This life is dangerous. Even if he gets out, how long will it be before someone tries to come after me again when he tries to take back his place? I don't want to live the rest of my life in some kind of gilded cage." It wasn't a lie, just not the whole truth. That would have to be enough for him.

Dante appeared thoughtful for a while, watching me so closely it sent a shiver up my spine. Why was he still looking at me like that? "You're safer with protection there than you are here. They already know where you are."

"We don't know that. That rat was just that. A rat. It doesn't mean anything. It's not like my uncle went government witness or anything. Isn't it supposed to be symbolic or something?"

He looked confused for a moment, then pinched the bridge of his nose and cursed under his breath. "Fuck, Michael…"

"What?"

He stood up without answering me. "Nothing. Go home and lock your door. Don't answer for anyone or anything unless it's me."

And just like that, he was closed off again, in complete authoritarian mode. There was clearly something he wasn't telling me. He appeared rattled, and it would have been somewhat unnerving from anyone else—but for Dante to be disturbed was much more concerning.

I followed him as he strode into the kitchen, gulping down a glass of water like he was dying of thirst. "You're hiding something, Dante, and I want to know what it is." I was talking to his back, and his shoulders tensed up immediately at hearing my demand.

"You're mistaken," he answered in a robotic tone, keeping his back to me.

I felt my anger bubbling over, and I tried to step around him to look at him. If he was going to lie to me, he could at least do it to my face. "Tell me, or I swear I'm going to go into my apartment, pack a bag, and no one will ever know where I went!"

That made him whip around and meet my angry stare. He closed the distance between us, his fingers firmly gripping my upper arms, but not quite tight enough to hurt. He tilted his head down so that his hazel eyes pierced straight through me. "Do you really want to test me, *principessa*?" he spat, face growing red from anger. "I've been doing this for a very long time. I will find you, and then you really will be living in a gilded cage."

His clenched jaw and harsh words had me completely frozen in place. "I—"

Dante interrupted me. "Go to your apartment; take Nero with you. Don't think he won't alert me if you try anything stupid."

I knew I wasn't going to get anything out of him, as angry as he was right then. And if I were honest with myself at the moment, I was a little afraid of him. Not so much that he would hurt me, but I didn't put it past him to lock me in his bathroom. At least I was being given leave to go back to my apartment, so I quickly ushered Nero to follow me, and I left the apartment without taking another glance at Dante.

I wasn't going to give up on this, though. I knew with every fiber of my being that there was something my uncle and Dante were keeping from me, and I was determined to find out what it was. I didn't know how I was going to do it, but I would figure it out. Parts of my plan were coming to me as I went back to my place and paced, Nero trailing behind me loyally. All I knew was that I couldn't let them drag me back to Manhattan. I didn't have a vast group of people here, but that was the way I liked it. Fewer people to let in, just so they could either leave, disappoint me, or die.

I thought about Eric. I knew I was going to have to talk to him soon and explain everything. He had called me several times today. I couldn't think of what to say to him, so I just didn't pick up. He was worried out of his mind, and I had spent the entire day trying to think of how to explain things to him in a way that wouldn't scare him off for good. It wasn't even just Dante and my past life that I was worried about, though. If he did have feelings for me, I was sure they would be dead and gone once he finally learned who I really was. Putting off the inevitable conversation wasn't going to work for much longer, and I knew that I might need him if I had to run away from my family.

I felt a stab in my chest when I thought about cutting off contact with my uncle. I loved him, and he was the only family I had left. But if he was going to force me back into the very life he wanted me to stay away from, I wouldn't have a choice anymore. Before I could even consider walking away from everything I had ever known, I needed some answers. And for that to happen, they had to trust me.

*Time to start going along with the program. At least for now.*

## Chapter Seven

*Dante*

The way Livia's eyes flashed with betrayal burned into my brain. The minute she left, I threw myself into a scalding shower to keep from leaving the apartment and heading for the first bar I could find, and guzzling vodka until I could forget the hurt look on her face when I sent her away. It wasn't just the fact that I realized Michael had kept something so huge from her, but also that I had actually scared her. That had never happened, not since I snuck up on her the first time. It bothered me to see the fear in her eyes. I didn't know if I could do my job effectively without instilling some fear, but if tonight was any indication, I realized with a jolt to my system that I truly didn't want her to be afraid of me. I wanted her to trust me.

*I shouldn't have put my hands on her.*

She was holding back something from me, too. I could tell by the way she shifted her gaze to look at the bridge of my nose rather than my eyes as she made her little confession. It was a classic tell, and I had played enough poker to see right through her.

Her fears were valid, I had to admit. Rival families didn't want Michael coming back, but it was more than that. The current acting boss, Augustine Lombardi, was a shifty bastard. In Michael's absence, he'd gotten very comfortable in the seat of power, and that made him one of the biggest threats to Michael and Livia. Michael trusted him and insisted that I was just looking for problems, but I knew I was right. The way he ran things was different, and I couldn't respect someone who allowed teenagers to peddle drugs for him.

It was the antithesis of what Michael set out to do. Yes, we were criminals, and ruthless at times, but we didn't screw with families or ruin kids' lives. Augustine knew that I didn't respect him, which was part of the reason why I accepted this job. It got me away from him and his snot-nosed junkies.

After my parents died and the restaurant was sold, I had a decent chunk of change of my own for the first time. And what did I do with it? I got wasted every day, dropped out of school, and started dealing for Augustine. He was only a fledgling back then, but he had the respect of enough men to have his own crew. When Michael took me under his wing and got me cleaned up, he tried to convince me that there would be no hard feelings with Augustine, but I knew that couldn't be further from the truth.

I did my best to stay away from taking drugs myself, but I wasn't about to tempt fate, either. It was hard enough to be part of this world without having some kind of vice. You get rid of one, and you replace it with another. For a long time, it was alcohol. Then it was women and smoking two packs a day, but I couldn't be trusted with the only thing that mattered to Michael with anything but a clear head. Not that I had one now, not with the way Livia wound me up every time I talked to her.

She deserved to know what really happened, and if

I had let her stay one second longer, I would have told her. I didn't know why I suddenly felt this surge of loyalty to her. This was just a job that I was doing for Michael. I told myself that over and over as I washed myself. I swore I could smell her floral perfume on my skin, and I wanted any trace of her gone. The thing that disturbed me more than any of this was that I knew that my mantra was a lie.

The second I stepped foot in Glendale, I told myself that I would have to let myself care at least a little in order to do my job. But the reality was that I cared more than just a little, and it had nothing to do with Michael. *Fuck me.*

When I got out of the shower, I threw on some jeans, not bothering with a shirt before I exited my apartment and strode across the hall. I wasn't going to bother her again tonight, but I wanted to make sure she was there. I leaned in and pressed my ear against her door, hoping to hear some sign of life inside. It was silent for a few minutes, but then I heard something that made me regret leaving my apartment.

Her soft crying was audible through the door, paired with Nero's whimpers. *Good boy, maybe you can comfort her, because I sure as hell can't.* Not without betraying Michael's trust. If he hadn't told her, then I knew it wasn't my place to do it. My loyalty would always be to Michael first, and that was how it had to stay.

I couldn't help but agonize about the reason for her sudden burst of emotion, though. Was it because I had yelled at her, or was it because of the real reason she didn't want to go back to New York? There was nothing more I could do for her tonight, and I pushed down the stab of pain I felt when I tore myself away from her door and went back inside. The only thing I could think of was to continue playing music and hope she could hear it and take it as an apology.

****

It was rare for Michael to call more than once or twice a week, but he had been understandably concerned about the warning that was left on Livia's doorstep, and he wanted to know if I made any traction with convincing her to go back home. I was honestly glad he called, because I had a huge bone to pick with him, and that bone was Livia's parents.

"She's hiding something from me. The complete and utter terror in her eyes at the idea of going back to Manhattan proved that something else is keeping her away. I tried to press her for answers, but she wouldn't tell me."

I recounted the events of the night before to Michael as I sat in my car in the campus parking lot. Livia was in class, and I picked a prime spot to keep an eye on her as she walked from one class to another across the courtyard. I left out the part about me playing the violin for her. I didn't know why, but it felt like I had crossed some invisible line. Michael trusted me with her life, but that didn't mean he would be happy about us being too friendly, either.

"I don't know what it could be. She tells me everything."

"Apparently not. You two are peas in a pod in that sense," I said dryly.

"What are you going on about, Dante? Stop talking in riddles."

I idly stroked my beard as I tried to think of a way

to ask him subtly. "You never told her about her parents."

I heard his sharp intake of breath. "You didn't say anything, did you?"

"No, but she knows something is up. She doesn't understand why people think you're a traitor. It's going to be hard to get her to cooperate with me if she knows I'm keeping something from her."

"Shit. Don't tell her anything. If she knows, she'll run for good. I know her. She won't be able to look past it." Michael's voice shook with emotion. Livia was the only thing that could render him weak, and I was beginning to understand how that felt. "Promise me."

I couldn't deny him, but it was the first time I was tempted to. I took a few deep breaths, trying to figure out how I could look her in the face and continue to lie to her, because I knew that yesterday wouldn't be the last time she would ask about it. "I promise."

When I hung up the phone, I caught sight of Livia's face through the windshield. She was walking to the studio when she spotted me. We locked eyes for a few moments before she approached the car. *Great, now she's going to guilt me for being an asshole last night.*

I unlocked the doors and let her in the passenger's side. She settled into the seat, and a few uncomfortable moments passed before she said anything. "I'm sorry. I'm really not trying to make this harder for you. I just don't want to feel powerless anymore."

Her honest statement had me reeling. She was apologizing? "You're not powerless. No one is making you do anything, okay? Tension was high last night, and we were just trying to come up with solutions to make sure you can continue to live your life the way you want to. Michael wants you to be free to do as you like. We're not ganging up on you."

When she turned to me, her eyes were shimmering. "Okay. I'll consider what my uncle said, but I really just want to finish my degree first. I won't argue when you follow me around. Just please don't interfere with my education. Art is the most important thing to me," she pleaded softly.

"What about your friend?" I didn't know why I cared, but I was curious to know what that little Irish boy meant to her. He was clearly into her.

"Eric? I'm sure he won't want anything to do with me once I tell him what's going on," she answered morosely, picking flecks of dried paint off of her jeans. "He's already suspicious because of your performance the other night, and I've been avoiding him ever since. I guess I should just be prepared to be alone for the rest of my life."

"Even if that's true, you'll never be alone. You'll always have your uncle, who loves you very much." I put my hand over hers and stroked it lightly. "And you have me to look out for you."

She stilled when my hand landed on top of hers, then she gradually relaxed under my touch. The comfort of the minimal contact surprised both of us, and neither of us moved for several minutes. "I won't do anything to harm you. If you believe nothing else I say, at least believe that."

Livia nodded slowly. "I know, Dante. Thank you."

Somehow it eased the tension from the night before, and I felt lighter as she slid out of the car and paced back to the studio. I kept myself busy on my phone trying not to obviously watch her through the window as she worked. When she finished, she waved at me as she passed my car to get into her own, and it was the first time she gave me no resistance. *Finally.*

When we got back to the apartment complex, Livia made sure to give Nero some love before she turned to leave. She surprised me when she willingly informed me she didn't plan on going out for the rest of the day before heading into her apartment for the night. I wanted to believe that she was subdued after our argument and the intervention with her uncle, but the shift had happened too quickly.

I wasn't convinced that everything had been bullshit, but I knew her sudden willingness to cooperate was. She was up to something, and I was going to find out what it was. My suspicion was cemented later that night.

I didn't want to leave the apartment as long as I knew Livia was home, so I had begun working out at home with a dumbbell set. Nero sat on the couch, his big hazel eyes following every rep I did. I chuckled to myself when I thought of him as my spotter. *That's kind of pathetic, Castellano.*

When I finished up with my workout, I went into the kitchen and guzzled some water before I jumped into the shower to clean up. I had been slacking for the past few weeks, as was clearly evident by the burning I felt in my arms. I couldn't afford to let myself get weak now. There had been no sign of any strange activity since the dead rat, but something had to be on the horizon, and I needed to be prepared for it.

I was only just getting out of the shower when I heard her soft knock on the door, and Nero's immediate pitter-pattering toward the door. I didn't know what it was about Livia that he loved so much, but I knew it was her just based on his reaction. Following the lovesick dog to the door, I wrapped the towel around my waist. But when I looked out of the peephole, no one was there.

I pulled the door open to look around, and almost stepped on what Livia had left on my doorstep. I knew what it was before I even looked at it from the smell that wafted up into my nostrils. Leaning down, I saw a plate wrapped in cellophane. *Lasagna, oh Jesus.*

I tried to resist the smile that spread across my face at that moment, but my stomach rumbled as soon as I felt the heat from the plate in my hand. Nero had no interest in the food. Instead, he raced across the hallway to shove his nose under the crack of her door, and I knew that meant she was probably watching me right now.

*I knew it. She's buttering me up. But why?*

I wasn't happy that my charge was trying to be devious, but I would gladly accept the food. I gave her a sparkling smile and a wave, knowing that she was on her side of the door watching. I laughed out loud when I heard her scoff from the other side. "Come on, Nero. I'm starving." I ushered him back inside with me and my dinner.

How could I have been so stupid to think that she was actually coming around for even a second? Livia was playing with me, and she had a pretty good idea about how to do it. The minute I dug into that lasagna, I was feeling lucky that she wasn't there with me. If she fed me like that, I would have been even more tempted to tell her everything I knew.

I could tell the sauce was homemade, and the spicy ground Italian sausage had just the right amount of kick. The lasagna noodles were perfectly cooked, and it gave me a rush of nostalgia. Memories of my parents' restaurant came flooding back to me, but it wasn't entirely unpleasant. Things were rough toward the end, but we had good times too. I wasn't sure if Livia was aware of what her cooking was doing to me, or if it was just a coincidence. Either way, I was glad that I was alone in my trip down memory lane, because I knew where it would ultimately lead me.

*You want to wear me down? Game on, Liv.*

## Chapter Eight

*Livia*

He saw right through my attempt to butter him up. *Dammit.*

Feeling defeated, I resigned back to my kitchen to eat some of the best lasagna I had ever made before wrapping up the rest and putting it in the freezer. I was sure he was enjoying it. I wasn't even trying to be cocky—I knew I was an excellent cook. It was probably half of the reason why my uncle's men needed to be constantly warned away from me. When I cooked, I cooked for an army, and inevitably they had all tasted my cooking at one point or another. They would have loved to have me as their good little housewife, not that I was interested in that kind of thing.

Maybe I had pulled out the big guns too soon, because he immediately knew I was up to something. His haughty grin once he realized it made me see that I was definitely not cut out for manipulation. I decided to tone it down a bit and hope that Dante would eventually forget about his suspicions. Obviously, I had no idea who I was up against, but it wasn't going to stop me from trying. I had to know what they were keeping from me, but unfortunately, I'd have to play the long game in order to get to the bottom of it.

I settled onto the couch and decided to tackle my

next problem—Eric. I had managed to get through the entire day without running into him, but I knew I couldn't keep it up for much longer. I found him in my contacts and dialed his number. It rang once before he picked up and gave me a frantic hello. "Eric...hey." I realized suddenly that I had no idea how to begin telling him everything. "Um...so we should probably talk about the other night." *Subtle.*

"Yeah, what was that all about? I was freaking out for days worrying about you! You just went radio silent on me," he said, making it perfectly clear that he was not happy with me at all.

"I know...It was shitty of me. Maybe we can meet up and talk. There are some things I haven't told you about me, and I think we should talk about it in person." I held the phone to my ear after I finished, nervously waiting for him to tell me to go to hell.

But he didn't. "Okay. I'm coming over right now." *Here? Oh no.* "Um..."

"What? Is he there right now?" Eric seemed to grow even more concerned. "Is he holding you prisoner or something? Who is he, Liv?"

"No, no, it's not like that at all. I'll explain everything when you get here. Just come on over." I didn't want to give him any reason to try his machismo act on Dante again, especially if I told him he was, in fact, just across the hall keeping a close eye on me.

He lived a little closer to the college than me, but it didn't take him long to get to me. I was sure he ran every red light on the way. His arrival was announced when I heard Nero doing his warning growl through Dante's apartment door, and I launched myself up from the couch to let him in before Dante came running to see what was going on.

When I threw open the door, I looked over Eric's shoulder to see Dante's door opening. I gave him a warning glare to tell him to stay where he was. Surprisingly, he backed off when he realized who it was in front of me. Eric was too busy taking in my frantic state to notice as I tugged him inside the apartment.

"You're acting really weird. Please tell me what's going on with you," he begged. "Do I need to call the police?"

"No! No police. Just sit down and I'll tell you." Eric gave a suspicious glance at my vehement refusal, but settled onto the couch and waited for me to start. I wiped my sweaty palms on my jeans and sat down beside him. "Okay. God... I don't know how to start. You know that I'm originally from New York, right?"

"Yeah. What does that have to do with anything, though?" Eric looked completely clueless as he studied my worried expression.

I took a deep breath. "It has everything to do with it. I never told you about my family because I was afraid that you would judge me for where I came from. Have you ever watched those old movies about Italians from New York...they're...you know..."

I couldn't even get myself to say the words, because even though I hated everything about that world, it felt like a betrayal to my family to admit the Mafia even existed.

His eyes widened when he finally grasped what I was trying to say. "Oh my God...your family is in the Mafia?" I braced myself for his judgmental stare and his inevitable departure from my apartment and my life, but he appeared more worried than anything else. "Are you in danger?"

"Maybe. I don't know. My uncle is in prison, and he has this idea that someone is threatening me because they don't want him to take back his place when he gets out." As I watched Eric put the pieces together, I sighed. I wasn't sure if I was doing the right thing by telling him all of this, but he was my best friend. I couldn't keep my history private forever. What I wanted more than anything else was to know I had a loyal friend who didn't judge me, knew everything about me, and accepted me for it all. Maybe Eric could have been that person for me.

"Now I understand why you never talk about your family. So...that man..." he trailed off, urging me to explain the giant who hauled me into his arms and carried me away that night.

I anxiously glanced at the front door, then back to him. "His name is Dante. He's a bodyguard, and my uncle's most trusted friend. He sent him here to protect me." He leaned back against the couch, and I fell silent for a few minutes to give him a chance to soak in everything I had just told him. I wanted so badly for him to tell me it didn't change the way he thought of me, but I couldn't even hope for that. Everyone else I told had practically run away screaming. After another minute passed, I couldn't wait anymore. "Eric, please say something."

He rubbed his eyes with the heels of his hands. "Why were you so afraid to tell me? Do you really think I would judge you?"

I willed myself to suppress my astonishment. "I...everyone else has in the past. I hoped you wouldn't. I'm sorry that I never told you. I just never thought that my past would come up. I never planned on going back to New York."

He jolted straight up. "You're going back there? With people after you? Are you insane?" His instant concern was heartwarming, and I felt myself tearing up in relief. He immediately gave me a guilty frown and softened his voice. "I'm sorry, Liv, please don't cry. I can't stand it."

His arms curled around me, and I instantly melted into his embrace. I cried freely against his shoulder as he rubbed my back. When I was able to speak without sobbing, I continued, "I don't want to go back, but I might not be able to avoid it. My uncle is convinced that he and Dante will be able to protect me better there, with their crew. But the last thing I want is to be locked in a mansion with no freedom."

"So, you are a prisoner. Tell me, what can I do? Do you want me to take you away somewhere? I have some money." He jumped up from the couch and began pacing, throwing his suggestions out to me. "But what about your degree? Maybe you can finish online, and we can go to Portland or something. It's nice, and there's lots of work for an artist out there."

I felt like I was getting whiplash as I followed his pacing back and forth in front of me. I had to squeeze my eyes shut. "Eric, slow down. I don't expect you to do any of that for me. I just wanted you to know what was going on. And maybe let me crash at your place if it comes down to that." I grabbed his hand to pull him back down to the couch. His pacing was only making me more nervous about what was to come.

He stared at me helplessly. "Why wouldn't I do whatever I could to help you? You have to know how I feel about you by now, Liv."

My worst fears were realized at that moment, because I saw a shadow over Eric's head, and met the steely gaze of Dante from behind him. I hadn't even heard the front door open. "Goddamn it," was all I could think to say.

He turned around and followed my eyes to the furious man behind him, his entire stance becoming stiff. "You! What right do you have to just bust into a single woman's apartment like this? What if she was indisposed?" Eric argued, but he fell quiet as Dante stalked toward him, seemingly becoming larger and more intimidating as he got closer. I was grateful that he left Nero in the apartment because this could only end badly.

Keeping his stare on Eric, Dante addressed me. "It's not wise to leave your front door unlocked."

I couldn't believe him. After I had mistakenly thought he would back off, he just walked into my apartment like he owned the place. "You can't just walk into my place whenever you want! What if we were doing something?"

Eric's cheeks reddened. I didn't know why I had said that, because I was just about to tell Eric that his feelings were very much not reciprocated. At the moment, I had the feeling that Dante's aversion to Eric had nothing to do with my safety, and everything to do with this strange connection we shared. A small part of me *wanted* to antagonize him.

I swore I could hear a low growl, but Nero was nowhere in sight. My eyes went wide when I realized the territorial sound had come from Dante. "See that window there?" he hinted with a snarky grin.

"What the hell? I thought you said he was just your

bodyguard?" Eric stammered at me accusingly, like I had kept something from him. Dante took a few long strides closer to him, until they were almost nose to nose. Well, nose to chin, more like. Eric straightened his back and glared at him. "You don't own her! She obviously wants nothing to do with all of this."

Dante cleared his throat and stared down at Eric with unbridled fury in his eyes. "Get. Out."

"No! Dante, leave him alone!" I shrieked, pushing my way between their bodies and giving him my own furious glare. He wouldn't dare push me aside to get to Eric. *Would he?*

"You can't trust outsiders. What did you tell him?" Dante asked me with a slightly softer tone.

I rolled my eyes and lied through my teeth. "Nothing. He knows nothing except that you're protecting me from someone who's stalking me." I turned back to Eric to give him a silent plea to go along with it. I was almost a hundred percent sure that Dante didn't buy one bit of that, but he took a step back and let his shoulders relax. Only slightly.

Eric chimed in. "Do you want me to stay?"

I darted my eyes between the two furious men. I couldn't very well continue our line of conversation with Dante there, so I slowly shook my head. "I'm all right, Eric. I have to talk to Dante. Just…thank you for being here for me. I'll see you at school." I outstretched my arms to hug him, and I could feel Dante's eyes burning into the back of my head the entire time.

Eric gave Dante a wide berth as he left the apartment. He was completely terrified. If my confession didn't scare him off entirely, I was sure that my bodyguard just had. Once the front door shut, I let out a breath and sat down again, my face buried in my hands. Dante continued to stand there watching me before he finally approached me, setting himself down next to me.

When several minutes passed, I finally broke the silence. "What was that all about? Eric wasn't doing anything wrong, and now he's probably never going to talk to me again." I peeked up at him, and he didn't look contrite at all.

He had the nerve to smirk at me. "Good. He's a lovesick little boy. Pathetic."

I jumped up and stood in front of him. "That's none of your business! Why do you even care?" I saw an almost imperceptible furrowing of his brows, as if he didn't even know the reason for his little outburst. Quickly, he raised himself from the couch and started to walk away. I shouted after him, "If I want to sleep with every man in California, it has nothing to do with you!"

Dante froze in place, his shoulders tensing up. He turned and closed the gap between us in two long strides. "You don't want to do something like that."

He slowed when he reached me, his eyes seeming to glow even brighter as he kept them glued to mine. Leisurely, he brought his hand up to cup my cheek. The sudden gentleness from him surprised me, even as his calloused palm touched my skin. I wanted to recoil, but his warmth held me captive. "And he doesn't excite you, anyway."

"And you think you do?" The words came out breathier than I had meant them to, and I couldn't help but notice his eyes darkening. *Is he...aroused?*

He laughed softly as he trailed his hand down from my face to the side of my neck, causing me to shiver under his touch. His thumb slowly brushed over the throbbing pulse point. I felt my heart racing, and the knowing look in his eyes told me he did, too. "Your body betrays you, Liv…"

*What is he doing to me?*

I felt myself physically quivering when his stare trailed down to my lips, and he leaned in. He was going to kiss me. *Oh my God, and I think I want him to.* His moist breath hit my cheek on his way to my ear. "Dante…what are you doing?" My voice shook, and I had to hold in my gasp when I felt his lips touch my earlobe.

He whispered into my ear, "Proving a point."

As soon as the words left his mouth, he turned around and quickly left, slamming the door behind him. I held in my breath until I heard his own door slam shut as well, then I ran to my door to lock it. I slid the deadbolt and the chain before I rushed into my bedroom, locking that door too for good measure. I didn't know what point he was trying to prove, but the only point he got across was that I would never leave my front door unlocked again.

The more I paced in my bedroom, the more confused I became. I knew we had become slightly more friendly as time went on, but what was that? Surely, he didn't care about me that way. He barely tolerated me most of the time. When he wasn't scolding me or laughing at me, he looked like he wanted to strangle me. And someone connected to the Mafia was the absolute last person I would have ever considered dating. And I didn't consider dating anyone, anyway.

*Oh God. That's it.* He didn't want to date me. He wanted to have sex with me. Did he think that just because my uncle had given him his permission to look after me whatever way he saw fit, that meant he could do what he liked with me? Nowhere in the realm of possibility did I think my uncle would give him permission to sleep with his niece.

I fell into bed and tried to go to sleep to forget about the insanity of the events of my night, but I tossed and turned for hours. I had never felt that visceral reaction to someone touching me before, and it scared me that the only thing I was mad about at that moment was that he stopped. As I struggled to find a comfortable position to fall asleep, the anger grew. Why couldn't he just keep his hands to himself? I was more confused than ever, and I hated that every time I tried to distract myself, my thoughts drifted off to him again. His rough palm against my cheek. His soft lips against my ear. What the hell was he thinking?

## Chapter Nine

*Dante*

What the fuck was I thinking? The minute I closed my door, I immediately launched my fist into the wall, leaving a splintered hole in the drywall. I didn't know what had gotten into me. I had only intended to listen in to make sure that she wasn't telling the Irishman her entire life story, only to hear him confessing his feelings for her. It was pretty obvious to anyone who had eyes, but for some reason, hearing it out loud made me irrationally angry. I was on autopilot when I jiggled the knob and shamelessly let myself in. On one hand, I wanted to be mad at her for not locking the door. On the other, I was glad she hadn't.

What would have happened if I waited ten more minutes? I shook my head to get rid of the unpleasant image of her in bed with him, his pasty hands all over her. What was the alternative? It wasn't like I could have her. I admitted to myself that some allure about her drew me in, but I couldn't go there. How could that work, anyway? Everything about me infuriated her. We fought all the time.

*Stop it, Castellano.*

This was not happening. I was thirteen years older than her. She was too young for me. I had to stop this line of thinking right away. Even if she were my age, and we didn't butt heads constantly, it couldn't happen.

The images ran through my head over and over like an old black and white movie. Her insistence when she tried to deny that her heart was racing, even though I could feel it hammering against my fingers. The way her lips parted when I leaned in closer. She wanted me to kiss her, but she was trying with every ounce of her being to hold in what I knew would be explosive passion. It seemed to scare her, and to be honest, my own feelings scared me too. My earlier impression that she had no fight in her was completely misguided. Livia was probably the most disciplined person I had ever met, and it only made me want to break down her defenses even more. What lay just below the surface?

The way she goaded me, practically threatening me with other men…it was everything I could do not to pull her in and claim her with a kiss that would make her forget that any other man had ever touched her. I almost did it, too. When I pulled back from her and looked into her dilated eyes, I saw those deep coffee brown irises, full of fear and arousal. I affected her. I knew that clear as day.

Then the ultimate cock-block. I thought of Michael. He hadn't made me swear not to lay a hand on her—that was how much he trusted me with her. He knew that I would never do anything to betray him, and yet I already had. If Michael had the slightest inkling of the filthy thoughts going on in my head right then, he would break out of prison and off me himself. Sure, I didn't even kiss her. But I thought about it. Many times. And if she had so much as let out a little moan of pleasure when I touched her, I wouldn't have been able to stop myself from taking her to my bed. I knew she wanted me, but I could see the turmoil in her every muscle, fighting it. Her determination was enviable.

I told myself at that moment that I had only been doing to break down her walls, just like she was trying to do to me with her agreeableness and her delicious cooking, but that was bullshit. It may have started as a game, but it only revealed the truth of what I had felt since that first moment I saw her through the studio window. I was in awe of her, and I saw something in her that reminded me of myself. We were such different people, and somehow, we were cut from the same cloth.

I wanted to go back there right now and make her see it, but my loyalty to Michael stopped me in my tracks. I was overcome with despondence when it hit me that this was the first time I felt such a powerful pull toward a woman, and there was nothing I could do about it.

I snapped out of it when I heard the whimpering at my feet. Even Nero was sad. He lapped at my bloody knuckles, gazing up at me with his cartoony eyes. "Don't pity me, Nero. I know I'm fucked."

Suddenly, I wondered how I was going to face her from now on. The second I touched her and all but made my declaration, I crossed a line, and things could never be the same again. Every time she looked at me, she would know that I desired her. And her, being the vindictive little brat she was, she knew exactly how to drive me crazy. *She better not test me.* Unless she wanted to attend an Irish wake before I dragged her back to New York.

I went into the bathroom to bandage my wrecked hand. As I looked down at the broken skin and blood dripping into the pure white porcelain sink, reality dawned on me. The only thing I could do was keep my distance. If I did that, maybe the feelings she stirred in me would go away. This could only end in disaster, anyway. She would hate life with a brute like me, and we would destroy each other. I was halfway there already.

By the time I had the wound covered, I was resolute. I would go back to what I did that first week. Follow her to school, follow her home, make sure no thugs went near her, and that was it. *Don't talk to her, and most definitely do not touch her.* Touching her again would be the end of me in more ways than one. How ironic that I grazed her beautiful face, feeling sparks like fire on my skin, and then I punished that hand by smashing it into a wall. It was like that Bible verse from my old Sunday school days. *If thy right hand offends thee, cut it off.* And I didn't even believe in God.

I had never felt more tempted to drink in my life, and that was saying a whole hell of a lot. I wanted to quell my anger at the situation, and this was the first time since arriving in California that even my violin wasn't good enough. I was too afraid that if I picked it up right then, it would splinter and break in my hands. Obviously, I couldn't trust myself with anything, so I continued to sit there and stew in my anger for hours, facing the wall while Nero stared at me with his tail between his legs.

Eventually, I knocked out on the couch into a fitful sleep, but I couldn't even escape Livia in my dreams. Her hooded eyes, her trembling under my touch, those soft pants she couldn't hold back when I leaned closer to her face. That moment of weakness was going to haunt me for the rest of my life. Those two minutes before I stormed out of her apartment played on a constant loop in my subconscious, and when I woke at seven the next morning, I felt like I hadn't slept a damn wink.

I waited until Nero alerted me to her presence in the hallway, and I watched her until she disappeared down the hall into the elevator. I didn't think I could stand to see her looking at me with those *how could you* eyes. Once I allotted enough time for her to get in her car downstairs, I headed down and followed her to school. I was being a goddamned coward.

In the parking lot at my usual spot, I watched her walk to class with bundles of art supplies in her arms. She looked like she hadn't slept either, and another pang of guilt rang through me. I did that to her. Hopefully, after some time passed, we would both be able to forget that moment and go on as usual. The threat would pass, and then I could go back to New York, back to my usual work and routines, and forget that I had ever touched her silky olive skin. *Yeah, right. I'm screwed, and I know it.*

This was how it went for the next two weeks. I was careful not to run into her in the hallway at home, and I kept my distance on campus. The Irishman was nowhere to be found, which I was extremely grateful for. I didn't think I could stop myself from intervening if I saw him sniffing around her again. I knew it was selfish.

Livia didn't seek me out either. I wanted to be a little offended that my sudden absence didn't seem to bother her, but I realized that she was finally getting what she wanted from the beginning—for me not to interfere with her life. Only two more weeks until graduation, and then Michael would reassess, deciding whether or not he wanted me to sweep her back to Manhattan, kicking and screaming. At this point, I would have preferred to leave her in California, as far away from me as she could get. Out of sight, out of mind. The part of me that I was desperately trying to suppress secretly dreaded the idea of leaving her behind, even if I knew that it was the right thing to do.

\*\*\*\*

It wasn't until the following week that I noticed a strange car that I hadn't seen before in the parking lot, at the far end near the street. I had painstakingly taken down the license plates of every car that frequented the school to make sure that there were no other strange people following her around, aside from me. I was so lost in my mental maelstrom that I didn't take stock of the vehicles in the parking lot that day, and I was kicking myself when I looked across the courtyard and saw the beat-up green sedan. It did almost too good a job blending in, that somehow it stuck out like a sore thumb.

I reached down and touched my gun in my holster to make sure it was ready and accessible as I got out of the car and stalked across the courtyard, moving slowly with crowds of students and any obstacle that would obscure my approach. I darted across the center of campus until there was only a building between me and the mysterious car, and the moment I rounded the corner, the car screeched as it backed out and sped away. I hadn't even gotten a chance to see the face of the driver, but I didn't need to. If he was so suspicious that he somehow managed to see me coming for him, it was definitely not a student. That meant he knew exactly who I was and why I was there. Was he just waiting for me to let my guard down so he could grab Livia? *Over my dead body.*

When I started heading back to my car, I saw Livia leaving the studio. She hadn't caught sight of me yet, and I saw her peering into my windshield, noting that I wasn't inside my car. That seemed to put her on alert immediately, and she nervously scanned the area.

When her eyes fell on me, she sighed in what looked to be relief. I tried to suppress the smile that wanted to break out across my face. I told myself it most likely had nothing to do with me personally. She probably only got comfortable with having me as protection, and when I was suddenly gone, she was wary. I knew she was attracted to me, but I scolded myself for thinking even for a second that she felt anything more than that. *She doesn't know you, Castellano.* If she did, she would never want anything more to do with me.

Knowing it would be odd to ignore her now, I walked toward her as non-threateningly as possible. I wanted more than ever not to frighten her, especially not with what was definitely a thug in disguise tracking her. There was no more doubt about it. They knew exactly where she was, and it was only a matter of time before leaving wouldn't be just a possibility anymore, but an inevitability.

I wanted to be all business, but I couldn't help myself, seeing her pale face and wide eyes on me when I reached her. "Are you all right?"

She hesitated. "Hey…I was just confused when I got out and saw you weren't in your car. Where were you?"

I didn't want to tell her just yet about her new stalker, and I wanted things to go back to normal between us. As normal as a relationship between a bodyguard and his charge could be, anyway. "Did you miss me, *principessa*?"

With a scoff of derision, she turned away from me. "Never."

*And we're back to basics.*

## Chapter Ten

*Livia*

These last two weeks have been absolutely miserable. Ever since the night of Dante's confrontation, I never felt more alone. Eric hadn't spoken to me since, just as I had feared, and Dante was nowhere to be seen. I knew he still watched me, but he rarely ventured to speak. I couldn't understand his actions at all.

The most frustrating thing was that I hadn't realized how comfortable I had become with Dante's presence until it was gone. I caught sight of his car behind me every day like clockwork as I went from home to school, and then from school to home. A few times I had even gone into the hallway when I had no reason to be there, just hoping he would come out to talk to me. I didn't know exactly what I expected him to say to me, but I needed some kind of explanation. What was he trying to do? Did he regret what he did?

His jealous argument with Eric, our near kiss, and his hand. I noticed the scabbed and bruised knuckles on the steering wheel of his car, and it took everything in me not to ask him about it. I didn't know what was going on anymore. I should have been used to it, this stoic mute man act—but even though it had been so normal for me growing up, it only felt unnatural coming from him now.

Maybe he fought with Eric, and that was why I

hadn't seen him anywhere for two weeks; but I pushed that thought aside immediately. Surely, he wouldn't have actually done something to him just because he confessed to having feelings for me. Did he even care? He looked to me like the type of man who had women hanging on him wherever he went, and he probably had lots of experience. Dante hadn't seemed too lost without me around, so I couldn't imagine that moment had him as confused as I was.

I had no idea how to go about getting answers from Dante, because the few words we had exchanged only told me that our strange moment was just that—a passing moment that meant absolutely nothing. Maybe I had been reading too much into it and bringing it up to him could only lead to more awkwardness. *Grow up, Liv. He was just playing with you.*

I thought perhaps I could at least fix things with Eric. I was sure he could tell that I didn't reciprocate his feelings, and that was why he had been ignoring me. He just needed some time to lick his wounds, but I thought that two weeks was more than enough to get over it. We couldn't let this ruin our friendship forever.

I called him the next day when I was getting ready to leave the studio for the day. It wasn't as if I was getting any meaningful work done, anyway. Mostly I had been staring at a canvas and splashing paint on it haphazardly in an attempt to encourage some kind of inspiration, but none ever came. This was the longest slump I had ever experienced. I had suffered from creative block ever since Dante came into my life, and the loss of my best friend only made it worse. I was completely stumped, and something had to give soon. Luckily, he picked up right before the call went to voicemail.

"Livia," he said in a stoic voice.

"Hey, Eric. Can we talk?"

"I don't know. Can we? Or is your bulldog going to be waiting around a corner to jump me?"

I deserved that, I thought with a sigh. "Look, I'm sorry about how we left things a few weeks ago, but I wanted to give you some time to process everything. Honestly, I kind of expected to at least see you around campus, but you've been a ghost." I paced in front of my failed attempt at a painting while I waited for what felt like an hour for him to respond.

"I've been busy," he said in a noncommittal tone, as if he didn't care that we went from seeing each other every day to zero contact. He cleared his throat. "If you want to talk, you can come to my place. I'm not going to your apartment with that guy hanging around."

"That's kind of unavoidable. He follows me everywhere. That's his job." I put it as nicely as possible. I didn't want it to look like I was defending Dante and his actions from that night.

Eric let out a frustrated exhale. "So, lose him. Just for an hour or two so we can talk without being interrupted."

I took a quick look around the studio. I supposed I could dip into the bathroom while he was looking, then try to sneak out the back door when he wasn't, so he would think I was in the bathroom while I made my escape. "Okay…I think I can manage that, but I won't be able to get to my car without him seeing me."

"I'll get a cab and wait for you on the other side of campus…" he paused for a moment before he continued, "I hate this. It shouldn't be like this."

"I know. I'm sorry."

After ducking into the bathroom, I waited, peeking out of the bathroom door for a moment when Dante was distracted. The moment I saw his eyes drift down toward his phone, I grabbed my stuff and ran out the back door. I darted across the campus and scanned the area for Eric. I finally spotted him near the back building, standing next to a cab. He waved me over, and we climbed in and sped off.

Looking out the back window, I didn't see Dante or his car behind us. I was surprised to find that I had finally managed to dodge him. I couldn't help but feel a little guilty, but how else was I going to finish a conversation with Eric when Dante was always showing up and spewing his testosterone all over him?

A wave of relief came over me when we got to Eric's apartment, and he locked the door behind us. "Just in case," he said with a ghost of a smile on his face.

I was grateful for the slightly lightened tension between us, and we sat down in his kitchen to have a cup of coffee. "So…what have you been up to? You said you were busy, but I can't imagine what with, seeing as you haven't been around taking photos of me as usual."

He sighed and slumped down in the chair across from me, as if he were hoping I wouldn't bring it up. "I had to find some other subjects for my work since things between us got so…you know. I didn't feel right about showing up like nothing happened. Do you really not see why I was so bothered after that night?"

I did, but I was hoping that he would have been able to look past it. I decided to feign ignorance. "What do you mean?"

The tension grew thicker with his every breath. It was as if a switch had flipped, and now he was angry.

"You left me hanging! I told you how I felt about you, and then Dante showed up, and I was quickly ushered out like you were taking out the trash." He rolled his eyes and ran his fingers through his curly locks. "You never even gave me a response, and when you didn't call, I figured it would be best to stay away from you."

"You were just never going to talk to me again?" As I glared at Eric, I noted that he wasn't denying it. He wasn't saying anything at all. "So that's it then? If I don't return your feelings, then you want nothing to do with me? What kind of friend does that?"

"We were never just friends, Liv. I could see that you had been through some shit, and I was trying to be patient and wait for you to come around."

I couldn't believe my ears. He was admitting to being the epitome of that nice-guy-finishes-last act. *Unbelievable.*

I let out a nervous chuckle. "For four years? Eric, I never gave you the impression that I wanted anything more than friendship!"

He went on as if I hadn't even said anything. "And then this guy comes out of nowhere, basically acting like you belong to him. He might as well have pissed on you in front of me!"

I physically recoiled at his harsh language. Eric had always been so mild-mannered, but that man was suddenly nowhere to be found. His fair skin was red with anger, and his attitude told me that he was done playing nice. "It's not like that with him. But even if it was, I don't feel that way for you. I'm sorry! I wish I did, honestly. It would make things so much easier."

He got up from the table and began to pace back and forth in front of me. "Girls like you always pull that line.

You string along guys that actually give a shit about you, but in the end, you always go for the men that treat you like garbage. You do know he's just going to screw you, hurt you, and then leave you, right? I feel stupid for thinking you wanted to be with me."

My fury reached its boiling point. "Did you not hear what I said? This has nothing to do with Dante. I didn't love you before, and I certainly don't now! Here I thought you were the best friend I've ever had, but you were only waiting to get me in your bed!" I slammed my hand onto the table, making my cup of coffee shake and tip over. The hot coffee poured onto my hand and splashed up onto my shirt.

The tears fell freely now. What else could possibly go wrong? My life was a mess, my friendship with Eric was as good as over, and I didn't even have Dante. Not that I had ever really had him to begin with. My hand stung, my shirt was drenched, and yet he just stood there staring me down like I was the one in the wrong.

I left Eric standing there and ran into his bathroom to try and clean myself up, but it was hard to see what I was doing with angry tears blurring my vision. I heard a soft knock on the door, and then Eric's voice, slightly subdued. "I'm going back to school. You can let yourself out when you're done."

I thought he was going to apologize, but this was really it. Still dabbing coffee from my shirt with bits of toilet paper, I swung open the bathroom door. "You're just going to cut me off?"

His anger had subsided a little, but his voice still had an edge of pain to it that only made me feel more guilty. "I don't want to, Liv, but I can't be around you right now. It hurts too much. I'm sorry."

I couldn't believe he was so angry with me that he left his own apartment to get away from me. I fled out of the bathroom to look for another shirt to wear. After opening his closet, I grabbed one of his shirts and chuckled at myself. A last parting gift from my only friend, who was never really my friend in the first place.

I threw my own shirt, which was covered in paint and coffee, into the trash. It wasn't really necessary to steal one of his shirts, but part of me wanted Eric to see it when he came back. I wanted him to realize what a huge mistake he made by rebuking my friendship just because I couldn't give him what he wanted. Slipping on his shirt, I walked back into the living room to grab my things and leave, but immediately a merciless banging started on the door.

Stepping up on my tip toes to peer into the peephole, I saw an infuriated Dante on the other side. "I know you're in there, Livia. Open the door. It is not a good idea for you to be running off without telling me right now." His voice had a certain warning to it that I knew was best not to ignore. He almost sounded worried.

I opened the door and was taken aback when I took in his disheveled, heavily breathing form. Dante pushed himself inside immediately, forcing me to take several steps back. "Sorry," I responded in a shaky voice. "I just wanted to talk to Eric without you interfering."

If it was possible, he became even more enraged. "Why are you wearing his clothes?"

I avoided his eyes and leaned down to grab my things. I really didn't want to talk about it, knowing that it would only make me cry again. The last thing I wanted was to be vulnerable again in front of this man. "It doesn't matter. Let's just go home."

He stopped me, standing between me and the door as he extended his hand toward me. I gasped when his palm touched my face again. The same sparks I felt two weeks ago came back with a vengeance, but it made me angrier than aroused. He traced his fingers down from my cheek to my jaw, holding it in his large hand. He tilted my head back and forced me to meet his eyes. "Tell me you didn't fuck him."

I pulled away from him. "No, of course not! Not that it's any of your business. How dare you?"

He let out an offended scoff, taking a step back. "How dare I what? Show concern when you run away from me, and I find you in another man's apartment, wearing his clothes, and looking like a wet rat? What did he do to you?"

The way he said "another man", as if that would have been some kind of betrayal. Who the hell did he think he was? Dante seemed to realize what he said, and I could have sworn I saw a hint of embarrassment in his angry gaze.

I was so tired of arguing. Even though I had so few people in my life, I was still always fighting with either Dante, my uncle, and now Eric, too. The frustration was driving me crazy, and I wanted to stop being confronted by everyone.

"Yes, how dare you? You have no right to be angry with me. Everyone is so concerned about who I'm messing around with, which is so ironic because I've never even had sex! Happy? You and every other man in my life have scared off any potential sex for twenty-two years, so let it go already!"

I hadn't meant to let that slip, and I slapped my mouth shut immediately when it registered in Dante's mind. His mouth fell open from shock, which was a novel look for him. He didn't seem to know how to respond to my confession and responded in a low voice, "You've been crying. Did you have a fight?"

"Yeah, so what?" I gathered up my stuff and started to open the front door. Dante stepped in front of me and pulled my supplies out of my arms and put them down again. "What do you want from me?"

"I want to know what happened. Where is the little shit?" He softened his tone slightly, but something in the back of my mind told me that my confession pleased him.

Clearly, I wasn't getting away with not telling him anything. "I'll tell you, but can we please go home first? I don't want to be here when he comes back. Please…"

He gave in, gathering up my things for me and driving me home, speeding like a demon the entire way. I didn't care that I had left my car at school. I just wanted to go home and forget that this entire day had happened. I already dreaded the idea of going back there tomorrow and possibly seeing Eric again. The way he looked at me like I had ripped his heart out without a care killed me.

Dante stayed silent beside me, his hands gripping the wheel so hard that I thought for sure he would snap it in half. I turned my face away from him, looking out the window so that I could let the tears fall without him seeing.

Chapter Eleven

*Dante*

My mind swirled with a thousand questions as Livia got into my car and we promptly fell into a deathly silence. I wanted to berate her with questions, but she looked as if she were ready to pass out from the stress. I didn't want to be the one to send her off the deep end. Something happened between her and Eric that she didn't want me to know. Maybe she was worried for his safety, and she would have been right to be worried. If he hurt her, I would eagerly and happily tear him apart.

Most of all, I wanted to know that she was okay. Selfishly, though, I was curious about her accidental confession. It had shocked me at the moment, but the more I thought about it, the more sense it made. Michael had chased men away from her for her entire youth. It was no wonder she didn't have any relationships under her belt. However, it was a surprise to find out that she hadn't gone through a wild phase over the past four years without Michael to chase away those horny guys she went to school with. She was still a virgin at twenty-two years old.

That blasted my previous suspicion out of the water. When she hinted that something had happened to her, even with all of Michael's protections, naturally I had assumed it meant something of a sexual nature had happened without her consent. If it wasn't that, then what was it?

I pulled into the apartment building, and Livia was so dazed that she kept staring out the window even when I got out of the car. Coming to the passenger side, I knocked on the window lightly to alert her. "We're here. I don't want you to fall out when I open the door."

She seemed to appreciate it, giving me a small smile before she took her forehead off the glass and allowed me to open the door. She climbed out and waited while I retrieved her things, then we went upstairs. I was growing more concerned for her by the minute, because when I led her to my place instead of hers, she didn't argue. She only followed me inside and fell onto the couch beside Nero, who was understandably excited after barely seeing her for two weeks. He settled down after a few minutes, resting his head on her lap while she stroked his head and stared off into space.

"Will you please talk to me now? I'm worried about you."

I sat on the coffee table in front of her, leaning down to meet her eyes. I wanted so badly at that moment to take her hands in mine, but something stopped me from touching her. That was a lie. Michael was in my head, stopping me from touching her. Livia took several deep breaths but didn't say a word.

Just when I was about to give up, she blinked back her tears and spoke. "If you must know, Eric told me I'm a tease, and that he wants nothing more to do with me. You got what you wanted."

I couldn't lie to myself, I was happy about that. But I couldn't let her see that. She was obviously distraught over the loss of her only friend, and she didn't need me rubbing it in. "I'm not happy that you're upset. But you have to understand, I've been around a while, and I've known way too many guys like him. They pretend to be nice, but turn nasty when they don't get what they want. I pegged him as one of those guys the minute I saw him leering at you." When Livia scowled again, I lowered my voice. I didn't want her to think I was getting any pleasure out of this. "I'm only trying to protect you. Don't make me the villain."

"How long is *a while*?"

Why did she care about my age? "I'm thirty-five."

"Oh."

"Why?" I asked her when she fell silent again and continued petting Nero.

She shrugged nonchalantly. "I don't know anything about you, and I'm completely alone now. I might as well get to know the only person I'm allowed to talk to."

She sounded so defeated, and I felt a pang of guilt in my gut. "We're a lot more alike than you think, Liv."

Her eyes widened slightly. "How?"

"We grew up in the same environment, more or less. We're both artistic. I'm no mystery," I offered, hoping that would be the end of the line of discussion. But she wouldn't be the Livia I knew if such little information satisfied her.

"I don't think that's true. Your parents owned Castellano's, didn't they? What happened to them?"

I wanted so badly to change the subject, but the way she was imploring me to level with her, with her soft brown eyes and deflated stature. I couldn't say no. Not to her. *Time to open up, Castellano. She needs it.*

I took a deep breath to steel myself for this. I had never told the details of that night to anyone in my life, and I didn't think I was ready for it. Not even Michael knew everything. He only came after it was over. "It's a long story. I don't want to unload something so heavy on you after the day you've had." It was my last-ditch attempt to delay this conversation, but she wasn't having it.

She was the one who made the first move, taking both of my hands in hers. "It would be a relief to tell someone, wouldn't it? Please, Dante. It's not like I would tell anyone…I have no one else."

Her soft hands in mine did something to me that I had never experienced before. I felt myself relaxing as long as her skin was in contact with mine, and I knew she was right. It would be a relief to tell someone, but what would she think of me once she knew everything? I couldn't deny that if she looked at me like I was a monster, I would be broken. Anyone else, and I would have welcomed it. But not Livia. I cared what she thought of me more than I wanted to admit. I cared about *her* more than I wanted to admit, and it was almost as terrifying as the prospect of exposing the darkest secret I had. I held on to it like a treasure for eighteen years, but it was no treasure. It was like a cancerous tumor that ate at me every moment I continued to keep it inside. No more.

*Speak.* "My childhood was normal for the first twelve years of my life. My parents had the restaurant, and it was doing pretty well. Unfortunately, when I turned thirteen, we fell on hard times. We were at risk of losing the restaurant because my parents couldn't pay the rent. They were friends with some of your family's associates, and they offered to help us out. But you know what that means by now."

She nodded slowly. "They were indebted to the Mafia."

"Exactly. They expected my father to cover up crimes as payment because we had no money to pay them back. I won't describe it to you, but I'm sure you can imagine. I heard more than they thought I did. I used to play violin for the restaurant band, so I was around when they would come with heavy bags after closing." I paused to rub my eyes tiredly. I hadn't even gotten to the worst parts, and I was already weary.

Surprisingly, she reached out to take my hands again. "Go on," she urged.

Livia looked at me with such compassion, I felt my tense muscles loosening with every word I spilled. "The things my father had to see on a daily basis drove him crazy. He started drinking and taking out his frustrations on my mother and me. I wasn't strong enough at the time to protect her. I started rebelling, which didn't make things any easier on them. My mom jumped on the bandwagon, too. They had drunken fights almost every night. I remember falling asleep with my pillow bunched up around my head to drown out the screaming."

She squeezed my hands. "I'm sorry you had to go through that...If you don't want to continue, you don't have to."

I shook my head, shocking myself with my refusal. "I need to get it out." She only nodded and stroked her thumbs across the backs of my hands. Somehow, it made it easier for me to continue. "One night when I was seventeen, I came home from a late shift at the restaurant. He was beating her again, and I was so fed up with it, I decided to confront him. Kick his ass if I had to. But it wasn't just his normal beating. My mom was lying on the floor, unmoving, as he repeatedly wailed on her. I ran to him and tried to pull him off her, screaming that he was killing her. That seemed to get him to snap back to reality, and he backed off. I fell to the floor and held her in my arms, trying to wake her up...but she didn't. I heard her breathing become rattled until it stopped completely."

I heard Livia's light sniffling, and knew she was crying for me. "Oh, Dante...I'm so sorry..."

"You won't feel that way when I tell you what happened next." For a second, I met her tearful gaze. Unable to mask it anymore, I let her see the emotion in my eyes. I was terrified, and more vulnerable than I had ever allowed myself to be in front of another person.

She stayed silent for several moments. I felt naked as she seemed to read me like a book. "I won't judge you. You can tell me."

*She knows where this is going.*

I closed my eyes and took a deep breath. "I saw red. My father was as shocked as I was when I came at him. I had never tried to fight him before, and that was to my advantage. After he realized what was going on in his drunken stupor, he tried to fight me off. But I was younger and stronger; I couldn't stop myself." I paused, forcing myself to get out the words I knew she was expecting. "My father was the first man I ever killed."

I was afraid to peer up at Livia, knowing that she would have a horrified look on her face, and I couldn't bear to see it. "Dante...look at me."

I lifted my head to meet her willful gaze. "I know I'm a monster, Liv. You don't have to tell me."

She pulled my hands into her lap, forcing me closer. For such a petite thing, her strength was surprising, but I didn't have the will to resist her. "You did nothing wrong. You were stopping him from hurting anyone else. You've been carrying around this blame for too long…" I almost felt her breath on my face when she inched closer to me. It was startling how natural it felt to have her this close. "I tried to ask my uncle about the Castellanos, but he told me that no one really knew what happened. He helped you cover it up, didn't he?"

I was completely taken aback that she not only didn't look horrified, but she thought I did the right thing. I shook my head in disbelief. "He did. He tried to help me afterward, but I wasn't ready to accept help at the time. I beat myself up for years. It was only when I started drinking and hanging around with Augustine Lombardi's crew that Michael finally stepped in and told me that enough was enough. He took me under his wing, and that's why I feel like I owe him my life now. I wouldn't have one if it weren't for him."

Her gaze hardened when she heard Augustine's name, but she didn't speak on it. "Thank you for trusting me with this. It means a lot."

I squeezed her hands. "There are only two people I care about. Michael, and now you. I'm telling you this so you know that you can trust me with anything. I won't let anyone hurt you—not even myself. Which is why I've been so absent lately." I didn't know why I admitted that, but something about the compassionate hold she had on me broke the dam, and I couldn't stop pouring my soul out to her.

She cocked her head. "What do you mean?"

"Michael would never forgive me if he found out I so much as laid a hand on you. But I couldn't stop myself. I had to keep my distance. I didn't expect to feel so territorial when I heard Eric confessing his feelings for you, and it took me by surprise…" I trailed off, not knowing how to continue. "All I knew was that I needed to touch you. I had to see if the connection I felt was real, and if you felt it, too."

"You do care for me…" Livia said in a hopeful voice, and my eyes snapped up to meet hers.

I nodded slowly. "It can't happen, Liv."

She frowned. "I know."

Once we both acknowledged that fact, it set us into motion. My hands flew up to cup her face, and I slowly inched closer until my nose was touching hers, and we were breathing each other's breath. Livia's lips parted, and her hands landed on my chest, the warmth of her palms sinking into my skin. "What are you doing to me? Why do you affect me this way?"

"I could ask you the same thing," she panted.

I leaned in closer. Every nerve ending screamed for contact; I couldn't help myself from slanting my mouth over hers softly. When our lips touched, it was like nothing I had ever felt before. Her lips were like velvet, pliable, and warm. So warm. Her quiet gasp when my tongue poked out to taste her lower lip sent a shockwave through my body, and I was rock hard in an instant.

Livia trailed her hands down my abs and curled around my torso to pull me closer. I wrapped my arms around her, cupping the back of her head with one hand as I deepened the kiss. I couldn't believe how smooth and supple her lips were. I had slept with many women in the past, and never in my life had a simple kiss made me so ready, so fast.

"Oh, God," she moaned. "I never knew it could be like this. Don't stop."

"We shouldn't," I whispered as my lips met hers again like magnets. Her tongue poked out to touch mine, and almost without being aware of my actions, I hoisted her up from the couch into my arms. I kept my hands and lips on her while I walked her back against the wall. I needed every inch of her touching me, her warmth seeping into me to calm the storm that raged inside.

When she was pressed between my body and the wall, she tilted her head back and I immediately ran my tongue up from her collarbone to the lobe of her ear. Livia shivered, reaching up to slide her hand under my shirt. Her palm felt like fire against my bare skin. Not taking my lips away from her neck, I traced the curves of her body, and cupped her breasts, making her whimper in pleasure. *Holy fuck.* "Jesus…Livia…"

When my mouth closed over her throat and I lapped at her taut flesh, she let out another breathy moan that had my cock twitching. "Dante…please. I need you."

I felt her arch her back, and my hardened bulge made contact with her heated groin. That snapped me back into reality. I immediately slapped my hands against the wall next to her head and took several deep breaths. I had to calm myself before I reached the point of no return.

Livia gazed up at me. "Why did you stop?"

Pushing away from the wall, I rasped, "I can't. I have to respect you, Liv. Don't tempt me again." I started to walk away from her. I couldn't see her like this without losing myself in her. Her hooded eyes and heaving breasts were so captivating that I couldn't trust myself to stop if I looked at her again.

"Maybe I don't want you to."

She didn't know what she was saying. I couldn't

betray Michael, and I certainly couldn't be her first lover. She was too young, too innocent. Her first time should have been with someone who wasn't a murderer. "You don't mean that. That's not the kind of woman you are. I won't taint you."

She laughed humorlessly at me. "So, I'm the holy virgin now? How could you be so backward?"

"It's not just that, and you know it. Michael would never approve. He would kill me himself if he knew that I touched you." I shook my head. "I'm sorry."

It was silent for so long that I risked turning around to look at her. She wasn't there. Livia had quietly snuck back to her own apartment, leaving my door wide open. Maybe it was an invitation to come after her, but I was frozen in place. *Let her go.*

## Chapter Twelve

*Livia*

I couldn't believe he would kiss me like that, then send me away as if nothing happened. Clearly, he wanted me just as much as I wanted him. I admitted that freely to myself now, and to him as well. Shocked that he actually opened up to me, I found myself overcome with emotion and warmth for him. But more than that, it gave me hope. Hope that I could truly be myself with someone one day. Maybe even with him. The fact that I was even considering it was a shock to me, but we had well and truly crossed a line at this point.

We were intimate in the most meaningful way. I had never felt closer to someone in my entire life, and the physical aspect had surprisingly little to do with it. When he pulled me close and I could feel his panting breaths tickling my lips, I was completely lost in Dante—physically and emotionally.

Somehow, his story didn't surprise me. I knew just from the way he carried himself that he had been through some darkness in his past. And I had yet to see him do anything that made him come across like a monster, as he feared. He could be a little intense at times with his angry outbursts, but he had never hurt me intentionally. I doubted he ever would. As the hole in his wall testified, I knew without a doubt that he would rather hurt himself than me. When I passed the cracked drywall as I left his apartment, it only confirmed what I already suspected about him. He was self-destructive, and the story he told me solidified that theory. When Dante hurt, he would make himself hurt even more as punishment. He truly believed everything that happened to him was his own fault and that he deserved it.

He couldn't even look at me when I left. That was how affected he was just by having me close to him. I knew that because I felt the same way. When he pushed away from me, I wanted to cry. My whole damn life, I had never found someone who made me feel the way Dante did, but because of his undying loyalty to my uncle, nothing could ever happen between us. And again, I was losing someone else to this cursed life I was born into.

I felt my heart stab with pain for both of us, because now we were both being punished. He could tell himself this was about my uncle all he wanted, but I knew the truth. Dante believed with every ounce of his being that he didn't deserve happiness.

I knew I meant something to him now, being one of the few people he cared about in this entire world. But his loyalty would always be to my uncle first, and me second. In a way, I understood where he was coming from. On the other hand, what just transpired between us couldn't be swept under the rug. I couldn't possibly classify him as just a family friend after he shoved me up against a wall, plunged his tongue in my mouth, and ground his hips against me.

I wanted to be angry that he ever let himself touch me, but every time I thought about it, I felt my face heat with excitement. And then I remembered his tragic upbringing and my heart ached again. I didn't know how to comfort him without making it look like I pitied him. One thing was glaringly obvious—he hated looking weak.

With his confession, he gave a piece of himself to me. In one heartfelt talk with him, I learned more about Dante in one night than I had in the month I had known him on a semi-personal level. All I wanted from that moment was to give a piece of myself back to him, but he wouldn't let me.

*Am I falling for him? Oh my God...*

****

I had one last assignment to complete before graduation. Luckily, I didn't need to be on campus to do it. After the way we left things, I was not looking forward to the idea of running into Eric at school. Or more accurately, the way *he* left things. I barely caught even a glimpse of him for days and concluded he was avoiding me.

The canvas on the easel in front of me had just a few strokes of paint lying across it. I was still in such a rut that I didn't know where to start. I knew I needed to finish this if I wanted to graduate before Dante decided it was too dangerous for me to stay here any longer.

Of course, that got me thinking about him again. I did not need this distraction right now. Still upset with him for shutting me down, my mind swirled with conflicting emotions. Anger, sympathy, arousal, and another emotion that I didn't even want to think about. I couldn't help but replay our kiss over and over in my head. Never had I felt such an explosion of arousal before, and it had me reeling still. Every time I touched my lips, I remembered how his felt pressing against mine. Mostly, it was the desperation of his kiss that threw me.

Without realizing it, I snapped back into reality and saw that I had been lazily sweeping my brush with deep blue paint across the top of the canvas. A memory immediately popped into my mind of that first night I officially met Dante at the fountain. His intense hazel eyes almost glowed against the moonlight as he stared down at me with curiosity on his face, like he was trying to figure me out. Even then, the fascination had been there.

I painted some stars into the night sky, and a flowing fountain in thick, abstract brushstrokes. Then, the silhouette of a man and a woman, almost touching. I painted layer over layer of paint to give it texture. In my mind, it signified the almost tactile sensation whenever I knew he was near, like sparks of electricity in the air. I smiled to myself when I took a few steps back to take in the finished product.

I felt like I had come to some sort of conclusion with the painting. It was cathartic because once I cleaned up my brushes and left the painting to dry, I was exhausted. Not just physically, but emotionally. I fell into a deep sleep, only waking after five in the evening when my phone rang.

I jolted awake with a start and reached for my phone, answering it before I even checked to see who it was. When I heard the automatic recording, I let out a breath and accepted the call. "Hi, uncle. How are you?"

"I'm doing well, sweetie," he announced. "I have good news."

I perked up immediately, sitting up in bed and turning my light on. "Tell me."

He did a drumroll on the wall with his knuckles before making his announcement. "I'm getting out next month."

"Oh my God! I'm so happy…Did you tell Dante already? I'm sure he's thrilled."

I leaned back and let out a giant sigh of relief. Even though going back to New York was the last thing I wanted, at least I could visit Uncle Michael with no glass between us. Or—he could come to California to visit me.

"Why would I tell him first? You're my baby. I'll let you give him the good news. He tells me you two are finally getting along, and I can't tell you how relieved that makes me."

I was suddenly overjoyed that he couldn't see the flush of embarrassment on my face. Uncle Michael didn't know just how well we were getting along. Over the past week, it had been nothing but longing looks and terse conversations in the hallway. The angry tension had gone, but it was replaced with sexual tension. I couldn't decide which one was more maddening.

Every time we spoke, even if only for a few minutes, I would catch his eyes drifting down to my lips. Almost instinctively, I would start to lean in before he realized where we were and pulled away from me again. He was determined to resist us, but I was done fighting it. I didn't know what kind of future we could possibly have together, but all I knew was that I wanted the chance to find out.

When I hung up with my uncle, I went to check my mail before heading up to Dante to tell him the good news. I collected the stack of letters and jumped back into the elevator. During the short ride, I mindlessly flipped through the envelopes and saw one that had no return address on it. It only had my name written on the front in the center of the envelope.

Weird. I slid my finger underneath the seal and broke it, reaching inside to feel a rigid piece of paper. When I tipped it over, a photograph fluttered out and onto the floor of the elevator. I looked down and froze in place. I almost didn't want to touch it, so I picked it up by the corner to get a closer look. It was a photo of me sleeping in bed. In my own apartment. Not through a window, but *in* the bedroom. How the hell had someone gotten inside to take a photo of me?

I stomped out of the elevator and straight to Dante's door, banging on it loudly. It must have spooked Nero because he began frantically barking. When Dante opened the door, Nero calmed down, realizing the loud noises had been coming from me. I looked up at Dante's alarmed face.

"What's wrong? Are you okay?"

I shoved the photo at him. "Did you do this to scare me so I'll agree to leave?"

He took it from me and glanced down at it. His brows knitted together in confusion, and then his face contorted in what I could only describe as intense fury. "I didn't do this, Livia, you have my word on that. I will find who did, and he will fucking pay for it with his life."

My eyes widened at his fervent promise of revenge. "Dante…they only took a photo. Whoever did it could have killed me if they wanted to."

That only seemed to alarm him more, and I was kicking myself for it as he visibly tensed up in front of me. He shook his head, finally meeting my eyes. "They violated your privacy, and that is unforgivable. You can't stay here any longer, and I think you know that."

I shriveled in front of him. "I know…And I'm sorry."

"For what?"

"For accusing you. I just don't understand how someone could get into my apartment when I only have one key. And with Nero around…It doesn't make sense," I explained, hoping that he would understand.

He looked almost guilty for a second, and then he became alarmed again when a flash of realization crossed his face. He frantically checked his pockets. "I'm sorry, Liv. I have a duplicate key. But…now I can't find it. Fuck!"

He ran back inside his apartment and straight to his couch to lift up all the cushions. "But how would anyone else have gotten it off of you?" I wanted to be annoyed that he had a secret key to my apartment, but it was the least of my worries right then.

"I must have dropped it that day when I saw that suspicious car on campus. This is my own fault. *Coglione*!" He straightened up and swiftly kicked the couch with his boot once, twice, and a third time while letting out a string of furious curses in both Italian and English. "If something had happened to you…*Cazzo*!"

I strode over to him quickly and grabbed his hands. "Hey! Stop! I'm not hurt. Don't worry about it now. It can't be helped." He leaned down to get closer to me, pressing his forehead to mine gently. He was almost vibrating with rage, but it soon seemed to melt as we stood there for several minutes. His heavy breathing slowed when I extended my hand and stroked his bearded cheek. "I'm okay, Dante. Just calm down. I'm here."

I felt his warm breath against my lips when he spoke

again in a whisper. "I need to get you out of here. Go pack your things."

I stayed where I was. "Kiss me first." It would calm him down if he would have stopped being so stubborn.

His eyes widened slightly. "No."

"Please. I know you want to," I said as I inched slightly closer to him, my lips a hair's width away from his.

"Of course, I want to. I can barely stand to look at your face without thinking about the way your eyes glazed over when I had you in my arms. You don't know half of the things I want to do to you. But that doesn't mean I'm going to do them," he whispered against my lips before pulling away again.

I felt myself shiver at his sensual tone, but I let it go. At least he admitted it now. "Fine. I'll go get packed."

Dante shooed Nero to follow me back into my apartment. And like the good boy he was, he guarded me while I packed as many clothes and essentials as I could into my one rolling luggage bag.

*Oh shit, my painting!*

I covered it with a piece of cloth and rushed back to double-check that I had everything. I swung my purse over my shoulder and halted when I found Dante in my living room. "Are you ready? Do you have your license and passport and everything?"

I stared at him. "Yeah…"

"What's wrong?"

"I'm scared to go back," I admitted, hoping that he wouldn't ask any follow-up questions.

He touched my arm comfortingly. "I know. But you won't be alone. I won't let anything happen to you." His eyes trailed behind me to the covered painting in the kitchen. "New work?"

"Yeah. I just finished it." I blushed under his intense gaze. "I need to drop it off at school. It's my last assignment. Do you mind? I know I'm going to miss graduation, but I at least want to complete my last class."

He started walking over to it as he responded back to me, "I think we can do that quickly on the way to the airport. Can I see it?" He sensed my hesitation right away and frowned at me. "I've been watching you for a month. I know how talented you are by now, Liv. Don't be shy."

He didn't wait for me to answer as he swiftly lifted the sheet covering the canvas. I closed my eyes when I heard his sharp intake of breath. I felt like a pathetic girl doodling his name in my notebook. He had to know he inspired this painting, and the thought was embarrassing.

My eyes flew open when his lips smashed into mine. "Oh!"

I let out a gasp of surprise, which he quickly swallowed as his hands slid up into my hair and he pressed his body to mine. The fear I felt a moment ago dissipated as the tingles took over. His hands fisted in my hair, holding me in place. As if there were anywhere else I'd have rather been. I kissed him back eagerly, holding onto his biceps as my knees buckled from the pleasure of his sudden onset of passion. When I gently sucked on his tongue, he let out a throaty moan and pulled back slightly.

"What the hell are you doing to me?" he groaned against my lips.

I flashed him a wide grin. "I take it that means you like my painting?"

"I love it," he whispered sincerely as he tried to gain his composure from the brief, but powerful kiss. "You got your kiss, you stubborn girl. Let's go." His words came out casually, as if he had been doing me a favor, but I knew damn well he needed that as much as I did.

He pulled out his phone and snapped a quick picture of the painting before grabbing it and my luggage for me and heading out the door. I smiled to myself as I followed him out, locking my door behind me. Not like it mattered. Whoever had broken in had the key, anyway. Dante slipped into his apartment one last time to get what little he brought with him, and Nero's carrier for the flight.

I should have been more upset about leaving, but I felt like there was nothing here for me anymore. I was missing graduation, but at least I knew I would get my degree like I had wanted to. Eric was done with me and I had no other friends to miss me. And the more I got to know Dante, the more I knew that I wanted to be wherever he was. Going back to Manhattan terrified me, but I trusted Dante. I was sure he would deliver on his promise to keep me safe.

Once we got to campus, I rushed into the classroom to hand over my painting and give my teacher a hurried, mostly bullshit explanation. I told her it was a family emergency, and once she wished me luck with a concerned gaze, I ran out before she could ask anything else. Dante kept his eyes on me like a hawk, with his hand strategically placed inside his jacket. He kept his hand on his gun as he scanned the area for threats.

I jogged back up to him by the car, where he immediately pulled me into his arms and escorted me to the passenger's side. I thought we had gotten over his fear of being too close to me, but then I realized he was only using his body to shield me in case anyone was about to pop out of the bushes. I rolled my eyes as he pushed me into the car and ran back to his side, before taking off like a demon, as usual.

I didn't think I had ever made it to the airport so quickly in my life, not even when I was fleeing Manhattan all that time ago. I had seen Dante protective before, but never in full bodyguard mode. He was tense and alert, his eyes catching every little detail about our surroundings. His arm didn't leave my waist for the entire trek through the airport, his other hand holding all of our bags while I rolled the carrier with Nero inside behind me.

"You know, I can carry something if that'll help," I offered, only to get an abrupt one-word answer. No.

He had already bought us tickets on his phone, and he had them ready to scan when we got to the gate. I really hoped he would at least calm down while we were on the plane. He was so tight and controlled, it only served to make me more nervous. Did he really think they would come into an airport and shoot at us or something?

Even at the last minute, he somehow managed to get us first-class seats. Once we had settled into our adjoining seats twenty minutes later, I decided there was some benefit to his intimidation tactics. Finally, it looked as if Dante had let out the breath he had been holding in ever since he saw the photograph in my hands.

Chapter Thirteen

*Dante*

I was accustomed to the stress that came with my line of work, but the fear I felt as I rushed Livia to the airport was unmatched. I found myself struggling to keep my composure so that she wouldn't know just how worried I was. I didn't quite manage it, because she was the one who kept comforting me during the run to the gate. That had never happened to me before, and it was a novel feeling for me. Usually, I was confident in my ability, never second-guessing myself to the point of uncertainty. With Livia, that veil of self-assuredness was absent. She made me feel vulnerable, and frankly, it scared the shit out of me.

During takeoff, she slid her hand across the armrest and intertwined her fingers with mine. I closed my eyes, trying to will myself to pull my hand away or make some move to get her to stop touching me...but I couldn't. It startled me that I couldn't resist her, and it stymied me even more that I felt my jaw unclenching the moment her warmth seeped into my skin. *How is she able to calm me so easily?* I shouldn't have been able to be rendered so weak just from a simple touch. And what was worse, she knew damn well the power she had over me. Something told me that this was going to be a very long trip.

We fell into a numbed silence, hands interlocked on

the armrest between us for the first two hours of the flight. I was sure she had a million thoughts going through her mind, as she usually did when she stayed quiet like that. That was one more way we were alike. Meanwhile, I agonized over my stupid mistake. I came to California to protect her, and yet, I had essentially opened the door as if to say, "She's right here, come get her!"

If she had been hurt because of me, I would never forgive myself. I wouldn't even need Michael to kill me—I would just go ahead and jump off the Brooklyn bridge myself. How could I have been so stupid as to just walk around with her spare key in my pocket? I would have noticed its absence sooner if I had just hooked it onto my keyring with the others. I could have had her lock changed and stopped all of this before it was too late.

I wished more than anything that Michael had a contraband cell phone right now. I hated that this sequence of events was set into motion, and I had no way of telling him what was going on without him calling me first. I didn't believe in any of that juju crap, but I wished I had as I tried to telepathically send a message to him— telling him to call us as soon as possible.

What I just couldn't understand was, how the hell had that guy gotten the key from me? When he spotted me from his car, he had been at least thirty feet away. Was this asshole's vision good enough to spot a key falling from my pocket, assume it belonged to Livia, and then backtrack later on to retrieve it? It didn't make any sense to me, but it was possible. Lots of things were possible. They could have bribed the landlord or picked the lock. Even if the latter was true, I knew without a shadow of a doubt that I blamed myself. How could I not?

I had originally thought it absurd to move into the apartment across the hall from her, but even with me being that close, it still wasn't enough to keep her from being left vulnerable. And what had Nero been doing that he didn't alert me to someone in the hallway? I felt a gentle squeeze of my hand and caught Livia watching me with a nervous expression on her face. I turned to her and tried to slip on my expressionless mask before she caught on. Of course, she did anyway. *I'm losing my touch.*

"Are you all right?" she asked in her soft voice. I wished she would stop being so sweet to me and gazing up at me with her compassion and…I couldn't even think of it. There was no way.

I scoffed at her to break the train of thought. "Shouldn't I be asking you that?"

"Maybe you should stop worrying about what we should and shouldn't be doing, and just work together to get through this," she retorted stubbornly. It was obvious she was talking about more than just the idea of her comforting my frazzled senses. "I wish we could call my uncle right now and tell him what's happening."

"Me too." I squeezed her hand back, and I looked down at her to see her gnawing on her lip. "What are you thinking about?"

"Where are we going when we get back to Manhattan? Isn't it a bad idea to go back to my uncle's house?"

"Originally, that was the plan once Michael got out. But that's not ideal right now." I lowered my voice so that the people across the aisle couldn't hear us. "I would take you to my apartment, but I'm not sure that's wise either, since we don't know who's behind this. They might know where I live."

When she chuckled, I turned to her in confusion. Why the hell did she think this was funny? "I just assumed you and my uncle had a million safe houses ready."

"What makes you think we don't? I hadn't intended on it becoming necessary to use them, but we always have a backup plan," I informed her with a slight smirk, and she rolled her eyes at me in derision. "Don't ever second guess my ability to look after you."

The smile faded from her face at my serious tone. "Sorry..." She pulled her hand from mine and sat back in her seat, slightly subdued. A few minutes of silence passed before she spoke again. "I trust you with my life, Dante."

I had to use every ounce of will in my body not to pull her into my arms in front of all the passengers on the plane. She had no idea what her statement meant to me, and yet she had thrown it out there so willingly. I took a few deep breaths before I could answer, trying and failing to keep the emotion from my voice. "Thank you. And I hope you know that if I have to lay down my life for yours, I will. Gladly."

I hesitantly met her eyes then, and I saw the shimmering golden flecks in her irises that held me captive every time I looked into them. "I hope it doesn't come to that. I would never forgive myself..."

Her voice shook with emotion, and I couldn't stop myself from doing something to comfort her. I took her hand in mine again and brought it up to my lips, just brushing them across her dainty knuckles. "Don't worry about that. I'm tougher than you think. And we have

Nero, too." I said it to comfort her, even if I found myself being slightly irritated at Nero right then for missing the threat that had been right under his nose.

A flight attendant walked up then and took note of Livia's hand in mine. I quickly dropped it like it was on fire. "How are we doing? Can I bring you and your wife anything to drink?"

Livia's eyes widened into saucers as she turned an ungodly shade of red. I was a little embarrassed, too, but her reaction was so extreme that it caused me to let out a rumbling laugh. I turned to the flight attendant and flashed her a wide smile. "Yeah, I think me and the missus will have some water."

She let out a nervous cough, and the flight attendant gave us both a confused stare. "Flat or sparkling, sir?"

"Baby?" I asked her with a devious smirk on my face.

"Um…sparkling," she whispered, avoiding my eyes and gnawing on her lip again. When the flight attendant handed us our drinks and walked away, Livia gave me a mighty scowl. "I have to beg you to kiss me, and now we're married? You're such an ass."

I laughed at her and let go of her hand. "I made a judgment call. We're incognito."

With the tension lifted for a while, we settled down and fell into a comfortable silence. I pulled out a book and read. While Livia dozed off on my shoulder, I reminded myself that we were basically running for our lives, even though I felt more content than I had in longer than I could remember. Her soft, even breaths, her long waves falling into her face. She looked like an angel to me, and I reached out to push her hair behind her ear. She was out for the count, so I allowed myself a gentle brush against her cheek.

"What I feel for you terrifies me…" I whispered.

As if to tell me to rein myself in, it was then that the pilot came on over the intercom, disturbing the peaceful few moments I spent staring down at the most beautiful woman I had ever seen. Livia stirred halfway through the announcement. "What was that?"

I threw my head back and groaned in frustration. "God fucking dammit. There's a snowstorm in New York. We have to take a layover in Illinois."

She thought about it for a minute, then shrugged. "Well, no one would think to look for us there, right? It might actually be a good thing. They might be expecting us to be back in New York by tomorrow. Instead, we'll be in another state entirely."

It was obvious that the only reason she didn't seem bothered was that it postponed our arrival to what was probably the last place on Earth she wanted to go.

"That's true, but this is a sudden unknown variable. I don't like it," I argued, rubbing my beard with my hand. "I haven't had time to scope out somewhere safe for you."

"Well, we can't do anything about that now. As long as you're there, I'm not worried." I didn't know where her sudden confidence in me had come from, but I wasn't about to pretend it didn't make me feel ten feet tall.

I couldn't help but grin back at her. "All right then, *principessa.* Buckle your seatbelt."

Livia buckled herself in and gave me a shy giggle as she did it. "I guess that makes you the *principe* then, since we're married now."

I let out a laugh, and when her eyes sparkled at me, I felt my chest tighten. "I suppose so."

124

We landed in Illinois, and once we had our baggage and Nero, I immediately went to the front desk to inquire about when we could get on the next flight. I didn't like the idea of being somewhere I wasn't familiar, and I really didn't want to end up in a hotel room with Livia. My restraint was so close to breaking, I didn't think I could take being in any more enclosed spaces with her without giving in to what I knew we both wanted.

The clerk checked her computer as a line formed behind me. "Oh, I'm sorry, sir. It looks like all flights have been canceled for the next two days due to inclement weather. However, there are a few hotels nearby, and a rental car station outside. Although, I don't recommend trying to drive into New York tonight," she informed me with an apologetic smile.

I turned back to Livia, who gave me a questioning look. "So? What do we do?"

I sighed and ran my fingers through my hair. "It looks like we have no choice. Let's get a car and head to a hotel."

While I rented us a car, Livia waited at the curb with Nero and our luggage, looking up nearby hotels on her phone. Once we got into our inconspicuous compact vehicle, I shook my head. How the hell was I supposed to drive over ten hours in this thing?

She didn't seem to notice my discomfort, or she ignored it as she showed me the results of her search. "It looks like a lot of flights have been canceled, so there aren't many bookings available. This one has a room that accepts dogs, so maybe we should hurry."

I paused for a moment. "Just one room?"

She immediately rolled her eyes at me. "I'm not that terrible of a roommate, and it's just until tomorrow, anyway. I'll sleep in the tub if it makes you feel better."

"What kind of man would I be if I let you do that? I'm perfectly capable of controlling myself." I wasn't sure if I was trying to convince her or myself more.

"I'm aware," she responded with a sardonic tone as I pulled out of the airport and headed to the hotel.

When we arrived, we managed to snag the last available room, and I quickly ushered Livia and Nero into the room while I brought in all of our bags. She opened hers and started digging through it with shaking hands. "What are you looking for?"

"Something warm to sleep in. It's freezing in here!"

I padded over to the heater and cranked it up as far as it would go. "I guess you're not used to the northern climate anymore. Go take a hot shower. By the time you get out, it should have warmed up in here."

"What about you?"

"I can handle it. I'll go after you," I offered, sitting on the edge of the only bed in the room. I needed her to leave me alone for a minute so I could get my bearings and figure out how I was going to spend the night with her without touching her. *I could make a pillow divider. Ugh, stop being a pussy, Castellano.*

Livia left to go shower, and I considered forming a makeshift cot on the floor with extra blankets and pillows, but I knew she would think I was being ridiculous. It wasn't that she was purposely doing anything to tempt me, but just her mere proximity sent me into a tailspin. The smell of her floral perfume, the way she smiled at me, and her smooth skin. Everything about her was intoxicating to me. Even the tilt of her lips when she scowled at me turned me on. *Get a grip.*

I hadn't come up with any viable solutions by the

Treasured

time she got out of the shower. I avoided looking at her while I grabbed some clothes and headed into the bathroom. Maybe a hot shower would calm my raging hormones. I felt like a teenager. It was ridiculous. I had more pressing things to worry about.

Chapter Fourteen

*Livia*

Dante ran from me like I had cooties. I wasn't doing anything, yet he got into such a panic about the prospect of spending a night with me in a hotel. It only convinced me more that he didn't trust himself not to cross the line again. I made sure to put on my most chaste pajamas, mostly because I was still cold, but also so I couldn't be accused of being some kind of devil temptress.

Settling on a baggy sweater and a pair of leggings, I curled up on the bed with Nero, idly scratching behind his ears while scrolling through my phone. With a naked Dante less than ten feet from me, I tried to distract myself, but nothing worked. I involuntarily bit my lip and tried to imagine it. The peephole in my apartment door allowed me to see his bare chest once. I hadn't gotten as good a look as I wanted, though. I had convinced myself at the time that I didn't want to see it and was kicking myself for it now.

As if he heard my thoughts, the door cracked open. As steam billowed out, I got a full view of his chest in the mirror's reflection above the sink. The tattoo on his chest was an enormous owl with its wings outstretched across his pecs, all in dark ink. The light smattering of hair partially obscured it, but it only made me more curious. One bicep sported a crowned Italian horn with intricate black knotwork going up his arm and almost up to his neck.

I tried so hard not to stare, but I couldn't help my eyes trailing up and down his firm body. He was so…broad. Not overly muscled, but solid and strong. He didn't have a six-pack, but his stomach was flat and toned, slightly narrower than his chest. My eyes followed the downward trajectory, and I felt the heat in my cheeks as I caught just a tiny glimpse of his hip bones where he had a towel firmly wrapped around himself.

I only managed to tear my eyes from him when he caught me peeking at him, his gaze flicking up to mine in the mirror. For just a brief second, every bit of his yearning was apparent on his face. When I noted his clenched jaw and darkened eyes, I blushed furiously and quickly snapped my attention back to my phone. The searing stare was too much for me to handle. I avoided looking directly at him when he finally exited the bathroom in sweatpants and a plain black T-shirt.

He didn't say a word about me ogling him as he sat down in bed beside me, with Nero between us. "You should get some sleep, Liv."

"I'm too wired," I answered, feeling the anxiety beginning to creep back in.

This was the closest I had been to New York in four years. Even Illinois was too close for comfort, and I felt the knot in my stomach tightening. Every minute that passed was a minute closer to when we would drive into New York, and I'd have to face my old life again.

"I can get us something to eat if you're hungry," he offered. It seemed like he was doing everything he could to make me comfortable and distract us from our closeness.

I shook my head and flopped down onto my back. Nero instinctively nudged himself closer to me and laid his head on my stomach, and Dante fell silent as he lay down next to me. It felt like hours of silence passed. Every time I glanced over at him, his eyes were open, but he looked like he was a thousand miles away from me. How could we be sitting inches apart and still feel so distant?

"Dante?"

"Yes?"

"What are you thinking about?"

He turned his head to me and expelled a gentle sigh. "I want to ease your worries about going back home, but it's hard for me to do that when I know there's something you're not telling me." I stayed silent for a moment, hoping he would let it go. "Livia. Does it have something to do with Augustine Lombardi?"

My flinch at hearing his name was involuntary. I prayed that Dante hadn't noticed, but he immediately sat up in bed and set his piercing gaze on me. "I can't…Dante, please don't do this now." I sat back up and pulled my knees to my chest.

"You have to know there's nothing you could tell me that would make me see you any differently."

*Can I do this?* Dante had opened up to me about the worst night of his life. Maybe I owed it to him to tell him about mine. I didn't think he would judge me, but the fear of having to relive it, and say the words…Maybe if I could do this, he would see that I truly opened up, and he would let me in again.

I sighed deeply. "I'm not worried about you seeing me differently. I'm worried about you treating me differently. You already act like I'm this untouchable princess. I don't want you to be afraid to be near me once you know what they did to me…"

He stiffened. *"They?"*

"I can't do this." I launched myself off the bed and started heading to the bathroom. An escape. Anything. I felt a sob traveling up my throat, but I was quickly spun around to face Dante. I was afraid to see his face, but I felt nothing but tenderness emanating from his light grip on my shoulders. He wasn't going to let this go.

He took both of my hands in his and pressed them against his chest, his intense stare boring into me. "Livia Rossi, I swear to you that I will not treat you differently. You know more about me than anyone else alive, even more than Michael. Let me be a relief to you, like you were to me. You deserve that."

I couldn't bear to move from the spot, so I stood in front of him and let my hands fall from his chest before I started talking. Letting out a shaky breath, I steeled myself to relive my worst nightmare. I started at the beginning, desperately trying to give myself time to gain the strength to reveal everything for the first time.

"When my uncle was arrested, I was angry with him. He put these insurmountable walls around me for most of my life so no one could get too close. I didn't realize how sheltered I was until he was gone. I was suddenly alone in a big house with just a few of his men watching me round the clock. I planned to go to an art school in New York at the time, and I had already applied. But I wanted to have one last hurrah before I went to school, and I knew with him gone, there would be no consequences."

Wordlessly, Dante led me to the chair beside the bed and sat me down. He waited patiently, sitting at the edge of the bed with his expression straight. I could tell it was a struggle for him, but I had to give him credit for it. "I can only imagine how hard it was for you," he said as he kept his compassionate gaze glued to me. "What happened?"

"I did what any other eighteen-year-old girl would do. I rebelled. I wanted to see what I was missing out on, so I started going out at night, drinking, and going to clubs. That kind of stuff. Because my uncle had warned his crew not to get too friendly with me, they didn't know what to do with me. They couldn't stop me from going out, and I was always dodging them when they tried to follow me. Maybe if I hadn't done that, I could have avoided..." I trailed off, unable to spit out the words.

Dante shook his head, stopping my train of thought in its tracks. "You can't think about what-ifs. They'll just drive you crazy, and it won't change anything."

I nodded slowly in agreement. "I know..." I couldn't stall anymore, blinking back tears when I gazed up at Dante again. "I wanted to know what was so special about this world that my uncle always kept me sheltered from. I found myself at...Augustine's club." I barely managed to choke out his name without throwing up. "Uncle Michael used to talk about him, and I was curious. I knew it was stupid and that it was obvious I was looking for trouble, but I couldn't stop myself. I ran into some men, who I later found out were part of the Leone family. They invited me to party with them, and I stupidly accepted."

Dante closed his eyes, but stayed silent and let me go on. "I...I drank a lot. But not enough to be as dizzy as I was only twenty minutes after I got there. They took me to the VIP room where dancers were stripping for the men. I thought that they only wanted to shock me, but they expected me to join in. The way those men looked at me…it still turns my stomach to think about it."

I felt Dante reach forward and grab the arms of the chair, sliding me closer to him. He took hold of my hands. It was only when he pried them off my knees that I realized I had been digging my nails into them. "What did they do to you?"

He was desperately trying to conceal the shakiness of his voice. He was angry, upset, or a mixture of both. I couldn't force myself to meet his eyes. "They drugged me. By the time I was in the back room with them, I was so disoriented I knew I couldn't fight my way out of there. This one man in a suit…I can't remember his name, suggested that I showed up there because I wanted to be one of his whores. All the men egged him on and they ordered me to 'audition'. The more I tried to refuse, the angrier he got. He told me that if I wasn't good in bed, then maybe I could be a stripper for Augustine now that my uncle was gone. When I tried to wiggle out of his grip, he trapped me against the wall…he pushed his gun against my head and said that if I didn't choose, he would blow my head off and send it to my uncle in prison."

"Livia…" Dante's voice came out broken, but he said nothing else. I couldn't blame him. What could you say after hearing something like this?

I let the tears fall because my head ached from the strain of keeping them inside. I clenched my hands around Dante's, and he didn't wince, even though I was sure it was uncomfortable. I needed to grip something to force myself to continue talking. "They weren't going to let me leave. My choices were to either let them have sex with me or strip and dance for them. And I just couldn't…"

Dante couldn't hold back his anger anymore. I felt his hands shaking in my grasp, and I risked glancing up at his eyes. I was terrified of what I'd see in them, but when I did, I saw nothing but unbridled fury and pain.

"I chose to strip. Anything to keep them from touching me. They all laughed at me while I danced for them, crying and shaking. The suited man told me that if I ever told anyone, he would get one of his incarcerated men to kill my uncle, and then me. They tossed me out onto the street after they were done being entertained by my humiliation. I took a cab home, and I never mentioned it to a single soul—until now."

Now that it was out, I was numb, and I reached up to wipe the wetness from my cheeks. Dante seemed to vibrate from anger, but he was trying with much difficulty to hold it in, if only to keep from upsetting me further. "This does not reflect badly on you in any way. This is all on the disgusting men who go to Augustine's club. They're the ones who should be filled with shame. Not you, Livia. Never you." His passionate words shocked me, and my gaze flew up to his again. His stare bore into me when he made his next declaration. "Nothing like that will ever happen to you again, I promise you that."

I felt myself begin to shake at his threatening tone. "What are you going to do?"

His face was the picture of determination and barely restrained vengeance. "I'm going to find out the names of everyone who even knew of your presence there that night, and then I'm going to kill them all. And I need to have a talk with Augustine."

I felt my blood run cold, but I couldn't muster up the moral outrage to tell him not to avenge me. Those men had humiliated me, and it gave me a tingle of satisfaction knowing that Dante would kill anyone who harmed me.

Even though Augustine himself hadn't been there, just hearing his name reduced me to a trembling mess. I had no illusions that he took issue with the way his "friends" treated me—it was par for the course in this world, as I learned. But I didn't want Dante to cause trouble with our rivals for my honor either. "Wouldn't that start a war, though?"

"I don't fucking care. We've been working with these people for years, not knowing that they violated the boss' niece. There is no excuse, and it ends now." He stood, pulling me up with him. Before I could say another word, he swept me up into his arms as if I weighed nothing and laid me on the bed. "I just want to hold you. Is that all right?"

I couldn't help my eyes from welling up again, and I reached for him desperately. "Yes…please." He still wanted to touch me after knowing my greatest shame. And beyond that, to comfort me, and forgo his fear of crossing the line again.

He slid under the blankets beside me, coaxing me to cuddle against him. I laid my head on his chest and wrapped my arm around his torso, snuggling closer until my entire front was touching his side. He enveloped me in his warm embrace, saying nothing for a long time, only stroking my back with his fingertips and repeatedly placing soft kisses on the top of my head. After a while, he spoke. "So that's the real reason you left."

I nodded against his chest. "The very next day I applied to an art school in southern California, and when my uncle called, he somehow seemed relieved that I wanted to get away from New York. I don't know if he had an idea that something happened, but he let me go."

"Trust me, if he knew what Lombardi let happen in his club, he would not still be acting boss right now, but in the Hudson."

I closed my eyes tightly and buried my face in his chest. "Do you still promise to treat me the same way?" I asked him. I didn't want to talk about those monsters anymore. I only wanted to feel his gentle hold on me and his deep voice reassuring me. I needed to know that he still saw me for who I was, and not by my trauma.

"I promise. And I'm sorry…" he spoke softly into my hair.

"What for?"

He took a deep breath. "For making you relive it. I knew there had to be a reason why you were so scared when I touched you…"

Shaking my head, I backed away and sat up. "No. I was only scared because I've never felt anything like that before. I didn't know how to take it. For four years, I didn't even feel sexual arousal because it was repulsive to me. It only reminded me of that night. But…when you touched me, it was the first time I felt that intimate connection without the immediate disgust. I felt…treasured."

I heard his gasp, and he tilted my head back to face him. "You are treasured. I would rather die myself than ever hurt you. You know that, right?"

I nodded through my tears. "I know."

He pulled my face toward his and slowly leaned in to give me a gentle kiss on my forehead. "Livia…"

"What?"

"You have no idea how much you mean to me…come here." He opened his arms again to let me in, squeezing me tightly to his chest. "You need rest."

As much as I wanted to keep talking, I was exhausted, and his gentle stroking of my back quickly lulled me into the most peaceful sleep I had ever had. My last thoughts as I drifted off were of him. My feelings for him were growing stronger every day.

*Had he been about to tell me that he loved me?*

## Chapter Fifteen

*Dante*

I woke up, slightly disoriented. I was used to waking up in my New York apartment, sometimes alone, sometimes with a random woman from the night before. Waking up alone in California with Nero at my feet was something different. Now I felt a warm ass against me, and Nero's wet nose touching my feet. I was still half-asleep, remembering the dream I had the night before.

As the details slowly faded in my memory, I tried to hold onto the sensation of Liv's warm lips on my chest, her soft moans of pleasure, and her fingers entwined with mine. I smiled to myself and ground my morning wood against her before reality rushed back to me.

*What am I doing?*

I jolted back from her, then peeked over her shoulder to check that she was still asleep. Her eyes were closed, and her breathing was even, so I tried to pull myself away without waking her. I shook my head as I headed into the bathroom to deal with the stubborn erection that felt like it would never go away. I had made another promise that would be very hard for me to keep.

In no way did I judge her for what she went through that night, but as I became more alert, washing my face and brushing my teeth, the details from the night before sank in. I couldn't even fathom the terror she felt, being forced to entertain those disgusting pricks, not even knowing if she would get out alive. She was violated, humiliated, and tossed aside like trash. What person could go through that and not have some severe hang-ups afterward?

I wanted so badly to keep my promise not to treat her any differently, but every time I caught myself looking at her in a sexual way, I remembered the revulsion on her face describing those men. Would she think I was just as bad as them if I gave in to my desire for her? I couldn't even believe I was considering it. Something between us had changed, and I knew it would be impossible to go back to the way it was before. We now knew each other on a deeper level than anyone else did, and I couldn't keep telling myself that it was just physical chemistry or professional concern. Her confession last night only cemented what I had known for weeks.

I loved her. And I would kill for her.

Sure, I would have killed for her before, because it was my job to protect her. But putting an end to the men who hurt her would give me a pure satisfaction that I wouldn't have felt if I were just doing it for me, or for work. I wanted to avenge Livia on a deep, possessive level. Not only to make her feel safe again, but to rid the world of any other man who had touched her.

She was mine, and I was done fighting it. *I'm sorry, Michael.*

As I finished sorting myself out, I tried to calm the storm of thoughts swirling through my mind before I went back out to Livia. I hadn't realized how agonizing resisting her affections had been until I made the decision to stop fighting it. A ten-ton weight was lifted off my shoulders.

At some point, the reality of it would kick in, and the guilt would eventually settle in. But for now, I was just going to put it from my mind and make sure I did everything to keep her alive. Everything else could come later. I wasn't going to touch her until I declared myself to Michael.

When I went back out to the bedroom, Livia was sitting up in bed with Nero splayed across her lap, begging for belly rubs. The sight of her in the bed we slept in together made my heart ache, and I had to get the frog out of my throat before I could speak.

"How did you sleep?"

She smiled shyly up at me. "Better than I have in years, surprisingly. You?"

I gave her the widest grin. "Me, too."

I left her in bed while I ordered room service. We had vegetable frittatas for breakfast, and then Liv scooped out some kibble for Nero while we checked for news about the weather in New York.

"It's not looking good for us today," I told her with an insincere frown. After her admission and my revelation, the last thing I wanted to do was bring her back to her own personal hell.

She shrugged, not appearing too disappointed by the news, either. "So, we'll stay another day. It's not the worst thing ever." She climbed out of bed and walked to the window to look outside. "It's not snowing here yet. Maybe we can get out of the room for a while and do something. Nero's getting restless. You know, he was nudging me all night," she said with a smirk on her face.

*Devil woman!*

I wanted to throw her in the bed right then, but I bit

down hard on my lip and looked away. She was going to be the death of me. I just knew it. After sneaking away like the coward I was, I got dressed in the bathroom. When I came out to grab my jacket, I froze in place when I saw Livia just pulling down the front of her sweater as she got dressed. I only got a quick glance of a strip of her midriff, where I thought I saw a scar. Her eyes nervously drifted up to meet mine. She knew exactly what I was looking at, and she blushed. "Um…"

I stopped her. "I'm sorry, Livia. You don't have to say anything. I shouldn't have been looking."

She shook her head at me and walked over to me. "It's from the car accident. You knew I was in the car with my parents that night, right?"

She gazed up at me inquisitively, and I expelled a deep sigh. "Yes, I did…" I was praying she wouldn't ask me what exactly I knew about that car accident. I willed myself not to tense up, and I let out a breath of relief when she didn't ask.

Livia smiled sadly. "It's okay. I wasn't badly hurt. It's a cut from a shard of glass."

She seemed to be deliberating about something to herself, then I felt her take my hand and gently slide it under her sweatshirt. My mouth went dry when she pressed my palm against the warmth of her bare skin. The scar was thin, slightly raised, and paler than the rest of her skin, from what I had seen in that split second. I couldn't resist peeking at it again. Her smooth skin, slightly marred, only helped me justify myself further.

*You're no untouchable princess, Liv.* She didn't just have physical scars, but emotional ones, too. I wondered many times if being with her would only bring darkness to her life, but it looked like that darkness was already there.

"It only makes you more beautiful to me. I have plenty of scars, too," I told her with a genuine smile that crept across my face, keeping my hand where it was. *Control yourself, Castellano.* "I am a bodyguard, so it's bound to happen."

She giggled lightly, and when she felt my fingers gently stroking her under her sweatshirt, she paused. Reaching up to graze my cheek, she whispered, "I think you're beautiful, too."

*God, those fucking eyes.*

I wanted to kiss her so badly, but I stopped myself. I was already breaking my promise to Michael. At the very least, I could hold myself back until I spoke to him about my feelings for her first. I doubted he would ever give me approval, but it was the right thing to do.

Her face fell, and she backed away to finish getting ready, not saying another word. We had decided to take a short walk over to the nearby park and let Nero get some exercise, as well as some much-needed air. I needed to put some space between Livia and me, because I didn't know how much longer I could take the torture of being so close and repeatedly denying myself.

It wasn't just that she was beautiful and so goddamned sexy. It was her compassion and the effortless way we opened up to each other. Somehow, I'd slept better beside her than I had in the longest time. It felt like unfamiliar territory for both of us. I had dating experience, but not at this level of intimacy. It felt so natural with her.

"I've got Nero. We should go before it starts snowing." Livia walked up to me with the leash in her hand. "Hello? What are you thinking about so hard?"

I shook my head, a little embarrassed that she caught me smiling like an idiot to myself while staring at her. "Nothing. I'm just in a good mood. It happens sometimes."

"Oh, I thought you were about to be sick," she teased back. "Let's go, whoever you are." I couldn't stop myself from lightly swatting her ass when she said that, and she squealed. "Dante!"

I laughed and opened the door for her to go outside. So much for keeping my hands to myself. I was in agony, but I quickly pushed it down. "Out you get, *principessa*."

We strode out onto the street after I made sure that the door was locked at least five times. We couldn't be too careful now that we knew people were actively stalking Livia. She seemed to think I was being ridiculous, and she huffed at me. "Come on! No one knows we're here."

I checked one more time just to annoy her, and then followed her as she stomped away from me with Nero. I tried to resist the urge to be an annoying ass, but it was the only thing stopping me from putting my hands on her for five seconds. "Are you warm enough?"

"Yeah, the walking will warm us up. I need to get some winter wear again."

"I guess we'll need to go shopping then," I threw out casually.

We fell into a comfortable pace, with Nero stopping every once in a while to jam his nose into the dirt as we talked about nothing in particular. It was odd to me how normal it felt. *I could get used to this. Just being with her every day.*

Nero caught a whiff of something, and he bolted suddenly. The shock of it caused Livia to jump and drop the leash, and Nero took off after a cat. "Nero, get back here!"

I started to run after him, but she stepped in front of me and shouted out, "Nero, come!"

And that damn dog actually stopped his chase and turned back around. He trotted over to her side like a lapdog, and she patted his head affectionately. "Good boy."

Staring at her in disbelief, I sputtered, "He listens to you better than me. Damn traitor."

Livia shrugged and laughed at me. "I give him belly rubs."

We made a few more laps around the park before I noticed she was shivering. It was definitely colder than it had been the night before. "Maybe we should go back and warm up."

I hadn't meant that to come out the way it sounded. I didn't even realize the undertone until I saw a flush cross Livia's cheeks, but she didn't call me out on it. I draped my arm around her shoulders and we walked back to the hotel room with Nero. We didn't say another word until the hotel room door closed behind us.

Livia stripped off her coat and swung around to face me. "You're acting strange today. Is this about last night? Please, don't make me regret telling you."

*What?* "No, it's not," I assured her. I met her wary eyes, and I could see every ounce of fear and insecurity in them. When I saw her lip quiver, I immediately took her hands and pulled her to the bed to sit down beside me. "I'm glad you told me. It doesn't change the way I see you. If anything, it made me see how fucking strong you are. I'm in awe of you, honestly." I reached up to wipe a lone tear from her cheek. "Don't cry, beautiful.

I'm not going anywhere. Even if you don't need my protection anymore, I'll always be there for you."

She shocked me when she wrapped her arms around the back of my neck and yanked me toward her. I didn't stop her when I felt her lips crash into mine. "I need you. Please, Dante."

I broke the kiss and closed my eyes, burying my face in her neck. "I need you too." I couldn't help the words tumbling out of my mouth as I stuck my nose in her hair and inhaled deeply. Everything about her was intoxicating. I wanted her all over me, and I grew more exhausted every second I continued to beat the feelings away.

She almost looked surprised, but her face broke out in the most beautiful smile. "You do?"

I was speechless, just staring into her dark eyes, full of desire and…love?

I answered her with a ferocious kiss, my hand at the back of her neck, holding her to me for dear life. How could I continue to deny myself when I felt like I needed her, like I needed air? If she only knew the spell she had on me. I couldn't think straight when she was around me, but somehow it just felt right to let our powerful bond draw us together. I didn't care where it would lead us anymore. It was inevitable from the moment I laid eyes on her. *She's mine.*

## Chapter Sixteen

*Livia*

Dante swallowed my gasp with a passionate kiss. I was grateful that we were sitting down because my knees would have buckled. His hand slipped up into the hair at the back of my head and held me in place. The thought of being held this way had never turned me on until him. I felt his other hand on my chest, slowly drifting down toward my breasts, and I knew he could feel my heart hammering against his palm. I responded immediately, taking every opportunity to taste and tease his tongue. He groaned into my lips, "You have no idea how long I've wanted you."

"Me too," I said as I felt his lips drifting up and down my neck. "I never expected to feel this way, but it just happened."

He retreated just enough to look into my eyes and cupped my face softly. In a low voice, he uttered, "It feels right between us, doesn't it?"

"It does."

He stood up to rip off his jacket and his shirt, almost as if they had been on fire. He wanted this just as much as I did. My stomach fluttered nervously as I watched him undress in front of me. I was more than ready, but I suddenly felt so vulnerable. The way he regarded me as he removed his pants made liquid heat spread between my thighs. His eyes were dark and his breath came out in heaving pants. I'd never felt such a craving before, and not even my nerves could stop me from letting Dante make love to me. He finished when he was down to his boxers. I could already see his hardened bulge, and my eyes widened in shock.

Luckily, he didn't see my reaction to his size, and he pulled me up into his arms to kiss me again. They were so gentle that I felt myself melting into his embrace. These weren't hungry kisses, but sensual ones. His hands drifted down to my sides, and he gripped the hem of my sweater, only breaking the kiss while he quickly lifted it over my head. I blushed heavily when his eyes roved over my body. "Livia…you're so goddamned beautiful."

His ardent words gave me the courage to reach behind my back to unhook my bra, letting it fall down my arms. I watched his gaze travel down to my already erect nipples in the still chilly air of the hotel room. "And I'm yours, Dante."

That seemed to please him, because he pushed me down to the bed and rested on his forearms, his body hovering on top of mine. "Yes. Only mine." He devoured my lips in another heated kiss, biting on my lower lip and sucking it while he gently stroked my thighs. My skin felt tingly everywhere his hands had been. "I need to feel you."

I nodded and lifted my hips while he tugged both my leggings and panties down. When I lay back on the bed again, he gazed down at my naked body with a look of pure desire in his eyes. They almost seemed to glow, and he kept them glued on me while he pulled down his boxers. I couldn't resist stealing a glimpse of his arousal and immediately felt my core aching with need. I'd never felt anything so powerful in my life, and I was ready to let it overtake me.

He got back in bed beside me. His shaft bobbed against my stomach, the tip wet from his arousal, marking me. "Oh, God…" I tentatively reached down between us as we kissed and wrapped my fingers around it, squeezing lightly. Dante groaned and his hand drifted up from my thigh to the already soaked flesh between my legs, letting out a gasp when he felt it.

"You're already so wet for me. Oh, Jesus Christ." He traced slowly from my entrance up to my clit, over and over, while brushing soft kisses all over my breasts. I didn't think it was possible to be as wet as I was, but his expert touch sent me into delirium. His fingers slid back down to my center, and he pushed gently inside. Dante kept his eyes on me, assessing my response to each sensual touch. "How does it feel, beautiful?"

I cried out, "Oh my God…you feel so good."

"Those moans are going to be the death of me, I swear," he muttered as I felt his fingers curl inside me, hitting a spot that had me suddenly clinging to him for dear life.

"Dante! Do that again…"

He quickly repeated the motion and leaned his head down again to suck a stiff bud into his mouth, teasing it with his teeth. When my legs began to shake, he used his thumb to stroke my clit as he continued his motions inside me. I felt a powerful orgasm come on suddenly, and he flew back up to my lips to swallow my scream of pleasure.

Dante slowly pulled every last bit of pleasure out of me with gentle, slow strokes. When I finally came down, he reached into the nightstand to grab a box of condoms.

He turned back to me. "Are you sure you want to do this?"

I met his hesitant gaze with my determined one. "Yes, Dante. Make love to me, please."

He slipped the condom on and climbed on top of me, resting himself between my legs. "I'm glad you say that, because I don't think I can resist you anymore." Dante met my fervent kisses while he positioned himself at my entrance, slowly pushing the tip inside.

It wasn't extremely long, but it was thick. I had no idea how this was going to work. I had obviously masturbated in the past, but never experienced anything close to his girth. After a few minutes of his gentle thrusts, he eased himself farther inside me. Even though I could tell it took considerable effort to hold himself back, he moved with such tenderness and care; I felt no pain. I was in awe of his control. When I felt the stretching sensation as he sank to the hilt inside me, I felt completely possessed by him. My emotional gaze shot up to his with a loud gasp. "Ah, God!"

Dante stilled for a few minutes, giving me a chance to adjust to his size. There was no doubt he had experience in pleasing a woman, because he kept a careful eye on me, waiting for my face to relax. When I loosened my vise grip on his upper arms, he resumed with gentle motions of his hips.

"Are you okay? Am I hurting you?" he asked me, continuing his slow, measured thrusts, and peppering my lips with soft kisses.

"You could never hurt me. You make me feel so safe." I uttered my declaration, taking in his intense gaze on me and the sweat dripping down his chest. I felt a fluttering in my lower belly, and it urged me to move my hips with his.

We bucked together, every inch of our skin touching. I could feel the spasms in his lower abdomen as he pumped into me, and I let my hands trail along his body as he worshiped me. The tension was building inside me with his every stroke. Listening to his deep, throaty moans every time I clenched around him only sent me closer to the edge. He groaned as he slowly started to thrust a little deeper, and I wrapped my legs around his hips to urge him on. "God, you feel so good…"

His hand came up to caress my thigh, and he pulled out of me almost all the way, before giving me a harder, uncontrolled thrust. I cried out, then bit his neck to muffle my scream. "Oh! Yes!"

He chuckled and repeated the move. "You are a vicious girl, Liv."

"You love it!" I shouted out when I felt him hit my core again, and I knew I was about to explode. Dante was close, too. I could feel his cock twitching inside me as I contracted involuntarily around him. He kissed me hard, hungrily sucking on my lip.

"Yes, I do," he responded, reaching down between us to rub my clit. "I want to hear you moaning my name when you come for me, baby."

I writhed in his arms as the pressure I felt inside reached peak capacity, and I was desperately panting against Dante's neck. I clung to him, feeling the waves of pleasure crash over me. "Yes, yes, yes! Dante!"

Dante slowed his strokes, drawing out my orgasm as long as possible. He quickly followed my climax, stiffening and letting out a low growl into my mouth. "Liv…God."

I felt sated, but as he eased me down from my intense orgasm, reality began to set in. *What does this mean?* Dante must have known that I was feeling vulnerable, and he reached up to stroke my face comfortingly. He withdrew carefully to avoid hurting me and rolled onto his back, bringing me closer to him into a tight embrace. I stayed quiet in his arms for a few minutes, waiting for him to say something.

"How do you feel?" he asked me sincerely, tilting my face up to look at him.

I shook my head in disbelief. Wasn't it obvious with the way I was still shaking in his arms? "It was…amazing."

I gazed up at him in wonder. On the outside, this man looked like a toughened criminal. But now, all I could see was the man I knew him to be on the inside. Warm, caring, and loyal beyond anyone I'd ever known. I wouldn't ever have expected such gentleness from a man like him based on first impressions. He blasted my every judgment about him out of the water, and even though he drove me crazy, he still stole my heart completely.

Dante tipped down his head to press a soft kiss on my forehead. "I don't know what I did to deserve you, *tesoro*."

I blushed furiously to hear the term of endearment from him. My heart squeezed almost painfully, and I had to bite my lip to stop myself from crying. He felt like he wasn't good enough for me, and that my uncle wouldn't approve. That much was clear to me. But I was happier than I had ever been. How could it be wrong if I felt this way? "You deserve me, Dante. My uncle will understand."

"I'm not so sure about that. But he'll have to deal with it because I'm not leaving you."

"Do you promise? I can't lose anyone else..." I couldn't stop the tears from coming out. Dante quickly rolled us onto our sides and wrapped his arms around me, and I let myself relax in his warmth.

He peppered soft kisses all over my face while he whispered to me. "Yes. I promise. Nothing is going to stop me from being with you. I'm done fighting with myself when I have everything I want right here. Just you, Livia."

Dante's firm declaration told me he meant business. He was going to fight for me. "Thank you," was all I could think to say. Well, I knew what I really wanted to say, but I held back the words. As much as I wanted this, I couldn't help but feel a little overwhelmed. I loved my uncle, and I hoped that he would have wanted me to be happy. On the other hand, I still craved his approval. He'd been my sole parental figure for the last twelve years of my life, and if I didn't have him, then I would be completely without family. I had to ask myself if Dante was worth it—but I already knew the answer to that.

I loved him.

****

We spent a few hours lounging around in the hotel room. The weather gradually got worse as the storm passed through, and it was freezing. I suggested we leave early to try to beat the storm, but Dante looked at me like I was insane. "Ab-so-fucking-lutely not. It'll clear up soon. I'm not putting you at risk to get there faster. Why the sudden rush, anyway?"

I shrugged. "I guess I'm eager to see my uncle. It's

been four years since I've been back."

"I know. He missed you, too. If we're not talking about work, we're talking about you. The man never shuts up about his wonderful niece. It's actually quite annoying," he teased. I was sure he was trying to cheer me up. I had to appreciate the effort he put into trying to ease my worries.

"Oh, poor you," I mocked him with a grin. I didn't know how, but he was always able to calm me down. I snuggled closer into his arms. "I could probably stay right here forever. Let's just live in Chicago."

"All right. Fine by me."

I knew he was joking, but I secretly hoped he wasn't. I got my answer when the weather cleared up in the afternoon and we were free to continue our journey. Dante and I silently repacked the few things we had unpacked, and I waited in the hotel room with Nero while he loaded up the car.

We had napped for most of the day, being so comfortable in each other's arms—so we'd probably be driving through the night into New York. Dante said that would be preferable, anyway. If we got to Manhattan before it got light in the morning, we could avoid being seen. He had told me we were going to a little studio apartment, which was one of the designated safe houses he had at his disposal.

Part of me wanted to just get there and break past my fear, but the other part of me wanted to stay in my safe bubble with Dante. I loved everything about it. It was so easy to be with him and talk to him. It felt so normal, like this was how it was always supposed to be. Dante and I together. The idea filled me with such happiness that I started to giggle to myself.

I snapped back to reality when he lowered himself in front of me. "Now who's acting strange, *principessa*?"

And that was the first time his little nickname didn't piss me off.

I threw his words from earlier back at him. "I'm just in a good mood. It happens sometimes."

Dante followed me out and we got inside the car, buckled up, and pulled out of the hotel parking lot. We drove for a few minutes before I took a quick glance at him, and he was carefully gnawing on his lip like he had something on his mind. I tried to decide whether to question him, but he startled me when he finally spoke. "Are you happy, Liv?"

"Beyond happy." I beamed at him, causing him to look almost shy. I couldn't hold back my giggle. "What is it?"

He shrugged nonchalantly. "I mean, could you be happy like this? Being in a relationship with someone like me?"

I blushed. "I know you. And what you are is a wonderful, loyal man. There's something special between us. I feel like I'm the lucky one. I look at you, and I wonder what the hell you see in me."

Dante took my hand in his, keeping his other on the steering wheel. "Don't worry, *tesoro,* you're never going to doubt your worth with me. I'm going to make you see what I see when I look at you. You're so much more than your beauty…" he trailed off as if he had more to say, but he stopped himself.

"What were you going to say?" My curiosity got the better of me, and I couldn't help myself.

Dante shrugged. "The first time I saw you painting through the studio window, it wasn't even your beauty that struck me. It was the pure artistic passion in your eyes. It's the same way I feel when I play music. I couldn't tear my eyes away from you."

It embarrassed him to admit to leering at me from outside, but the idea was comical to me, since it was basically his job to do just that. I kept that thought to myself. "That's how I felt when I first heard you playing the violin. It captivated me."

He laughed lightly. "I needed to do something to calm down after I got a swift kick to the balls."

"Oh God, don't remind me. That was awful of me."

Dante vehemently disagreed. "No. Especially considering what happened to you, your response was completely understandable. I should never have approached you like that."

I squeezed his hand. "Thank you for understanding. I still wish I hadn't done that. I wish I had been nicer to you in the beginning. You probably thought I was such a bitch."

He chuckled back at me. "Oh, I thought you were a pain in the ass, but I was so attracted to you, I didn't care. It was like foreplay to me."

I let out a gasp. "Oh my God! You're ridiculous." Dante reared his head back and let out a rumbling laugh. The complete look of happiness on his face had me staring at him with astonishment. *He's so handsome when he smiles like that.*

"You make me fucking crazy, Liv. But at least I'll never be bored," he said as he pulled my hand up to his mouth to kiss it.

After a giggling fit, we settled into a contented calm as we listened to soft classic rock on the radio. I didn't even care anymore that we were going back home.

Wherever Dante was, would be home to me.
If that place was Manhattan, then so be it.

## Chapter Seventeen

*Dante*

We were actively fleeing from people who wanted to hurt Livia, and likely take me down at the same time. But somehow, I felt completely content as I drove us into the mouth of the beast. After our night together, Liv seemed to open up in a way that she hadn't before, and she looked visibly more relaxed. At first, I couldn't put my finger on why—then it hit me. Before, she might have trusted me to do my job—even when we didn't get along. Now she trusted me to protect her for reasons beyond obligation.

Telling her I was in love with her felt like the last nail in the coffin. She had yet to say the words, and neither had I. I was pretty damn sure she knew how I felt, but I held back. I had already betrayed Michael by not trying harder to resist her, then went as far as to take her virginity. Maybe it was wrong to consult him before she knew the depth of my feelings, but it seemed like the last option to prevent me from losing either of them.

Sure, telling him over the phone would have been safer. He couldn't hop out of his cell and kick my ass. It would be cowardly to hide behind a phone, so when he called a few hours into our drive, I had to have a hurried discussion with Livia.

"That's him calling. I recognize the caller ID of the

prison." Her face went white in an instant. "Are you going to tell him about us?"

We hadn't had much chance to discuss our plans going forward, and there wasn't time for it now, either. "Not over the phone. When he gets out, I'll tell him in person."

She started chewing on her lip, a sure sign of nerves. "Okay…but I want to be there with you when you talk to him."

"I'm not sure if that's a good idea. We'll talk about it, Liv…" I waited until she nodded her agreement before I picked up the call and put it on speaker. "Yes, I accept."

Michael's voice rang out through the car. "Dante, what the fuck is going on? Is Livia alright?"

I shared a confused look with her before I answered. "She's fine, Michael. But I had to get her out of California. How did you know already?"

He expelled a relieved sigh. "I have L.A. newspapers sent to me regularly. There was an article about a break-in at an apartment building, and I immediately recognized it as Livia's place. What happened?"

I braced myself for two things. Number one, to tell him they, whomever *they* were, had gotten close enough to take a photo of her while sleeping. And two, to lie by omission. It came across as weird to me that someone would have needed to break into her apartment when they already had a key, but there wasn't time to think about it now.

"Someone managed to get into Livia's apartment, with me and Nero across the hall. I don't know how they did it, but they sent her a photo of herself sleeping in her bed. The minute she showed it to me, I got her out of there."

Livia leaned closer to the phone to explain. "I'm okay, Uncle Michael. I was just a little freaked out, but Dante is making sure I'm safe." She knew about his hot-headedness and probably wanted to take the heat off me.

I reached over and squeezed her hand, mouthing, "Always."

Michael cursed loudly. "*Cazzo*! Sneaky pricks. Do you have any idea who it could be? Where are you two now?"

He sounded more frantic than I had ever heard him. It only made me feel more guilty for not protecting her well enough, leaving her vulnerable, and being too distracted by my insane desire to possess her. *Get it together*.

"It's a long story, but no. I told you about the suspicious car, but it sped off before I could ID them. After we got the photo in Livia's mail, we took the first flight out. But a snowstorm put us in Illinois. They've canceled most outgoing flights for the next few days, so we're driving the rest of the way. Just leaving Indiana now."

By the tone in his voice, Michael seemed to calm down. "Good, because I'm sure you were followed to the airport. Hopefully, no one will know that you're not already in New York." He paused for a minute, then continued, "I need you to do one more thing for me. Just until I'm out of here."

I nodded, even though he couldn't see me. He didn't have to say it. "Don't leave her side. Please. I know this goes beyond your comfort zone, but I need to know she has protection day and night."

I didn't need to glance over at Livia to know that she

felt just as guilty as I did in that moment. Thick tension filled the inside of the car until I couldn't breathe. If only he knew what was in my comfort zone. I tried to keep my voice as straight as possible when I answered. "Of course. I haven't left Liv's side since we left. Don't worry about that."

I heard a quick hum from him, followed by silence, until I realized what I had said, but he said nothing about it. "Thank you. I knew I could trust you with this...I'll call again as soon as I can. Be careful, both of you." He called out to Livia, "And sweetie, I love you."

"I love you, too. I can't wait to see you again." Livia's voice came out shaky, which quickly put me on alert. I looked for a place to pull over the minute I hung up the phone.

Pulling into a gas station, I turned the car off and reached over to undo her seatbelt. I coaxed her into my arms just as she let out a choked sob. Pecking the top of her head with soft kisses, I whispered to her, "What is it, beautiful? You know I can't stand to see you cry."

"It's just everything. Hearing the panic in his voice, knowing I'm in danger...." she trailed off as she wrapped her arms around my neck, squeezing tighter. "Us. What are we going to do?"

I hated that my lack of restraint was the cherry on top of everything else that she had to worry about. This wasn't how it should be. "I'm sorry...I know I should never have let it go this far."

She gasped into my neck and pulled away. "Are you saying...that you regret what happened?"

I hadn't meant for it to come out that way, and she was becoming even more upset. "No! Never. I'm just saying this wasn't the best time for this to happen. We have so much else on our plate right now. And now I'm lying to Michael every day that I don't tell him I'm sleeping with his niece."

This wasn't the way I usually handled myself, but this petite, tenacious woman always managed to put me off-guard. With our luggage and Nero piled into the back seat, there was nowhere else to go. I didn't want her to see me like this.

"That's not all we're doing, and you know that," she answered sternly.

I couldn't bring myself to look up at her, but I could feel her burning stare. "I know. But that's all he's going to see when I tell him the truth. It's a betrayal."

"I'm a grown woman. I can make my own choices without his approval. And I want you. Not just your skill in bed, or your protection. I want the man who shares my life experiences, who listens to me, and who inspires me. If he doesn't want that for me, then he's the one who doesn't deserve loyalty or respect!" By the time she finished her rant, she was out of breath and trembling. "I…" She stopped abruptly. I waited for her to finish, but she kept her mouth firmly closed and looked away from me. What was she about to say?

She was right. It shouldn't have been this way, but I couldn't think of a way out of this situation that didn't hurt either of the people I cared about. A part of me wished I would have just told him over the phone to get it over with. But it would have been the easy way out. He had to know that I was serious, and the least I could do was tell him face-to-face.

I held her close to me again. "Liv…you are the most important thing to me. Don't ever doubt that. We just have to tread carefully while we deal with the threat."

"I want to believe that, but I wonder what you would do if my uncle told you to stay away from me. Would you do it?" she asked as she turned her determined eyes to me.

She was only asking me the same question I'd been asking myself for weeks. What meant more to me? Livia, or my loyalty to Michael? If he told me that being with her would mean a betrayal, I would have to make a decision that I almost couldn't bear to think about. Michael could be a cruel man when he was fucked with. Disobeying him wouldn't only mean losing his friendship, it could also be the end, period. I didn't even need to ask myself if Livia was worth it. I had been ready to lay down my life for hers for longer than I wanted to admit. She tensed up when I opened my mouth to speak.

"If you have to think about it, then maybe we should just stop what we're doing," she answered with defeat in her voice. "I'd rather have you in my life as a friend than to lose you completely. I don't think I could take it…"

Defile her and then break her heart? *Friend?* Oh no, that was not happening. "No, Livia. I'm not letting you go. I made you a promise, and I intend to keep it. You are mine."

Livia's face broke out in a huge smile that took the air right out of my lungs. Then she leaned across her seat again and softly brushed her lips against mine. I instinctively let my hands draw upward to cup the back of her head, pulling her closer to me as I explored her soft, warm mouth with my tongue. She let out a light sigh of pleasure, and I started to feel myself stiffen up instantly. *How does she do this to me so easily?*

She was the one to retreat this time. "We should get back on the road before it gets too late. I can drive if you want…if you're tired, or something." She was almost babbling, and I smiled to myself. She was just as flustered as I was, but we couldn't very well pounce on each other in the car. Well, we could have, but it would have been very difficult.

"You're not driving. I'll be fine. When we get to Queens, I'll sleep. Promise."

We got out to take bathroom breaks and let Nero stretch his legs for a minute before we got back on the road. I tried to keep my hands to myself while I was driving, but looking over at Livia and seeing her flushed face was driving me crazy. We had only slept together once, and she was already a fiend, roving her dark eyes over me shyly and biting on that damn lip. I had to keep shifting because of my nagging erection, which I was sure she'd noticed.

I sped up almost involuntarily. In a few hours, we'd be there, and all of my resolve from earlier would go out of the window. I wanted to rip her clothes off, make her come until she begged me to stop, and mark her so that everyone would know she was mine. The way she looked when she lay limp and satisfied underneath me; it was a sight that I would never forget. Her heaving breasts and glazed eyes. That flush that ran from her cheeks, down her neck, and spread out across her chest. Just the lurid image had me on the edge. If a swift breeze blew by, I was sure I would have spontaneously ejaculated.

I had never felt this primal need when I was with a woman in the past, and my filthy thoughts were surprising, even to me. This innocent girl had awoken the beast inside of me, and I didn't know if I could ever go back to the way I was before. And I didn't want to, either.

I finally got a little relief when Livia dozed off next

to me as we drove through Pennsylvania. She looked so calm and peaceful while she was asleep. I sneaked a peek at her just to take in the sight of her slightly parted lips and her long eyelashes fanning out against her cheeks. In the soft moonlight shining through the windows, she looked like an angel. It was a sight I could definitely get used to. *I love you, Liv.*

## Chapter Eighteen

*Livia*

I'd been more exhausted than I realized. Maybe I was just overwhelmed from the sudden chaos in my life, that even a good night's sleep wasn't enough to calm it. Once the high of making love with Dante wore off, fear set in. I had been worried about my safety before; now I had someone else to worry about.

Dante had sworn many times he would give his life for mine. I knew he was an experienced bodyguard, but he wasn't made of steel, either. What if those people found us? After twenty-two years of living a nearly solitary life, I finally found someone with whom I could picture a real future. Because of the world we both came from, it could slip through our fingers in the blink of an eye. I knew I'd have to fight to hold on.

As the silence filled the car, I fell into a fitful sleep, only waking up just as we left Pennsylvania and passed the Welcome To New York sign. I immediately groaned my displeasure, alerting Dante.

He stretched one arm across the console to brush a few strands of hair from my face. "Sleep well, beautiful?"

"I'm sorry. I didn't think I would knock out like that. You must have been bored." When he frowned, I asked, "What is it? What's wrong?"

"I don't want to take you back."

I reached out for his free hand. "I know. But you must; I understand that."

I wasn't happy about any of this, but I wanted him to know that I didn't blame him. It was nearing four in the morning, so when my phone chimed to alert me to a new text, I cocked my head. "Who would be texting me this late?"

Dante made a "gimme" motion, but I shook my head. Surely it could only be an emergency, and I felt my stomach tighten with anxiety. With a deep breath, I assured myself I could handle whatever it was. I picked it up and opened the notification with shaky hands.

—*Do you want to know how your parents really died? Lose the bulldog*—

I stared at the words on the screen until Dante pried the phone out of my hand. He looked down at it when he stopped at a red light. His eyes scanned the two sentences so many times, I started to wonder if he was trying to burn the screen with that death stare of his.

"What are they trying to say?" I squeaked out. That wasn't the first time someone referred to Dante as a bulldog. I didn't understand why nobody saw what I did when I looked at him, but that thought soon fell by the wayside.

He didn't look at me. "I don't know, Livia," he spat out quickly and handed my phone back to me. The way he gripped the steering wheel told me he was full of it.

"You're lying! You always choke the steering wheel when you're nervous. I know you've been hiding something from me since the start. Does it have to do with my parents' death?" After everything we'd been through, I wasn't going to let there be any secrets between us.

Would he really lie to my face? The guilty expression on his face told me everything I needed to know. He knew something about my life and had kept it from me. It hurt even more knowing I had laid myself bare for him and given him…everything of myself.

After what felt like hours of waiting, he seemed to come to a decision. "Don't answer that text. I'll tell you everything when we get to where we're going. I don't want to have this conversation while I'm driving."

He spoke in such a grave voice, as if he felt guilty. Was it because he'd hidden something from me—or because he'd conceded? I had a feeling it was the latter and decided to call him on it.

"I swear to God, if you tell me that my uncle made you promise not to tell me, I'm going to go postal." I couldn't decide who I was angrier with at the moment—Dante or my uncle. Unfortunately, I couldn't tear Uncle Michael a new one, so all of my frustration then poured out on Dante.

He stayed quiet for a few moments before he responded in a defeated voice. "I'm so sorry, baby."

It was quiet when we finally pulled into a residential neighborhood in Queens that I didn't recognize. I didn't come here often, but it looked normal enough. I wasn't sure what I had expected, but I knew Dante wouldn't take me to a dump to hide in. We pulled up to a brownstone apartment complex, and he immediately jumped out to grab the bags. The question hanging in the air temporarily overshadowed my worry about being in New York.

I climbed out and walked Nero up to the grass while Dante stacked everything else in his arms. "I can carry something."

"I got it. Just take the dog and get inside," he said, handing me a key to the front door.

While I focused under the flickering light of the front door, I dropped the leash. Nero didn't budge, content to stay at my side and guard me. *I wonder who he learned that from.*

Once I got the door open, fluorescent lights illuminated the cramped lobby. Mailboxes lined the right wall; a wide stairwell took up the center. Looking down at the key, I noted that it was for the third floor. I stood there nervously waiting for Dante, hoping to myself that no one would come down and recognize me. After a few minutes, he clambered in with our stuff and gestured for me to go up the stairs first. We wordlessly walked up the three flights of stairs, and I was surprised when I looked back at Dante and he wasn't even breathing hard.

He dropped his armload onto the floor beside me, then took the key and unlocked the door. "I'll go in first and make sure everything is okay. Keep Nero with you. I'll be right back." And then he leaned forward and kissed me softly before he rushed inside, his hand in his jacket.

The way he turned from just Dante to Protective Dante in zero seconds flat took me aback. Nero hadn't signaled that anything was off, yet Dante worried that someone was already inside, ready to jump us? The thought made me a little nervous as I stood in the hallway and waited. And yet, in my panicked brain, seeing him this way turned me on. Dangerous. It was startling to me that I liked even this aspect of him, when it had been the epitome of everything I wanted to escape from years ago.

Dante interrupted my train of thought when he

Treasured

suddenly popped his head out of the doorway. "It's safe. Come on." I followed him inside the little one-bedroom apartment and surveyed it carefully. He kept his eyes glued to me, as if he were waiting for my approval. "This is home for the time being."

It had large windows with gray curtains, drawn closed, and the basics in furniture: a couch, coffee table, TV. Off to the left side was a small kitchenette. It wasn't a bad apartment, but the idea of living in close quarters like this with a man...it was different when we were in the hotel. That was temporary. This was...I didn't even know.

"How long do we have to stay here?" I hadn't meant for it to sound so ungrateful coming out, and his face fell slightly.

"It's not that bad. Or is this about me?" he asked, as if he could read my damn mind.

"We're going to be living together...I don't know. It just feels strange."

"Liv, it's what we've been doing for the past few days. Was it that terrible for you?"

I hesitated, and he seemed to get irritated at that. I crossed my arms over my chest and reminded him that I still needed an explanation. "It might be if you keep lying to me."

Dante sighed and paced past me to gather up the bags from the hallway, then dead bolted the door. After a few minutes of silence, he slumped down on the couch. "All right. Come here. I need to hold you, beautiful."

He knew whatever he was about to tell me was going to upset me, and I almost didn't want to know at that moment. *No. I need to know.* Even though I was furious with him, I was grateful that I would have him to comfort me. I followed him, and as if I had been doing it for years, I naturally curled up under his arm, laying my head on his broad chest. "Please tell me. I can't wait any longer."

He cleared his throat as if he were readying himself to give a speech. *That's not good.*

"Before Michael was the boss, he and Angelo were in a crew together."

"My father?"

"Yes. They were making their way up. But things changed when your father married your mother and started a family," he uttered as he stroked my arm. "Having you made him realize that he wanted to get out. As you started growing up and entered grade school, he realized he didn't want this life for you."

I feared I knew where this was going, but needed to hear him say it. "What does all this have to do with the car accident?"

Dante held me closer as if he were bracing me for the impact. Or himself. "It wasn't an accident. It was a hit. This is why Michael's rivals don't want him coming back. They think he's a traitor."

Tears stabbed the backs of my eyes. Knowing the truth shocked me, even though in reality, it wasn't such a shock at all. That was how it went for people in this life. Prison or death. Every death was suspicious, even if it didn't immediately appear that way.

"Why would they think that?"

He took a deep breath and went on. I hoped he wouldn't hate himself for breaking his promise. I deserved to know what happened to my own parents. As I listened to Dante, I felt my anger melt away. "Because they knew Angelo was skimming money to make a getaway, and that Michael helped him cover it up. Or he tried to. Carmine Antonetti was Augustine's mentor years before he became the acting boss. When the boss at the time figured out where the leak was coming from, he sent Carmine to take care of it." He paused to rub his weary eyes. "As much as I hate Augustine, he offed Carmine for what he did."

Nothing I had heard of Augustine Lombardi in the past indicated he was a decent man, especially after hearing Dante's experiences working with him. A small part of me was relieved that Augustine avenged my parents.

Even though I was upset, being in Dante's arms made it a little more bearable. I tried to think back to the accident. What he said made total sense. At ten, I didn't understand we were running away; I thought we were going on a long vacation.

*Why does everyone lie to me?* "I can't believe this."

"It's the truth. You deserved to know," he said, echoing my own thoughts. "Michael wanted to tell you, but he was afraid that you would blame him for not trying harder to save them."

*What?* I tore myself back from his embrace. "Honestly, I'm angrier that he kept this from me than anything else. I would never blame him for my parents' deaths. I can't believe he lied to me. Although, I guess that's just me being naïve," I sputtered, getting more irritated the more I thought about it. "And on top of that, you knowingly kept this from me. I'm not so fragile that I can't handle myself. If there is anything else you're hiding, you better spit it out now."

When he said nothing, just staring at me with disbelief, I started to get up to leave. I was quickly frozen in place when I felt Dante's firm chest against my back, and his arm around my waist. "Liv, I won't lie to you again. Don't walk away from me."

The second I felt his skin on mine, I felt my anger turning into arousal. I couldn't believe how responsive I had become to his touch. His index finger barely grazed the small strip of skin right underneath my sweater, across my stomach, and I felt a shiver down my spine immediately. "If you do, you won't have to worry about my uncle killing you because I'll do it myself," I whispered when I leaned my head back against him so he could have access to my neck.

"My vicious girl," he crooned before he nipped my neck. His hands traced my torso underneath my sweater, slowly up toward my breasts. Dante cupped them gently, then reached for the front clasp of my bra. "Let me make everything better, *tesoro*."

I lifted my arms so he could pull off my sweater, and I let my unhooked bra fall to the floor before I turned to face him. "Please…" I begged, reaching out to press my bare skin to his. I helped him unbutton and shrug out of his shirt before I crashed into his arms. "Even though you piss me off like nothing else, somehow, I always feel safe with you. I know you would never hurt me."

He flashed me a bright smile before he bent down to kiss me. "Good. Now come to bed, beautiful girl." I was quickly swept straight off my feet and carried into the bedroom.

Chapter Nineteen

*Dante*

All I wanted to do was make Livia feel good, so she could have a brief break from the stress of hearing the truth about her parents' deaths. I couldn't go back in time and change it, so I settled on showering her with my affection instead. I swept her up into my arms and carried her like a bride over the threshold into the bedroom. When I caught myself smiling at the thought, I froze.

*Bride? Where did that image come from?*

Shaking the image of Livia in a wedding dress from my head, I placed her down near the foot of the bed. It was an old-fashioned one with a metal frame and a nice, sturdy footboard. A lovely thought came to mind. I gave Livia a smirk before I slowly sank down to my knees in front of her. She gave me a confused look when I pulled down her jeans and panties, but then I didn't get back up.

"What are you doing down there?" she squeaked.

I didn't respond right away, instead pressing my lips gently onto her mound, and she instantly shivered in front of me. "Hold onto the end of the bed, beautiful. I want to taste you."

I smiled to myself when I heard her light gasp. "No one's ever done that to me before…" she trailed off when I blew a cool breath up through her wetness. I could already see it. Gently spreading her lips, I kissed that tight little bundle of nerves, making her moan out loud. "Oh!"

After slowly lapping at her for only a few minutes, she was writhing against me. *So responsive.* I pulled back, teasing her. "How does it feel?"

"So good, Dante. Don't stop!"

I gave her my most wicked grin, then pulled her leg over my shoulder so I could get better access as I licked and sucked on her soaking flesh. "You're close already…" I wrapped my arms around her thighs to hold her steady as her legs shook. "I've got you. Let go, Liv."

And then, as if my words gave her permission, she let out a loud cry as she came, coating my face in her wetness. "Oh, God! Oh, God!"

She clung to my hair as I slowly decreased the speed of the strokes, easing her down. When she finally stopped spasming against my tongue, I rose to my feet and took her hand. Leading her to the bed, I gently nudged her to lie down.

I wanted so badly to have sex with her again, but she had to be sore from the day before. It was too soon. I lay down on my back next to her. My pants were still on, but my erection strained against the fabric. "Did you like that?"

Her eyes immediately fell to my cock as she nodded. And without another word, she got up onto her knees beside me on the bed, her fingers quickly working my fly open.

*Oh God, yes.* She was always as eager for me as I was for her, and I loved it. I shifted my hips to help her pull my pants off. I didn't think I'd ever get used to the sight of her gasping when she saw my shaft ready and waiting. She leaned over my groin and took my cock in her hand. She slid her fingers up and down the length a few times, then flashed me a smoldering look that told me words weren't needed. She swiped her tongue across the head without warning. I let out a loud bark of surprise and had to resist the urge to buck my hips at her face.

"Yes, use your tongue, baby."

She stroked her tongue along the length, and when it brushed the underside of the head, I let out a throaty groan. Livia gripped the base firmly and when I felt her hot mouth close around the tip and suck, I had to take deep breaths to stop myself from coming immediately. She slowly took me in farther. Maybe it was her enthusiasm, or maybe it was just the fact that we had an emotional connection. Either way, it wasn't long before her eager suction and the gentle caresses of her tongue brought me to a surprisingly quick finish.

She smiled shyly at me when she pulled back from my still semi-erect shaft. "Did you like that?"

I let her see my astonished expression. "Are you serious? I came so fast. How the hell are you so good at that?" I was sure she heard the twinge of jealousy in my tone.

"I've seen porn, Dante. Why do you ask?" When I didn't respond right away, she giggled at me. "Are you jealous?"

Her eyebrow raised suspiciously. She could read me like a book, so I didn't bother to deny it. "I just don't like the idea of other men touching you. Is that so wrong?"

"I like when you get possessive. It kind of turns me on," she confessed with a blush.

*God, she's killing me.* "Then in that case." I sat up against the headboard and pulled her onto my lap, facing me. I slid my hand around to her ass and pulled her close enough that my solid shaft was rubbing between her legs. How in the hell was I hard again? She instantly moaned, dropping her head onto my shoulder. I whispered into her ear, "I'm going to be the first and last man to ever touch you, Livia. It's just you and me."

Another grind against her clit, and her eyes flew up to mine. "I don't want anyone else. Make love to me."

I jolted under her at her quiet demand. "But aren't you sore?"

"A little, but I don't care. I want you to take me."

I couldn't deny her, lifting her up and slowly sheathing myself in her tight center. "This is what you want?"

She threw back her head and shouted. "Oh! It's deeper this way. Oh my God…" I worried for a minute that I had hurt her, but she wrapped her legs around my waist and eagerly ground herself down on me. "You feel so good."

I leaned her back a little, holding her around her lower back to give me access to her breasts. Pulling her nipple into my mouth, I began to tease it with my teeth. I sank deeper than I'd ever been, immediately letting out a ragged breath when I felt her tensing around me. I was almost blind from the ecstasy of being buried inside her, muttering my thoughts as I worshiped her eager breasts. "God, I don't think I'll ever get enough of this. You're so damned beautiful right now…"

She rose and fell in rhythm with my gentle grinds. "Me neither…"

I reached between us to swipe my thumb over her clit, causing Livia to throw back her head and moan to the ceiling. Just the sight of this sensual goddess in my arms heightened my pleasure. Even though I had already had an orgasm less than five minutes ago, I was close again. I could tell she was ready, too.

Livia's entire body began to shake, but I didn't let up my movements, stirring myself deep inside her while I rubbed her sensitive clit. Suddenly, I felt her walls clamp around me as she came in an explosion. She covered my mouth with hers to muffle her scream and threw her arms around my neck as she rode the lingering waves of her orgasm. That was the end of it for me. With a feral growl, I spilled into her instantly. It felt so good to fill her up, and that was when I realized it. *I didn't put on a condom.* "Livia...I didn't realize. I'm sorry."

I didn't know what else to say. The sex was mind-blowing, as it always was with her. I completely lost my head with desire. After carefully slipping out of her, I gently eased her onto her side.

She looked up at me, but not with anger. "It's all right, Dante. I actually fibbed a little. I, um...got the birth control shot. I didn't want to tell you."

I furrowed my brows at her in confusion. "Why not?"

She nibbled on her lip. "Because I didn't want you to think I was planning on being with someone else...I did it for you."

The admission only made me love her more. She wanted me that badly. "Don't be embarrassed, baby. You have no idea how long I've wanted you."

She let out a relieved giggle. "I do actually. The time you saw me painting. You told me that already."

I shook my head and turned to face her. "I've been watching you for longer than you know."

"What?"

"Before you get upset and call me a liar, remember

you would never know this unless I chose to tell you," I began slowly, desperately hoping I wasn't about to put my foot in my mouth. "I kept an eye on you from the time Michael was arrested, up until you left for California. Unfortunately, I didn't do a good enough job, but there it is.

"There was something about you that held me in thrall. You were a complete mystery, but I was trying to figure you out. I knew it meant something because I usually didn't care to get to know any woman. I told myself it was nothing. Just curiosity about the apple of Michael's eye. I pushed the thought away and sat on it for years. When I saw you again through the window of the studio, you were different...but there was a part of the you I used to know, too. My curiosity about you only grew from there."

By the time I finished my confession, her eyes were glistening in the dim lights. "Dante...so you always cared for me?"

She nudged in closer to me. I thought my admission would send her running, but I was starting to realize that opening up to her only brought her closer. I wrapped my arms around her. "I more than care for you, beautiful."

When I peeked down at her, I saw her gnawing on her lip again. I knew what she wanted to hear, but I couldn't get the words out. My allegiance to Michael still held me back. It was a few moments before she spoke again. "I more than care for you, too."

I felt my heart swell.

Livia was innocent and inexperienced. I wanted to believe that she could possibly love me back, but the fear in the back of my mind kept nagging me. *She only thinks she loves you.* I was a killer. Yet, in her eyes, I was some kind of avenger. The only killing she knew about was my abusive father. If she knew details about the others, where I killed for little reason other than to punish someone for giving information they shouldn't have, she'd never look at me again.

I didn't think I could do without seeing those beautiful chocolate eyes every day. I had to force the dark thoughts from my mind. She knew I would never hurt her, so maybe she could compartmentalize the ruthless beast side of me.

It was the least I could hope for.

\*\*\*\*

The next few days blended together as we settled into the shabby apartment that Livia had lovingly dubbed, "Heaven in Queens." Her initial apprehension about staying here with me disappeared after that first night. She'd spent the next day making an extensive list of things we needed for our stay. I sent one of my most trusted guys to fetch the items, including food, toiletries, and some warmer clothes for her. During the rush to get to the airport, she'd left most of her things behind, only grabbing a few outfits that were barely suited to the northern climate.

He stopped by my apartment to get more of my clothes, as well. I could have gone myself, but I was too paranoid to leave Livia alone. It wasn't just about her safety; I didn't want to be away from her. Every night, we would talk in bed for hours before she fell asleep in my arms. Even something as simple as walking Nero together quieted my mind in a way I'd never experienced before. I hadn't noticed the constant ache of loneliness until it was gone, but I didn't miss it.

I was sure my guy didn't enjoy spending his entire

day in a department store, but I cared more about making Livia comfortable. I'd asked him to purchase a sketchpad and pencils as well. During the first few hours of the flight, I realized she'd left all her art supplies behind. It wasn't much, but once we figured out where we were going long term, I could replace all the things that she had lost. *If she moved in with me, I'd make space for an easel.*

I kept that thought to myself when I presented her with the notebook. "It's just for now until we can replace the rest of your supplies."

One would have thought I'd handed her a diamond-studded watch. "That's so sweet of you…thank you." Liv quickly jumped up from the couch to hug me tightly. "I've been itching to draw. How did you know?"

I pressed a kiss to her lips. It felt so natural after just a few days of being in close proximity to her. My lips gravitated to hers almost without my knowledge, and at night she fit so perfectly in my arms that I didn't know how I'd ever slept without her. "You draw on my back with your finger when you're asleep. I'm not complaining, it feels nice. But I figured you missed doing your artwork."

I didn't want her to feel like a prisoner. We were basically on lockdown at the apartment, aside from the brief walks outside, but neither of us seemed to mind it. In the space of three days, I ravaged Livia on every surface of the apartment. The dam had broken, and we couldn't keep our hands off each other. For a few blissful days, it felt as if we were a regular couple living our lives together. She cooked my favorite things, which we shared every night. Since very few people knew where we were, I felt safe enough to let my guard down for a while. That gave us time to just enjoy each other.

I wasn't in denial that the bubble would eventually pop once the danger was over and we returned to our regular lives. Would she want to go back to California? I didn't want to live there, but I knew damn well that I would if she asked. If I had a long enough rope, I'd have strung down the moon for her. Although, I secretly hoped that she would choose to stay in New York with me. Since her uncle was close to his release date, maybe that would have made her more likely to stick around. Where would that leave us?

I'd never considered marriage in the past, but the second that flight attendant made the assumption that Liv was my wife, I couldn't get the thought out of my head. Just the idea of her being Livia Castellano gave me an unexpected wave of happiness that I didn't know what to do with.

*What is this woman doing to me?*

Chapter Twenty

*Livia*

There was only one more week until my uncle would be paroled. The closer the date came, the more anxious I got. On the one hand, I was excited to see him for the first time after four years. On the other, I dreaded the inevitable look of disappointment I knew I'd see after Dante and I told him about our relationship. That was the worst for me, anyway. My uncle had his reputation for being ruthless among his men, but he never raised his hand to me—and rarely his voice, for that matter.

I was infinitely more concerned on Dante's behalf. He tried to assure me that everything would be fine, but by now, I knew his poker tells like the back of my hand. I saw the slight twitch in his eye when he told me not to worry. When we discussed my uncle, he didn't smile once. He was almost incapable of smiling disingenuously, so when I couldn't eke any enthusiasm out of him, I knew something was wrong. I found myself wondering what he was more upset about. Was it the idea of losing my uncle's friendship, or having any barrier between us? I just hoped that he wouldn't regret it later.

*What if he realizes that I'm not worth the trouble?*

Dante had gone into overdrive trying to get me to put my uncle out of my mind. When we weren't rolling around in bed, he showered me with affection. I was sure that he was trying to rid unpleasant thoughts from his own mind just as much as mine. It was either that, or he was trying to get his fill of me before he lost me. That unwelcome thought was buried deep underneath everything else. I was not going to let that happen, even if I had to put my uncle in his place myself.

In the rare moments that I managed to forget about the coming confrontation, I was unexplainably happy. I couldn't imagine going back just a few weeks ago when Dante was nothing but a nuisance in my eyes. Here he was now, playing awe-inspiring music for me while I sat on the couch and sketched him. It felt right and unnerving at the same time. How had I met him so many times over the years, never knowing what he would eventually mean to me?

I smiled to myself as I took in his masculine form, gliding my pencil across the paper. I was in absolute heaven as I took my time examining his every feature to bring it to life on the page. He stood in front of the bay window with the curtains slightly drawn so that the sunlight streaming in draped across his handsome face. His angular jaw, his newly trimmed beard, the Roman nose I loved, and those glowing eyes. Every time he reached a crescendo, I mourned the loss of his eyes as he closed them and soaked in the vibrations of his powerful bow strokes. Dante was deep in the zone, and I had to stop drawing for a moment just to appreciate it fully.

I was proud of how the drawing was turning out, but I wished more than anything that I had my paints. I decided then that I would recreate this drawing once I replenished my supplies. A furious blush creeped up to my cheeks when I wondered if Dante would have the same reaction to this as he did to that painting the day we left California.

When he finished the song, he rewarded me with an adoring gaze as he moved to put his violin down. "What are you drawing, beautiful girl?"

I rose from the couch and walked to him, stopping at the window to open the curtain farther. "Don't make fun of me. I'm better with paints and canvas."

He took the pad from my hands and tilted it into the light to study his two-dimensional counterpart. A few long moments passed before he met my eyes with a piercing intensity. "You see me, Livia."

I didn't have to ask him what he meant. "I do...Dante, you're so much more than the circumstances that led you to where you are. This is the part of you that survived all of the tragedies, against all odds. It's resilience, and it's the most beautiful thing in the world to me."

As he looked down at the drawing again, I saw the storm behind his eyes. It was as if he couldn't decide which side of him was more authentic. His ruthless criminal self, or the softer side he reserved only for me. To me, it was obvious. The self you only trusted with a few people was the genuine version. The self you showed to the world at large was something completely different—a fabrication of expectations and self-preservation.

I took the sketchbook back from him and put it down on the coffee table, and was quickly hoisted into Dante's arms, my toes barely touching the carpet. I heard his voice in my ear, gravelly with emotion. "Thank you, *tesoro*."

"What for? Telling the truth?"

He shook his head before burying his face in my

neck, inhaling deeply. The warmth of his breath against my skin heated me all over as he spoke. "For reminding me."

I smiled as he nibbled lightly on my neck. He was overcome with emotion, and he hated for anyone to see it—even me. The only time I had seen him even close to crying was that night he told me about his parents, which felt like ages ago compared to where we were now. Dante and I now knew everything about each other, which was something no one else could say about either of us. I didn't have any desire to push him further, so I wrapped my arms around his waist and let him feast on me until he was sated.

****

The next day, Dante left to attend a meeting with some of my uncle's men. We had been back in New York for just over a week; it was now necessary for him to meet with them to get the low down on what was happening. I didn't know much about what was going on outside of Dante's bodyguard duties, but I knew better than to think that my uncle would have just one man dedicated to keeping me safe. Dante was only the last line of defense.

It surprised me how jarring the idea of being left alone was. I hated to come off as a needy girl, but I couldn't help but cling to him as he dressed to leave. "Are you going to miss me while you're gone?" I asked, trying to hide my face in his chest so that he wouldn't see my embarrassment at my sudden anxiety.

Chuckling lightly, he snaked an arm around my waist. "Every second you're out of my sight. I'll have my phone on the entire time, and I won't be far. I made sure we chose a meeting place nearby so that I won't have to be too far from you…" he trailed off as he shook his head. "When I leave, lock the door behind me. Keep your phone in sight."

"We went over this earlier. And I have Nero, too. He won't let anything happen," I told him if only to make him feel better. He didn't like the idea of leaving my side any more than I did, but I tried to put on a brave face for him.

Dante pulled on his coat and then leaned down to pat Nero's head. "You watch out for my girl, okay? Be a good boy and maybe you can have some peanut butter later."

Nero's ears perked up immediately at the promise of a special treat. I laughed at them. "He's going to be giving me puppy dog eyes the whole time you're gone now. You're a tease."

He swept me into his arms and kissed me hard enough to knock the wind out of me. "You weren't complaining last night, if I can remember correctly."

"Begging is kind of like complaining," I retorted with zero confidence. "Just wait, I'm going to get you back later."

Dante pulled away, giving me a sexy smirk that sent a tingle straight to my core. "Oh, I look forward to it, beautiful." He pressed one more kiss to my lips before he left.

I scoffed at him when he waited outside the door, checking to make sure that I locked it after him. I stood there with my arms crossed for at least thirty seconds while he repeatedly jiggled the knob. It only occurred to me then that he may have had a touch of OCD, because I counted him testing the lock six times exactly, and he had done it before. I wasn't sure if he realized he was doing it compulsively, but I didn't think it was the right time to call him on it.

When Dante finally left, I realized how alone I truly was. The apartment was decently sized, but it seemed so much larger with half of its occupants missing. As much as I wanted to distract myself from the fact that anything could happen to me while he was gone, I thought against watching TV. What if someone came and I couldn't hear it?

I eventually ended up settling in on the couch and thinking about the events of the past few weeks. And even though I wanted to put him out of my mind, I thought about Eric. He had been my most faithful friend for the last four years, and now he was gone. It really hit home at that moment that I would probably never see him again. I hated that it made me upset, but I hated it even more that he'd ditched me the way he had. I was sure he must have noticed my absence at graduation, and yet he hadn't even called or texted to see if I was okay. He knew I was in danger, but he never checked in once.

I hadn't completely ruled out the idea of going back to California once this was all over, but, in a way, I had. I couldn't imagine going back to my apartment, knowing that some psycho had been in there watching me sleep, and could have killed me if he wanted to. That, added to the stress of my situation with Eric, soured any happy memories I had made there. It struck me as odd how easily unpleasant experiences could overshadow happy ones. I just couldn't picture myself there anymore.

Dante hated California, and it wasn't that I was particularly drawn to it, either. It was only a means of escape back then, and it had served its purpose. I got my degree like I wanted to, and when I picked it up from the

P.O. box that Dante had procured for me, I felt like I had successfully achieved what my mother wanted for herself, and then me. It was a surreal thought. California was never home to me, but New York wasn't really home anymore either. Did home have to be a place, or was it more of a feeling? Or a person?

My phone pinged with a text, and I rushed to grab it, knowing that it was Dante.

—*Just finishing up, everything okay there?*—

I quickly typed out my answer.

—*Yes. Nero saved me from a spider just now. I'm all good here.*—

I decided to kill some time by sketching the good boy himself as he sat stationary at my feet. He had trained him well to look for threats because Nero seemed to know that without Dante there, he was on duty. Or maybe he just missed his owner. Either way, his eyes stayed glued to the door as he sat like a statue, which worked out well for me.

He was the perfect model until I finished the last stroke of my pencil, and my phone rang, causing both of us to jump to action. "That must be your dad," I said to Nero as I gave him a scratch behind his ear and picked up the phone. "Hey, are you on your way back now?"

"Yes, I'm just down the block, but I missed your voice," he admitted, making me blush instantly.

I giggled into the phone. "Sweet talker. Any news?"

I heard the smile in his voice. "I'll tell you when I get home. Do you miss me yet?"

"Of course I do," I said, feeling cheeky at that moment. "I might get naked and wait in the bedroom. You better hurry, or I'll get started without you."

He growled into the phone. "Now, who's the tease?"

"Only for you," I whispered into the phone in a husky voice, knowing that to be his weakness.

"Yes, beautiful girl. Only for me."

Chapter Twenty-One

*Dante*

Livia wasn't naked when I walked in, and I quietly
cursed to myself. I was looking for any excuse to avoid
having to tell her the bad news, but also knew sex
wouldn't distract her for long. "Why are you wearing
clothes?"

Tossing her hair over one shoulder, she just laughed.
"I only said that to get you back here faster. You're so
predictable, Mr. Tough Guy."

I leaned in to give her a hungry kiss, losing my
fingers in her dark waves. Lingering sunlight trickled in
through the window, bathing her in the late afternoon
glow. Just a few hours away from her made me desperate
to feel her skin on mine, and devour her soft sighs with
my mouth. "You only have yourself to blame for being
so irresistible."

With a roll of her eyes, she sank down onto the
couch. "You can have me as soon as you tell me
everything." She crossed her arms across her chest and
stared up at me. "Do we know anything at all?"

How could I tell her my guys had turned up nothing?
That all I had to go on was a suspicion that would likely
send her into a tailspin? If I was correct, there would be
a whole new meaning to the phrase "painting the town
red". I had broken a few promises since meeting her, and

wasn't going to make it a habit. If I couldn't be a man of my word, what redeemable quality was left for me to hold on to?

"I have several men keeping an eye on things. So far, no one has found anything suspicious."

"No clues as to who was in my apartment that night? Or who is responsible for all this?" She was growing more and more irritated and I couldn't blame her. "How can there be nothing at all?"

As far as the Mafia is concerned, when someone's coming for you, they have no shame about letting you know it's them. Either that, or you never see them coming at all. Nothing made sense, and my suspicions continued to grow.

"We thought it could be the Contis, but we've had a fairly decent relationship with them for years. A lot of them actually prefer Michael to Augustine," I finished, immediately feeling guilty when I saw her slight flinch at hearing Lombardi's name.

"What are you thinking, then?"

Liv was getting too good at reading me. I expelled a weary sigh. "That it's either the Leones, or it's coming from our side. And if I'm right about the latter," I said as I sat at her side, taking her hand in mine, "then we can't trust anyone."

She stared at me for a moment as she mulled it over. "I think you might be right...what are we going to do?"

I leaned back on the couch. "I think we should err on the side of caution. I have another place that no one but Michael knows about. I'm going to take you there. A few of our men know the locations of the safe houses, and I won't put you at risk."

Livia hadn't been fond of the idea of moving around

a million times, and I wanted to avoid making her feel like a fugitive as much as I could. Unfortunately, it wasn't an option any longer. If I couldn't trust my crew anymore, then we were screwed.

She sighed deeply. "I guess it's the only option. I trust you."

She would never understand how much it meant to me, knowing that she trusted me wholeheartedly. "Thank you, Liv. I guess we'll have to save the nakedness for later. Go get packed."

We spent the next few hours getting our things together, along with whatever food we still had, and loaded up the car. I couldn't help but keep a watchful eye on our surroundings as we got ready to pull out. Someone had to be watching us—I just knew it. You didn't get far doing what I did without having a keen sense of awareness. I tried to suppress my worry for Livia's sake. She was nervous too, and I knew how much she hated feeling weak. We were much alike in that way.

Getting to our location was going to take more time than it should have. I took as many odd turns and detours as possible to confuse anyone who might be following us. When the traffic thinned out, I was able to spot one recurring car. My growl of frustration put Liv on alert.

"What is it?"

"Don't panic, but we're being tracked." I hit the gas; the car jerked forward with the sudden increase in speed.

"How do I *not* panic?"

I took a calming breath. *Put aside your feelings. Your job is to protect her, and that's all.*

"I want you to unbuckle your seat belt and get in the back with Nero. Get down on the floor and pull as much of our shit on top of you for cover. Do it now."

"What? While you're driving at this speed? Are you crazy?"

I turned on her. "Do what I fucking tell you, Livia."

Her eyes flashed, but she quickly complied. Obviously, she wasn't pleased with my tone. At the moment, I really didn't care. I had to remember that my number one priority was her safety. Not my love for her, not her feelings—whatever they may have been.

None of it mattered if I got her killed now.

Once she scrambled into the back, I whipped my head back quickly to see her lying on the floor in between the back seat and the front, hugging Nero close to her body. His head poked out from behind one of the duffel bags to give me one of his looks. Even when her life was in danger, Liv was still worried about getting my dog out of harm's way. I felt another quick pang of guilt for yelling at her, but shook it off as I took us farther into the middle of nowhere.

I was hoping against hope that I'd imagined the car tailing us. Every time I flicked my gaze to the rearview mirror, it was still on us, far enough away that I couldn't see the driver's face. It felt like hours had passed and I wasn't even sure where we were anymore as we headed into upstate New York. Eventually, I would need to pull over and confront this guy, but how could I do that without putting Livia at risk? I couldn't just keep driving to the house with this guy tailing us the entire way, and I couldn't lose him on the back roads, either.

There was only one thing I could think of, but I knew Livia would never agree. I had to try. "Are you okay back there?"

I heard her answer, muffled by all the junk on top of her. "Yeah."

"I have an idea. I'm going to speed up and get some distance on this asshole. Then I'll pull over. I want you to get into the driver's seat and take off. Fast." The suitcases shuffled behind me as she jolted upright. "Stay down!"

"What? And leave you here? Have you lost your mind, Dante?"

I tried to offer as much reassurance as I could muster. "I'll take care of him, then call you to come back for me. Get back down!"

"Goddamn it! I can't do it. What if something happens to you?"

I pulled out my phone and continued driving with one hand as I shot a quick text to her. "Go on to the safe house. I just texted you the address. The key is in the glove box. Wait there until Michael comes for you."

I felt some of my resolve melting when she didn't respond, and then I heard her light sniffling. *Damn it all to hell.* "Liv, please don't cry for me. I'll be fine. I can't focus on getting rid of the threat if you're there. I'll be more worried about you than about myself."

There was a long pause before she finally whispered her answer, "All right."

"Okay. I'm going to speed up now. When I stop, climb up to the front and get the hell out of here. I'll call you as soon as I can."

"Please be careful."

"I'll do whatever I have to in order to get back to you. I promise." It was stupid to promise her that, but it was the only way I could see her willingly driving away without me. It was just one guy that I could see. I could handle this. "Okay! I'm going to stop. Get up here now!"

She clambered back up to the front seat as I skidded

the car to a halt. She jolted against the dashboard from the impact of my braking. When I reached for the door, I heard the back window shatter as a bullet narrowly missed Livia. At that moment, I swore my heart stopped. I surveyed her quickly for injuries before I met her terrified eyes.

*I need to get her out of here.*

"Go!" I yelled as I catapulted myself out of the car and she slammed herself down in the driver's seat. The acrid taste of fear in my mouth was unfamiliar to me, and I swallowed it down as I watched Livia speed off away from me, tires screeching.

I wasn't thinking straight. There was nothing stopping this guy from running me down and following Livia until she ran out of gas. All I could do was make sure that when he got close enough, I lined up my shot correctly. I reached into my jacket and pulled out my gun. It was the first time in my career that I ever feared for my own life. And the only reason for that was so I could go back to the woman I loved.

Usually, when people faced death, their entire lives flashed before their eyes. The last few weeks played like a movie in fast forward in my head. I wanted more memories with her. Making love to her every night, making her smile, and being a man she could be proud of. Putting a ring on her finger. The thought had scared me before, but now it was my saving grace.

The car drew closer, and I kept my eyes glued to the driver's side. It seemed to take forever as time slowed. As he fired off rounds, they hit the gravel, sending bits of dirt into my face. My eyes watered as I raised my arm and aimed. I saw red, and I fired until my clip was empty. My eyes stung, but I forced them to stay open as I saw blood splatter on the windshield of the sedan, and then it veered toward the forest. The car flipped as it tumbled over the embankment.

I took that moment to rub my eyes before I went to check the wreckage. Planning to interrogate him before I put a bullet into his brain, I sprinted across the road and hopped over the embankment. It was silent, but I still took a moment to reload before I got any closer.

The front of the car was wrapped around a tree, pinning the man in his seat. I rounded the back of the car to his side, taking careful steps to avoid sliding down the steep hill. His rattled breathing sounded through the open window and I leaned down to get a closer look. Through thick plumes of smoke, I saw the steering wheel crushed against his chest, just under where my bullets had landed. Blood spurted out as he struggled for breath. This guy wasn't going to last long. Between the collision with the tree and the gunshots, the car was a ticking time bomb.

*Now's my chance. Better hurry.*

Even though his face was covered with blood, I didn't recognize him. I aimed my gun at his head. "Who sent you?"

He coughed, sending spurts of blood onto the dash. "Get…fucked."

I fired a second round into the hood of the car. "See, I was going to be nice and put you out of your misery, but now I think I'll just let you burn. Or bleed to death. Whichever happens first."

I carefully made my way back around to the passenger's side to see if I could manage to get in and grab any of his personal effects. A wallet, his phone. Anything. But the door might as well have been welded shut. When a flame escaped from the mangled hood, I thought about Livia again. It wasn't worth my life to find out who this guy was.

I climbed my way back onto the gravel road and sprinted toward the highway, away from the blazing car. I'd lost my nerve back there and I let my fear for Livia's safety decide that this guy was better off dead than leaving him alive to interrogate him.

I was a safe distance away from the car when I heard the boom. It wasn't the first time I had seen it happen, but I winced when the sound reached my ears. *Now I know she heard that.* I reached into my pocket to take out my phone and call her back.

"Liv, I'm okay," I spoke before she had a chance. "Come back to me."

"I heard gunshots and then an explosion. What happened back there?"

"I shot him, and then the car veered off into the woods. He'll be dead soon, so mission accomplished. I'm going to walk toward you while you head back. Okay?"

It wasn't long before I saw Livia speeding toward me. The car screeched to a halt. Instead of throwing open the passenger door, she flew out of the car and ran toward me. "Dante, oh God. I almost had a heart attack waiting for you."

Only after she squeezed me did I realize I'd been shot. I buried my face in her hair to hide my wince. I had been running on pure adrenaline until I felt her arms around me.

*Goddamn it.*

Chapter Twenty-Two

*Livia*

Dante seemed hesitant to let me go when I tried to pull back, and when I saw the blood on my shirt, I froze. "You said you were okay. Where are you hit?"

He shrugged. "I don't know. I didn't realize until you hugged me."

I grabbed the lapels of his jacket and carefully pushed it away from his chest, surveying him. Blood bloomed from his side; I carefully tried to pull up his shirt. Pushing the fear from my mind, I saw a chunk of flesh was missing from his abdomen. "It looks like the bullet grazed you. Did you get hit anywhere else?"

Dante's level of concern was nowhere near mine, and he shook his head. "No, I don't think so. We need to get out of here. I'll deal with it when we get home."

"Um…you're still bleeding a lot. You can't drive like this. Shouldn't we go to a hospital or something? You'll need stitches," I countered, walking away from him to open the back door.

"We can't go to a hospital. Once the cops find the wreck, they'll connect the dots. We have to go now." He gave me his stern tone again, and I returned to his side with one of my T-shirts.

"Fine, but you better not bleed out on me. Hold this to your wound while I drive us to the house." I used my stern tone, and for once, he didn't argue. Following me back to the car, he slid into the passenger seat, and we sped off toward our location.

I had never been shot before, but I couldn't fathom how he had been hit without feeling it right away. His wound looked awful, and he vehemently refused to go to the hospital. I wanted to be angry with him, but I couldn't muster up the energy to feel anything but relief.

He was alive.

It wasn't long after I first drove away from Dante before I heard shots. I wanted to squeeze my eyes shut until it was over, but couldn't while driving at a hundred miles an hour. At that moment, I felt no fear for myself, even though I had never driven so fast before. I was only thinking of Dante and cursing myself for allowing him to bully me into leaving him.

The explosion seemed to echo throughout the surrounding forest, and a flurry of birds came soaring out from the trees. When the boom shook the car, I did squeeze my eyes shut for a split second. But I didn't cry. I didn't let out a single tear until my phone rang, and I knew he was alive.

We sat silently in the car, the only sound being the automated voice from the nav system directing me to our next location. Twenty minutes later, we finally reached some semblance of civilization. The houses we passed had nothing but woods in between them, and the odd deer. I snuck a quick peek at Dante. Sweat drenched his brow, and he clutched at his side, holding the bloody T-shirt to his wound while he stared straight ahead at the horizon.

When I pulled into the driveway of a beautiful house right at the forest's edge, I was surprised that Dante would have such a nice house and choose not to live in it. I wanted to appreciate it more, but there were more pressing issues to deal with before I geeked out over the real estate. I jumped out of the car and ran across to Dante's side to help him out, but he swatted me away. "I'm fine. I'll get the bags. You get Nero."

I stomped the ground like a toddler at his tone. "Forget the damn bags. Get your ass inside and take off your shirt before you bleed to death!"

Dante chuckled at me, even with his pained face as he got out of the car. "You don't have to ask twice to get me naked."

I had to resist the urge to slap him. I opened the back door to let Nero out and quickly shuffled inside the house. After running around turning on all the lights, I ducked into the bathroom and hurriedly gathered any medical supplies I could find. Rushing back out to the kitchen, I dropped my armload of first-aid stuff onto the table as Dante sank down into a chair. He had taken off his shirt and turned sideways for me to get access to his wound.

"We don't have antibiotics. What if it gets infected?"

"Liv, baby, this isn't my first rodeo. I'll be fine."

I had seen a few of his scars, and I wondered how many of them had come from gunshot wounds. Some of them were perfectly round, and others were more like slashes. I spent one night studying his naked body as he slept, and I couldn't help but try to decipher what each one meant. Gunshot, knife, surgery?

Every time I saw a new one, I hurt for him. Every wound could have been his last, and it pained me to think about what he must have been through before we met—

what he would probably continue to go through. *Surely, he can't keep this up forever.*

I instructed him to tilt as I opened a bottle of peroxide. "This is going to sting. Ready?"

He gave me a weak thumbs up before I poured it directly into the gash, and he groaned. The peroxide bubbled up when it hit his wound, and I got to work wiping away any residual gunpowder or other muck, trying hard to ignore his grimace. I hated hurting him more, but if I didn't clean it well enough, he could have died from infection. *He calls me stubborn? Look in the mirror.*

It was too jagged to even consider trying to close up with my sub-par sewing skills, so I packed it with as much gauze as I could jam in there, then I wrapped his waist with more gauze and an old ace bandage I found in the bathroom closet. Maybe it was overkill, but I needed to stop the bleeding.

Nero whined at Dante's feet. Once I was finished, the dog rose up to lay his head in his master's lap, looking up at him with his big, sad eyes. "I'm okay. Our girl fixed me up good. Don't worry," Dante rasped and gave Nero a rub.

I managed to wrestle him gently to the couch to lie down. "I'm going to get the stuff from the car, and if you move, I'm going to hurt you. Okay? Then I'm going to make something for us to eat. You need to rest."

He chuckled lightly. "So damn bossy. It kind of turns me on."

"How can you even think about sex right now? I'm still shaking like a leaf, and I'm not even the one who got hurt." I stalked back to the couch to stare him down. "You scared me."

The smile slowly faded from his face. "I'm sorry. Honestly, it probably wasn't the best plan, but all I could think about was eliminating the threat and getting back to you. I was more worried about him running me down and following you. I couldn't let that happen, and I didn't care if I got shot as long as I took him down."

I sank down to my knees in front of the couch and softly rested my head on his chest. "Please don't ever make me leave you again…all I could think about was all the things I'd never get to say to you if I never saw you again. It was terrible…"

He sucked in a sharp breath, and then almost whispered his reply, "Tell me now. I don't want us to have any regrets."

My heart felt like it stopped in my chest. Given what we'd been through on this day, my previous worries about looking too eager seemed unimportant. I lifted my head from his chest and met his glowing eyes. "I wanted to tell you in Chicago, but I was afraid. If something happens to you, or to me…I don't want you leaving this world without knowing what you mean to me. I love you, Dante."

He winced when he reached up to cup my face in his hand. "Livia, you're all that matters to me. I tried to fight it, but you forced your way into my heart, and you made it come alive. Of course, I love you, *tesoro*. Can't you feel it every time I touch you?"

"Yes…" I didn't realize I was crying until I felt his thumb swiping away my tears. "I'm going to the car now before I blubber anymore."

I got up from my knees, but Dante's hand reached out to grab my wrist. "Say it again."

I smiled through my tears and looked down at him.

He was showing me his vulnerability openly, his eyes pleading with me to love him the way he always needed but never received. "I love you, Dante Castellano."

"I love you, Livia Rossi. So goddamned much."

The words were finally out there, and even with an ailing Dante lying on the couch, and the horror of the car chase, I felt safer than I had since this whole series of events started.

No one knew where we were, and we were both alive. Nothing else mattered.

****

The house, one of Dante's properties, was immaculate; everything looked almost brand new. I couldn't imagine that he had spent much time here, or what it was even for. He worked in the city, so what use did he have for a house on the edge of the woods in upstate New York? When I questioned him about it, he gave me a very evasive answer that only left me with more questions.

"It's my retirement home," he answered with a little grin. "Although I wasn't sure I would ever have the chance to use it."

Dante gave me a wistful look that I had noticed he was using more and more over the past few days. I didn't know what it was about, but he dodged my every attempt to ask more questions about the house.

I came to the assumption that he had plans to leave the Mafia at some point to try to live a normal life. But in this world, quitting the Mafia just wasn't a thing that was done unless you went government witness. Usually, it was the other way around. The Mafia quit you, and there were no retirement homes or sunny beaches in Florida for you with a cushy nest egg to live off of. And

I doubted he would ever do it as long as my uncle needed him. As of right now, it seemed to me that Dante was one of the few he could still trust.

There was no telling whether one of his own men had turned on him. With each day that passed, I was more and more sure that Dante's suspicion had been right. Someone was conspiring against my uncle. Until we knew who it was, we would have to isolate ourselves more than ever.

My uncle called a week into our stay at the new house, and we filled him in on the events that led us there. He wasn't pleased to learn we were in the middle of nowhere, and he acted as if Dante getting shot was an everyday occurrence.

"It's not Timbuktu, Uncle Michael. There's a town like ten minutes away by car. We're on the edge of the woods here, completely safe. No one knows where we are but you," I assured him.

He seemed more annoyed than anything at my agreement with Dante's decision to bring me here. "Either way, it won't matter for much longer. I want you back at home with me when I get out. This way Dante can get back to doing other things."

His words would have given me relief just a month ago, but now I felt complete and utter dread. He wanted me to move back home with him? And then what? Be a single Mafia *principessa* forever? He sensed my hesitation and questioned me. "Sweetie? Or did you want to go back to California?"

I quickly looked at Dante, who shared my same expression of dread. "No, I don't want to go back to California." When I finished my statement, Dante visibly relaxed.

My uncle took that as an agreement, and he barked with laughter. "Well then, great! I can finally have my family back. I can't tell you how good this feels."

When I hung up the phone, I gently placed it on the counter, and a truly uncomfortable silence fell between us. I was so afraid that he would decide the confrontation wasn't worth it, and the fear forced me to avoid the subject until I couldn't any longer.

Chapter Twenty-Three

*Dante*

The day of Michael's parole finally came. He called a few hours before to let us know after one of his guys got him settled at his home, he would come to our hideout to "debrief" me and see his niece. Even knowing that I wasn't leaving Livia for anything, I still felt the dread in the pit of my stomach at the finality of his words.

It was as if Michael expected me to walk away from Liv now that he was out. From his perspective, he probably thought I would be eager to move on to the next job. He knew me better than anyone else—before Liv, anyway. Did he think I was so heartless I wouldn't have grown to care for her?

Even before I completely crossed the line, I promised to be there for her no matter what, and I couldn't do that if Michael sent me away. A small part of me feared he no longer trusted me around her. I knew I wasn't good enough for her, but the thought of Michael having that mindset stung. I wanted to be good to her. Good *for* her.

Michael had even gone as far as to tell Livia to pack up her stuff to go home with him. I never disobeyed him, but there was no way in hell that he was taking her away from me. As soon as she got off the phone with him, I knew it was now or never.

"Livia, we need to talk."

"I know," she responded in a quiet tone.

I sat down at the kitchen table and gestured for her to join me. When she did, she met my intense gaze with her own fearful one. "Don't you dare pack a single thing." I reached out for her hand and squeezed it firmly. "I'm going to tell him about us, but for me to do that, I need us both to be on the same page here. We need to be a united front if I'm going to defy Michael."

Livia fidgeted uncomfortably in her seat, but didn't let go of my hand. "So, what are we going to say?"

The way she asked made me wonder if she thought I intended to lie to him. "I'm going to tell him the truth. That we got to know each other, and we fell in love. That we're together, and he'll never have to worry about your safety with me around. That's what I'm hoping will sell it. He knows what I'm capable of."

I could see how nervous she was as she nibbled on her lip. "Then what do we need to discuss?"

I swallowed the fear in the back of my mind. The idea of her having second thoughts gave me a sense of dread that I had to face. "I want to make sure you really want this. Me. If he thinks I'm corrupting or coercing you, he won't hesitate to have me killed."

There was no time left for dancing around the subject. And I didn't think I could bear it if she told me that she changed her mind.

"Do you think after everything we've been through, and everything I've told you, that I'm not sure by now? I want you, Dante, and only you."

I felt myself let out the breath I had been holding in. *Thank God.*

"Good. Then maybe you'd like to move in with me

once this is over."

She laughed, and I felt the knot in my stomach loosen further. Her laugh was like velvet in my ears as she flashed me a smirk. "Aren't we doing that already?"

"I mean my apartment in Manhattan. Once it's safe, anyway," I answered with a little more vulnerability than I meant to show. My cards were firmly laid on the table and I was left with nothing to do but wait and hope she would lay down hers.

She was silent for a few scary moments, then said, "I wasn't sure that I wanted to stay in New York...but if it's where you're going to be, then we'll make it home again. Together."

I couldn't hide the broad smile that broke out across my face, and she met it with her own. "God, you have made me a happy man, Liv. I love you so much."

I stood up from the table to pull her into my arms and get my usual fix of her intoxicating scent, burying my nose in her chestnut waves. I backed off after a moment with a disappointed groan. It wouldn't bode well for me to present Livia to her uncle, looking tousled and harassed. "I want to throw you into bed right now, but we have to get ready."

Michael was already on his way. I knew we were cutting it pretty close with this conversation, but I had felt some resistance from Livia's side, which made me anxious to bring it up sooner. I didn't want to push her to make a final decision about us, and then give Michael the impression that we didn't know what we were doing. I felt like a pussy having to ask her the dreaded "What are we?" question, but the suspense of not knowing what her plans were was driving me up a wall.

Livia was a nervous pinball, bouncing around the

house, tidying up and getting herself all dressed up as if she were getting ready for a date. As if Michael would be any less furious if we both looked like we were going to have tea with the queen. Watching her amused me, and I felt myself calming down slightly. She was worried enough for the both of us, and she didn't need me falling apart, too.

I put on my usual dress shirt, black jeans, and boots in a few minutes at Liv's fervent demand. Then I sat in the living room as she paced around the entire house over and over. Eventually, I got tired of watching her zip around with Nero chasing behind her. Even when I turned away, I could hear her shoes clicking on the hardwood floors like the keys on a keyboard.

"Liv, will you relax now? You're giving the dog whiplash."

She paused in front of me, finally ready to relent, but then she suddenly frowned. "Oh my God, what if he sees that the guest bed hasn't been slept in?"

I couldn't hide my bemused reaction. "He's going into the bedrooms now? I'm not planning to beat around the bush for long. Just leave it alone."

She was starting to make me nervous again. I hoped Michael wouldn't be so bold as to ask if I had slept with her. I wasn't sure if he knew she had remained a virgin until I came along, but if he asked, I would tell him the truth. In as appropriate a way as possible. If I told him I had fucked her every which way to Sunday, well, that would just be asking for it.

She shrugged at me and ran off, most likely to mess up the sheets in the guest bedroom and make sure there was no trace of her in the bedroom we had been sharing for a week. A small part of me was a little wounded at the idea of her erasing her presence from our bed. I couldn't think of anywhere she belonged more.

When she came back, she finally slumped onto the couch next to me and exhaled. "What if he tries to force me to leave you?"

"I won't let him." I spoke confidently, keeping my eyes glued to hers. She didn't ask how I would stop him, and I was grateful for that, because I wasn't even sure. I just hoped it wouldn't come down to that.

Livia seemed to absorb a little of my feigned confidence, and she snuggled against me on the couch. I took her hand in mine and brushed soft kisses along her knuckles to ease her nerves. It had the desired effect on her, and me as well. As long as I was touching her smooth skin, nothing could plague my mind. She filled me with her beauty, her love, her gentleness, and her strength. Even when she was feeling weak, I could see the pure will bustling under the surface.

Livia jumped when there was a knock on the door, and she ripped her hand out of my grasp immediately. I had to suppress my eye roll as I lurched off of the couch. The moment had been a pleasant distraction, but now it was over. *Here we go.*

With my hand on my gun, just in case, I peeked out through the peephole to see Michael standing at the door, expressionless. I looked back at Livia and nodded, and she jumped up from the couch to join me at the door when I opened it. Michael came into view with a broad smile on his face the minute he set eyes on his niece. The three of us stood and stared at each other for a few minutes before anyone spoke. I supposed the surreal feeling was mutual. I never thought that we would have been here years ago. The three of us at my "retirement" home in upstate.

He darted his eyes between us a few times, then settled on Livia as he let himself inside. After he crushed her against his chest, they held each other for a long few minutes before they broke apart. She was already crying, and I could only imagine the conflicting thoughts swirling through her head right then. I clenched my fists to stop myself from touching her.

"Sweetheart! *Madonna mia*, it's so good to finally see your face again. Let me get a look at you!" Michael held her at arm's length and surveyed her carefully. What did he think I'd do, let her starve or something? I knew I had no right, but I felt myself growing irritated at his over-the-top concern for her. "You've gotten so tan! That California sun is brutal."

She scoffed at him in embarrassment. "I've always been tan, uncle. You're looking well too. You even lost that gut you were growing," she responded as she patted his belly in jest.

Michael barked out a loud laugh that seemed to echo throughout the house. "I had to whip myself into shape. Things are going to hell, my dear girl, and I need to get everything back in order." He glanced at me when he said that, and I raised a brow in confusion.

*What is that for?*

Livia gave me a nervous glance when her uncle started walking farther into the house, and I answered with a confused shrug. Michael didn't seem to notice our awkwardness as he continued to inspect the house. "This place is nice. I was worried you were keeping my little girl in a haunted house or something."

I understood his protectiveness of her before, but now it was only getting on my nerves. Did Michael think

I couldn't take care of her? I couldn't hold in my snort of derision. "Of course not, Michael. I wanted to be sure she was comfortable."

"Of course," he threw out casually. We followed him as he walked through the house, and I wanted to laugh to myself for questioning Livia earlier. He really *was* going to be a nosy prick. But why would he even think of checking the bedrooms?

Livia couldn't seem to stand the awkwardness anymore. "So, do you want to sit down? I made some pasta salad for us because I know how much you used to love it. I figured we could eat and catch up properly." She intercepted him before he reached the bedrooms and tried to usher him back toward the kitchen.

I wanted to kiss her or touch her in some way to get her to relax, but I had to will myself to keep my hands at my sides. She was flailing, and I was sure that Michael had picked up on it by now. He hesitantly gave up on his search of the house and followed Livia back into the kitchen like a puppy. I supposed her cooking had that effect on everyone.

Michael settled down at the kitchen table and patted his stomach. "I missed that pasta salad, sweetie. They had it sometimes in the cafeteria, but it tasted like fucking glue, and it only made me more depressed. I'm so glad to be back home."

Livia flashed him a genuine smile that weaseled its way through her apparent nervousness. She opened the fridge and grabbed the bowl of pasta salad she had prepared. "I'm happy, too."

The smile quickly faded when he uttered his next words, "Did you get all packed up?"

She noticeably froze in place with the bowl of pasta

in her hands and shot a quick glance at me beside her. "Um…"

Michael's face fell immediately. "So, it's true then."

*What the hell?* I didn't know if we had completely failed at acting normal, but there was no point in denying it now.

With my voice as low and unthreatening as possible, I said, "Michael…"

He held up his hand to tell me to shut my mouth. "Don't say a goddamned word, Dante. I had an extra guy on the previous safe house. I was hoping he misheard a conversation with one of your whores, and it was all just a big misunderstanding. But you really went there, didn't you? How could you, of all people, do this to me?"

Livia slammed the bowl down in the center of the table. The sudden thud took us both by surprise. "With all due respect, uncle, do *what* exactly to you?"

Already seething, Michael avoided her eyes when he addressed her again. "Defile you!"

His words mirrored my own thoughts all those weeks ago, and I felt a wave of disappointment flow over me. I knew he would likely think exactly that, but I had hoped he wouldn't. We had a friendship, but knowing he thought so little of me made me unbearably angry until I couldn't sit quietly anymore.

"I don't know what you were told, but it isn't what you think."

He interrupted me immediately. "So, you didn't fuck my niece?"

Livia flinched beside me at his harsh words. "Uncle Michael!"

"Shut your mouth, Livia. You don't know what you're getting yourself into," he responded angrily, making her tear up instantly. "All those years I protected you from the harsh realities…down the fucking tubes. How could you be so foolish?"

She had told me he had never yelled at her. Hearing him talk to her this way sent me over the edge, and I slammed my hand on the table to direct his attention back to me. I would be damned if I was going to let him berate her in front of me. "Listen to me! Michael, I never intended for this to happen, but it's not what you think. I'm not just screwing around with her like a stupid teenager. I'm in love with her!"

My passionate outburst made him slide back in his chair and stalk toward me with unbridled rage in his eyes. His fury seemed to come off of him in waves as he stood inches away from me, burning me with his glare. "Bullshit, Dante. I've never known you to fuck the same woman twice. What's different now? Because she's off-limits?"

Michael stepped closer to me. I didn't retreat, only forcing him to come nose-to-nose with me. I was going to stand my ground if it killed me. And the way things were going, that was certainly a possibility.

Livia tried to force her way between us, but when neither of us budged, she settled for shouting at Michael while he stared me down. "I've been in a goddamned cage for my entire life because of you, uncle! If I'm taboo, it's because you made it so. Dante didn't do anything wrong. It was all me. He kept pushing me away because of his loyalty to you, but I kept it up until he gave in."

He finally turned to face her, his astonishment apparent on his face. "Why?"

"Because I love him. I'm not leaving him, so you're

going to have to get over it. I'm a grown woman, Uncle Michael. I can make my own decisions."

She reached out to touch his arm, and somehow, he seemed to let go of some of his anger under her touch. His anger was quickly replaced with sadness, and I wasn't sure which emotion bothered me more. "I never wanted this life for you, sweetie. And you never did, either. You won't be happy with him…"

"Michael," I started slowly, forcing my voice to come out as calmly as possible. I felt anything but. "I swear to you that I'm serious about this. I would never do anything to hurt her. I want to marry her."

Livia gasped. I turned to her to take her hand in mine. I pressed my lips to the back of her hand as I watched her beautiful coffee eyes glaze over.

Michael soon reminded us of his presence when he shouted, "Jesus, Mary, and Joseph! I can't trust your promises anymore. And I don't know what you've done to my niece, but this is not fucking happening."

"Yes, it is," I informed him in an even tone. "You know me. I wouldn't defy you unless I had a good reason. There is no better reason than this beautiful woman you raised. She's strong-willed, and you know I could never force her to do anything she doesn't want. Without knowing it, you gifted me with the presence of the only person apart from you who made me feel like I was worth something. She's the one who changed me."

Still clasping my hand, Livia seemed to radiate strength into me with her next words. "It's true. He's told me everything about his childhood and his life. I wasn't under any false impressions about what kind of man he is. I love him because of it, not in spite of it. Even after a life of nothing but pain, he was ready to deprive himself of true happiness just to remain loyal to you. Could you do that to him? Could you take away Dante's happiness? And mine?"

Michael almost appeared to shrivel in front of her. "No. I don't want that." He turned to me, setting his green eyes firmly on mine. "If you hurt her in any way, I will kill you myself."

I stared back, unflinching. "If I hurt her, you won't need to kill me. I'll already be dead."

He scoffed at my declaration and sat back down at the table. "I get out of prison just to be given a heart attack on the same day. I don't understand this at all."

"You don't have to understand it. You just have to back off," Livia responded calmly, which caused both of us to turn to her in shock.

"Fine. I won't intervene, but I don't like this. I think it's a mistake." Michael shot a disappointed look at Livia, but she let it slide. At least she wouldn't be mourning me today, and that was the most I could hope for.

I had fully expected this confrontation to come to blows, but I was relieved when it didn't. Livia relaxed at my side, but still clasped my hand as we joined Michael at the table to eat. It was awkward to sit across from him while he stared at me like he didn't know who I was anymore. I would have been lying if I said it didn't hurt to know that he thought I would hurt Livia or make her unhappy.

Yeah, I used to sleep around. So did Michael. That part of the lifestyle was expected, but I secretly hoped one day I would meet someone who would make me want more. I was convinced that every step I'd made in this world brought me closer to where I needed to be, to make Livia finally see me. And now that she had, I was never letting her go.

Chapter Twenty-Four

*Livia*

Once I felt comfortable enough to leave my uncle alone with Dante without the risk of gunplay, I snuck to the bathroom to calm my frazzled nerves. I never thought I'd find the nerve to speak to my uncle that way without Dante there to support me. It felt like a weight was lifted from my shoulders—and it had surprisingly little to do with the topic of our relationship.

I didn't know how much I had needed to stand up to Uncle Michael until that moment. Once I did, I felt as if I had grown several inches taller. I wasn't defying him, but fighting for my future. For too many years, he had run my life. Even if it had been for the right reasons, that didn't make it okay.

The past four years played in my head like a movie. Every step I'd made since my uncle was arrested led me to where I was. If I hadn't made the decision to leave New York and become my own person, would I have stood my ground the way I did just now? I thought it was very unlikely.

I would have never had the chance to get to know Dante on a deeper level, and get to experience a love that went above and beyond what I had seen in movies and books. Every step I took was a move toward where I was meant to be, and it was at this moment I knew what home meant to me. If I knew myself, I was already there.

I looked down to see that my hands had finally stopped shaking, and I threw some water on my face before I went back out to the kitchen. My uncle was still giving Dante a disdainful look, and when he saw me, he got up from the table in a rush. "Well, I guess I'm out of here then. Dante says you're staying with him, so I'll see you back in the city."

He wouldn't even look at me; that was how disappointed he was. It hurt to see him regard me that way, especially since he always acted like I could do no wrong. It stung, but I had to brush it off. *This needs to happen, so he knows I can make my own choices.* "Is it safe to come back?"

My uncle approached me to give me a very limp one-armed hug, giving Dante the death glare as he passed. "Yes. No one will try anything now that I'm back. You'll be within our turf. Now I have to go see Augustine before anything else happens."

I ignored his comment. "All right, well, we'll have lunch again soon."

Acting as casual as possible, I hoped to calm him down enough to act normal with me. It was possible I'd have to accept the fact that he might never warm to the idea of Dante and me together. He gave me a tight nod and left without giving Dante a second glance.

Once the sound of his car had faded into the distance, I looked up at Dante as he sat across from me at the kitchen table. We had both been frozen in place, not speaking for several minutes, and the tension was palpable. His face was a little pale, and I felt a pang of guilt. "Are you okay?"

He frowned at me and picked at the last few pieces

of pasta on his plate. "I'm relieved that I don't have cinder blocks tied to my feet right now, but I don't think he's ever going to forgive me for this."

I reached out for his hand. "He just needs to get used to the idea. Once he sees how we are together, and how happy you make me, he'll get over it. You'll be even more special to him because you'll be…" I trailed off with a blush.

I couldn't make myself say it. I didn't know if he had meant what he said, or if it had been something that just came out in the heat of the moment. Maybe he had only made his declaration to make my uncle see that he was serious. I hadn't had time to think about it yet, but the idea of being his wife didn't fill me with the fear I expected.

Dante cracked a smile finally. "Family."

It struck me then how impactful that would be for him. We were both orphans, but at least I still had my uncle. I knew his anger toward me would wane with time—it always had. But if this ruined their relationship, Dante would truly have no one. I made up my mind then to do anything I could to make sure that their relationship was repaired. I wanted more than anything for him to know what it felt like to have a family again, starting with me.

I had to bite my lip to hold back my wide grin. "Did you really mean that?"

"You're the only woman in the world who can bring me to my knees. Of course, I meant it. I would prefer for your uncle to approve, but I don't think that's going to happen. Are you okay with that, Liv?" He met my eyes with his, and the flecks of gold in his irises seemed to shimmer with pure, unadulterated love.

I nodded and squeezed his hand. "I love you. I'm not going to put my life on hold anymore just to stay in my uncle's good graces. When it was just going to school and staying out of trouble, that was one thing. But leaving you? He's asking too much from me, and I'm not doing it anymore."

Dante gave me his blistering smile again and got up from the table, taking my hand in his. "Then come, get packed. I want to take you home, my beautiful girl."

\*\*\*\*

I forced Dante to sit still so that I could change his bandages again before we left. It was going to be a long drive back to Manhattan, and even though it was slowly healing, I wanted to make sure it stayed clean. "Does it still hurt?"

"Not nearly as much, thanks to you. I think I still need a kiss to make it better."

I took a few steps back from him and started putting away the medical supplies. "Oh no, you don't. That's a slippery slope. I want to get back to your apartment before it gets dark."

My sexual experience was limited to him, but I knew by now that a simple kiss was never just a kiss. Dante seemed to revel in how responsive I was to his touch, and he greatly enjoyed watching me melt into a pool of desire under his ministrations. He knew my every weakness, and he used them against me constantly. It never ended with just a kiss. The minute we made contact, the undeniable pull was too powerful to stop.

He smirked at me again and looped his arms around my waist as if he'd been able to read my thoughts. Or maybe he saw the flush rising on my cheeks. "I love it when you talk dirty."

"Now who's the fiend? It's only been a few days. You need time to recover." I pried his arms from my waist. "You're insatiable, Mr. Castellano."

"You only have yourself to blame, Ms. Rossi."

The conversation with my uncle had been productive on more than one level. It forced us not only to confront our fears about being an actual couple, but also forced us to talk about where we wanted it all to go. It was easy to let important discussions sit on the back burner while we were in a life-threatening situation, but with my uncle insisting things were taken care of, there were no more excuses. And now I knew where Dante stood. He wanted to marry me.

After dodging his affections through the entire house, we finally had the car packed up and ready to head back to Manhattan for the first time in four years. It almost felt like I hadn't really been in New York at all, because I'd been isolated in Queens and then upstate. After seeing my uncle again, I felt more ready than I had two weeks ago, and I held my head high as we climbed into the car to go home.

His hand rested lightly on my thigh while he drove, and he seemed more cheerful than I had ever seen him. "Dante?"

"Yes, *tesoro*?"

"I'm going to miss that house. Do you think you'll ever retire?" I asked, sounding like a nagging wife already. But with everything else out of the way, I wanted to know what his plans were for that house.

He shrugged a little. "Eventually, it would be nice. For now, it can just be a vacation home for when we want to get away. What do you think about that?"

I smiled at him. "I'd like that."

At least it hadn't been a hard no. I didn't push it further, not wanting to spoil his good mood. We fell into a comfortable silence as we drove. Dante knew I needed time to process all the changes happening in my life, and for that, I was extremely grateful.

When we finally drove over the bridge into Manhattan a few hours later, I felt a sudden wave of nostalgia that had me reeling, followed by a rush of conflicting emotions. He quickly took my hand. "You're okay, Liv. I've got you."

He hadn't even needed to look at me to know what I was feeling. I didn't think I could have made myself come back without him, and I squeezed his hand and held it in my lap. I hoped for some of his unwavering strength to seep into me through the mere contact of his skin. "I know you do. That's the only reason I feel like I can do this."

He turned to me with a reassuring smile on his face. "Don't give me all the credit. You could have refused at any time and run away, but you didn't. I'm proud of you."

Once we reached his apartment building, Dante parked out front next to a truly gorgeous car that had my eyes bugging out of my head. "Whose is that?"

"It's mine. I had to be incognito in California, but this'll be our ride from now on. You like it?"

"It's amazing. Can I drive it?"

Dante laughed and slid out of the car to unload our stuff. "Judging by your getaway performance the other day, I can't see why not. Just be careful not to run over any small animals or children."

I climbed out and gave him a mighty scowl as I reached to take my share of the bags. "Hey! I was under duress. You can't hold me accountable for that. I didn't crash the car or anything. Not a single deer was harmed in the making of my getaway."

"I suppose you're right. I didn't know I had such a little adrenaline junkie on my hands. I hope I won't get too boring for you." Dante threw me the keys for the building and refused to let me help as I ushered Nero out of the car. Not that he needed ushering; he was frantic to be able to move around again. Just like his dad, I laughed to myself.

"Life with you could never be boring. And besides, you owe me. We abandoned my car in California."

"Fair point, but I definitely wouldn't have wanted you to continue driving that death trap in the city anyway." The look he gave me told me that he was completely serious and not to be questioned. I raised my brow. "I'll replace it with something safer, Liv. Don't argue, please."

"Fine, I'll just take yours and you can buy yourself a nice minivan," I joked as I unlocked the front door and we filed into the lobby.

I felt a pinch on my ass, and I let out a loud gasp of surprise when I turned back to see Dante shaking his head at me with an amused grin. "You're going to be the death of me, woman."

When we made it to the second floor, Dante unlocked the door to his apartment and led me inside. I let Nero go running to find his many toys while I took a look around. With all of our constant moving around, I had yet to see any place Dante inhabited that actually felt like him—until now.

The first thing I noticed was a framed portrait of some famous violinist above his couch, which made me smile. His couch was a long black leather sectional, with a sleek all-glass coffee table in front of it. It was facing a large wall-mounted TV. I walked farther into the living room to take a look at the books on his table. They were all biographies of musicians and history books. I felt like I was getting a new glance into the inner mind of Dante, and I was surprised by how comfortable I was already.

I felt his chest against my back, his head perched on my shoulder. His deep voice rumbled in my ear as his hands rested on my hips. "What are you thinking about, Liv?"

I could tell that he was nervous about bringing me here, and he desperately wanted me to be happy. I took a deep breath. This place even smelled like him. So comforting and safe. I breathed out, "I'm home."

I didn't have to turn around to see his smile. I heard it in his voice. "Finally."

Dante took me on a brief tour of the rest of the apartment. The kitchen was obviously the least kitted out part of the place, as he admitted he couldn't cook to save his life. I told him that was going to change unless he wanted to remain a disgrace to all Italians. Dante seemed so happy to have me there, he didn't even fight me on it, assuring me that he would gladly learn anything I had to teach him.

The last place he brought me was the bedroom, which was minimal, but in a good way. No TV. Just a bed, lamps, nightstands, the closet, and dark gray sheets almost the color of Nero's fur. I laughed to myself and wondered if he had gotten those so that the dog hair wouldn't show up.

"I look forward to christening this bed as soon as possible," I whispered as I went up on the tips of my toes to kiss his shoulder blade.

He chuckled while he hung our things up in the closet. "Why do you think I'm unpacking so fast?"

I feigned ignorance with a grin. "Why is that? Are you so deprived, you poor man?"

Dante turned around and slid his hand into my hair at the nape of my neck, bringing my face close to his until I felt his warm breath against my lips. "You have no idea. I need to be inside you, baby. I need to hear you panting while I make you come over and over again until you beg me to stop." His voice came out husky and even deeper than usual. "And then, my beautiful girl, I'm going to lick every drop of sweat and arousal from your body. I want you spent, your wild hair across my pillows as you gasp for breath, knowing that I'm the only man who will ever make you feel that way."

I felt my knees wobbling from his sensual promise. "Oh God, Dante…hurry up and finish. I'll go walk Nero and then I want you naked and waiting for me."

I tried to rush away from him, if only to stop my heart from thundering in my chest. "Wait. I don't want you going out alone. I'll come with you." He stepped away from the suitcase to follow me.

"I'm just going to take him up the block and come right back. Get back to work." I giggled when he smacked my ass as I ran off to get Nero. He was already waiting at the door. I felt bad for the dog being cooped up in the car all day.

"Just a quick one, Nero. Your dad is very demanding, and he requires my presence," I joked. Nero eagerly bounded down the stairs, with me trailing behind. I threw open the front door to the building and smelled the city air I used to love, and hopefully would again.

I tried to ignore the throbbing pulse between my legs as I rushed up the block, willing Nero to do his business as quick as possible so I could get back to my confounding man.

## Chapter Twenty-Five

*Dante*

When I finished hanging our clothes up in the closet, I tore off my shirt as per my demanding temptress' request. I looked down at the wound on my torso, which was slowly getting better. I thought Livia was being too cautious. It had been almost a week since we had sex, and already I was starving for her. I kicked off my shoes and socks before I went to the window to check on her.

Both of us were being overly cautious of each other. Her for my safety, and me for hers. I peeked out the window to see her pacing down the block with Nero walking beside her, more dutifully than he ever did with me. Damn traitor he was. Seeing how he guarded her made me feel better, and I lay back on the bed to wait for her.

At that moment, I felt a wave of pure happiness. I was finally back home, where I felt most comfortable, and I wasn't alone anymore. I told myself I was okay with being by myself before, but it was apparent now that I had never been truly content. If I wasn't in bed with Nero, there was a random woman or a bottle of liquor that I would think about drinking, but never touch—to test my resolve. It wasn't until Liv that I found a temptation I couldn't resist. She was here, and she was mine. I intended to indulge in her every day until the end of my life, or as long as she would have me. I had never felt so helpless to another person since I was a child, and for the first time, I was relieved to let the wall tumble down.

It wasn't until I snapped out of my reverie that I realized it had been fifteen minutes since she'd gone outside. I looked at the clock to double-check, and then I started to get worried. Climbing off of the bed, I glanced out the window and saw nothing. She had said she was only going up the block…

As if to confirm my worst fear, I heard Nero's frantic barks from downstairs.

Not bothering with my shoes or a shirt, I threw myself out the front door and barreled down the stairs past the front lobby. I opened the front door of the building and my heart dropped when I looked down to see Nero on the doorstep, a bleeding gash over his right eye, and holding up an injured paw. He still had his leash on, and when I stepped outside, Livia was nowhere in sight.

*Oh, God. No. Please.*

I didn't care if I looked ridiculous; I ran out onto the street in my jeans, bare-chested, with no shoes, whipping my head around for any sign of her. I screamed her name until my voice came out rough and hoarse, only to be cursed at by my neighbors. "Shut the fuck up, man!"

"*Vaffanculo!*" I shouted back at my upstairs neighbor with a crude gesture before I rushed back inside. Nero limped behind me, still whining.

I knew someone had taken her. Nero had never been spooked like this before, and he followed me back inside guiltily, as if he knew he messed up. I wanted to comfort him, but I didn't have the patience for that at the moment.

Who was going to comfort me? I was the one who had to call Michael and tell him I lost her. Already.

What scared me even more than Michael's rage was knowing that every second I didn't find her, the less the chances were of finding her alive. I couldn't bear to think about it, and I took a deep breath to brace myself before I rang Michael. As pissed with me as he was, he still picked up on the first ring.

"What?" he spat out, clearly not pleased to be hearing from me at all. He was about to be much less pleased, if that was even possible.

I cleared my throat to stop the sob I felt crawling up my throat. "Livia...she's missing."

Angling the phone away from my ear in anticipation, I heard Michael's roar of anger. "What? You lost her? How?"

"I don't know. She insisted that she go alone to walk Nero, just up the block. I checked on her and she was fine...but then I heard Nero barking downstairs. He was there, and she just...wasn't. I don't understand, Michael..."

I couldn't think straight. I needed him to be the logical one for both of us as the fear clouded my mind from thinking like a bodyguard. I wasn't her bodyguard anymore. My ability to think rationally was gone the minute I laid my hands on her.

"God dammit. I'm coming over and I need your ass outside searching and interrogating everyone you fucking see. I knew letting her stay with you was a mistake." He hung up before I could argue or agree with him. At this point, I didn't even know whether he was wrong or not.

He pulled up to the building ten minutes later as I

was asking passersby if they had seen her, showing them the photo of her that I had kept in my wallet since Michael gave it to me. He walked up to me, his shoulders squared like he was ready to end my life, and I wouldn't have even blamed him. I knew I shouldn't have let her out alone, but I wanted to let her have a small piece of freedom back. She should have been able to walk outside in our area without getting dragged away. The more I thought about it, the more the anger welled up inside me.

And I turned on Michael before I could think twice. "This is Rossi territory. How the fuck did they come in here and grab her without anyone noticing? I would never have brought her back if you didn't tell me it was safe…She would have screamed for help. Why didn't she scream?"

As I felt my control slipping through my fingers, Michael looked suddenly lost, as if he didn't know what to do with me. This wasn't like me at all.

He furrowed his brow. "I don't know. But we need to find out, and fast. I thought if anyone was going to retaliate against me, they would have come at me directly once I was out. The fact that they're still going after her means it's personal. They don't want me dead, not yet."

"It has to be the Leones," I threw out. "They seemed to have some kind of obsession with her."

Michael set his suspicious gaze on me. "Why do you say that? We've been cordial with them for years. It doesn't make any sense."

It wasn't my business to tell him Livia's secret. Then again, she hadn't expressly told me not to. It was a matter of life and death, and I made the decision. "It's not like they haven't tried shit with her before."

Michael stilled. "What are you talking about?"

"It was after you got arrested...She went to Augustine's club, and some of the Leone's guys were there. They tried to mess with her," I answered carefully. I wasn't sure he would want to hear the details, but I also wasn't sure I could get the words out without going into a blind rage. I already wanted to make the streets run red with blood.

He stepped closer, forcing me to look into his eyes. "What. Did. They. Do. To. Her?" Michael's furious face mirrored my own, and I had to force myself to look away again. "And how do you know about it?"

"They drugged her, forced her to strip for them...she told me about it the night we were stuck in Illinois. That's what she was holding back from me when I first came to California," I explained, defeated. "It's why she didn't want to come back—she was afraid."

The only way to describe his face at that moment was brokenhearted. "Why didn't she tell me? I would have taken care of...any piece of shit that dared to leer at her!"

"That's why she didn't tell you. She didn't want to give you a reason to keep her on an even tighter leash. She felt trapped."

I barely got the words out before he stared me down with a hatred I had never seen, not since my father was alive. "You think because she told you one secret and let you in her bed that you know her better than me? That you know what's best for her? You. Know. Nothing."

"This is fucking pointless. I called you for help, but if you want to have a pissing match instead, I'll just go find her myself!"

I began to walk back inside to get dressed, but Michael grabbed my shoulder. "No. I may not like you two being together, but…at least I can trust that you'll do anything to get her back. We go together," he stated with finality, barely curbing the rough edge of fury in his voice. I could still see it in his eyes.

Once I threw on clothes almost without looking, we rushed back down to my car and sped off. I knew where those disgusting pricks liked to hang out, and a plan began to form in my head. I pushed the terror of losing Livia out of my mind and focused instead on the maelstrom of hatred to keep me going. Michael was seething next to me the entire ride to Lombardi's club. He grunted as we pulled into the parking lot of the seedy nightclub. "Two birds, one stone, I guess. I haven't seen Augustine since I got out."

The bouncer at the front door immediately fawned over Michael like a schoolgirl, and he looked quite disappointed at the response he got—a quick shove out of the way as we threw open the doors and walked in. I thought perhaps we should have tried to be a little stealthier, but it was unnecessary. As we surveyed the crowds of drunk and horny patrons, not a Leone was in sight. But this wasn't the only place they hung out.

"The VIP room," I whispered to Michael, who only nodded and walked ahead of me, making a beeline for the back room. I stopped him at the door. "They might recognize you. I'll go in and look for any of their men."

"Fine. Hurry up," he said as he started nervously scanning the crowd again in the main area of the club.

I slipped inside as quietly as I could, but barely anyone looked up from the dancers' tits to notice me. The wall was lined with plush leather couches for viewing, and tables in front, facing the center of the room where women gyrated against several stripper poles. I had been to a few strip joints in the past, but never got much from it. I had always figured it was a waste to pay women to strip for exorbitant amounts of money. All I used to do was buy a woman a drink and then take her home. It was much more efficient, in my opinion.

But looking at those poles now filled me with rage rather than indifference. I had to shake my head to rid myself of the image of Livia hugging that pole and crying as the pigs who came to this club humiliated her. I wanted to kill everyone in here, especially the Leones. I zeroed in on every piece of shit in there, and none of them were their guys.

I popped back out of the room after double-checking, and Michael glanced up at me hopefully. I shook my head at him. "Augustine?"

"No," he answered.

I gestured for him to follow me back outside, but there was a sudden influx of patrons coming in. Technically, no one knew why we were here, but we didn't want to arouse suspicion. We slipped out the back, and like a beacon, I saw Luca Leone pressing a woman up against the dumpster, sucking on her face. I approached, and the moron didn't even notice me until I snaked my hand between them and clasped his throat in my fist, pulling him away from the stripper.

"We need to talk, Luca."

"Can't you see I'm busy?" Leone groaned. His attitude disappeared the moment he clocked Michael behind me, glaring at him with pure fire in his eyes. "Oh shit, Don Rossi! What did I do?"

"We're going to find out."

I whipped out my pistol and smacked him across the temple. The stripper jumped at the sudden thud that rang out through the alley. I didn't look up as her heels clicked away from us. Maybe I shouldn't have knocked him out in front of a witness, but I didn't care at the moment. It had already been an hour since Livia disappeared. Dread sank farther into my stomach with every minute that passed.

He fell like a bag of rocks to the ground. I tossed my keys to Michael as he ran to get the car, and I hoisted the man up into my arms. By the time I had hauled him to the street behind the club, Michael sped up to the curb and jumped out to help me throw him in the trunk. I had been slacking on my workouts, and I felt a dull throbbing in my wound when I un-tensed.

"Fuck," I breathed out. I hated that I needed to be strong more than ever, and I was the weakest I had ever been. *Get it together, Castellano. Livia needs you.*

We drove to one of the safe houses in the city. Our men surrounded it, so there were no shocked looks as we dragged the unconscious Leone prick into the house. Michael and I worked in tandem. I grabbed a chair and put it in the middle of the room, as he went into the kitchen and grabbed some duct tape. I plopped the guy into the chair, and Michael got to work taping his hands together. I secured his feet to the chair legs in case he tried to get up. Once he was in perfect position, I landed a punch across his face to give him a little wake-up call.

He stirred, then coughed a little blood out before he opened his terrified eyes to see us both glaring down at him. "Why are you doing this? Augustine's is neutral territory! I didn't do anything wrong!"

I leaned over, resting my hands on the arms of the chair and bringing my face level with his. "Where the fuck is Livia Rossi?"

He furrowed his brows in confusion. He darted a fear filled look between Michael and me. "What are you talking about? Didn't she move to California?"

Michael and I shared a quick glance, and a sliver of hope died inside me. He leaned closer and growled in his face, "No, and I think you knew that. We know your people assaulted her four years ago."

Luca's eyes flashed with fear then. "No! I swear, the minute we found out about it, anyone who took part in that was dealt with. You have to believe me, Don Rossi."

I didn't trust this guy as far as I could throw him. "I think you're lying," I threw out in as casual a tone as I could manage. I scanned the area quickly, then walked to the kitchen. I heard him call out to me, but I said nothing until I walked back into the room holding a pair of garden shears. "Are you willing to bet a few fingers on that?"

Luca struggled in his chair, his eyes wide. "No, please. I'm telling you the truth. It's not us that's after you! You need to look a little closer. I can't say more, or they'll dump me in the river. You know they will."

I knew a man would say almost anything to get himself out of trouble, but for some reason, I was beginning to believe what he was saying.

We ended up letting the Leone guy leave with all of his fingers intact, swearing he wouldn't say anything to anyone. Then Michael and I spent the next few hours calling around, but nobody seemed to know anything, or at least they refused to tell us.

Things got eerily quiet as the night went on, and we had no news. By now, I knew without a shadow of a doubt that we were being betrayed. If Michael was ever going to forgive me for "corrupting" Livia, then he certainly wouldn't if she got hurt because I wasn't looking after her. *Which was your job, you stunad!* If I had to burn down Manhattan to find her, I would.

The sinking feeling I got in my chest had me reeling, and I turned to Michael. "I know who it is, and you're not going to like it."

That coward had stayed away on purpose.

Chapter Twenty-Six

*Livia*

I woke up confused and disoriented in complete darkness. The last thing I remembered was walking down the block with Nero. But I wasn't outdoors anymore, that much I was sure of.

There was hard ground under my feet. After a few minutes, the haze faded enough for me to make an attempt to move, but my limbs felt like they were made of lead when I tried to lift them. I felt weak and nauseated. Listening hard for any signs of life around me, I quickly lost hope when I heard nothing.

Wherever I was, it was almost unnaturally dark. Even outside, there would have been ambient light of some kind. A distant skyscraper, a streetlight, or the moon at least. But there was nothing. I felt myself beginning to panic. How had I gone from walking Nero to being somewhere else, unable to remember anything? I felt so sick. I tried to feel around for the dog, but when my arms didn't move, it dawned on me that someone had tied me up. *Oh, God.*

It took conscious effort to get myself to slow my breathing. I couldn't afford to freak out as I tried hard to remember what happened after I got outside. Playing back the last minutes I could remember like a movie, over and over. I stepped outside with Nero, I walked down the block, I glanced up to see Dante at the window before he turned away, I turned back…and then there was nothing.

*Oh my God, Dante!* He must have realized that I was gone by now, and he would be freaking out, wondering where I had gone. My heart began hammering against my chest. Dante would come for me. He always did. I just had to keep my head on straight and stay alive for as long as possible.

I jolted against my restraints when the lights in the room turned on in a blinding flash. They were those obnoxious fluorescent ones that flickered, making me feel like I was in a bad horror movie. I blinked rapidly to adjust to the sudden brightness and darted my gaze around the room, which only added to my dizziness. It looked like I was in a warehouse, but it was suspiciously barren, with nothing on the shelves surrounding me.

When I turned my face forward again, I saw a figure standing in front of me in a sleek gray suit and blue tie. The lights formed a blurry halo behind his head, obscuring his face from me. The voice I heard sent a shiver down my spine.

"It's lovely to see you again, Livia. How have you been? It's been…what? Four years?"

I continued blinking until his face came into focus. The room spun. All I wanted to do was close my eyes. *No. Not him.* I managed to croak, "What do you want?"

Augustine Lombardi just smirked, ignoring my question as he paced back and forth in front of me. "How's Michael?"

*Is that a threat?* I felt my hackles rise immediately. I may have been mad at him, but no one messed with my uncle. "He's perfectly fine. Why?"

He shrugged, content to ask all the questions and ignore all of mine. "And what about that guy...what's his name?"

"Dante? He's coming for me, I'm sure," I answered, keeping my focus on Augustine's smug face. I got a glimpse of that stupid rat tail and wanted so badly to rip it off as it swished back and forth as he paced the floor in front of me.

Augustine circled me slowly, his icy blue eyes trailing from my head to my toes as if he were getting immense pleasure from seeing me like this. For the first time, I looked down to take in the state I was in. I was tied to a chair with my hands behind my back, and my ankles were tied to the chair legs. There was dirt on my shirt, and tears all over my clothes as if I'd been dragged around like a rag doll.

"Oh, I'm counting on it," he sneered. "But I'm not talking about Castellano. I mean Eric. Spoken to him lately?" His voice trailed off; the leering grin made my skin crawl.

I had been trying to wiggle my hands free from the rope but the way he said that froze me to the spot, figuratively and literally. "Oh, my God. What did you do to him? He had no part in anything!"

Augustine chuckled, almost to himself. "You didn't know? Eric's been my assistant for a while now."

What was he talking about? "That's not possible. Eric had no idea who my family was. He would never help you!"

"While you had your little bulldog following you around, we went after Eric. He was able to keep an eye on you for me," he said with a suggestive wink. "He's a talented photographer, don't you think?"

He held out a photo in front of me, and he chuckled when he saw the blood leave my face. Everything snapped into place. I squeezed my eyes shut to stop the tears that threatened to come. I didn't want Augustine to see me cry.

I should have known Eric took that photo of me, and I felt stupid for not realizing it sooner; he hadn't even tried to mask his usual style.

*Bulldog.* He had used the same word to describe Dante. How long had he been reporting to Lombardi? Tears stabbed the back of my eyes, but I refused to let them squeeze their way out. Everyone always left or betrayed me. Why did I think it would change now?

Even knowing Dante was coming for me, Augustine had me right where he wanted me. This was a trap, and there was nothing I could do to prevent it from unfolding the way he wanted. I sagged in my chair and tried to steady my voice. "Why are you doing this?"

"Because you're Michael Rossi's most precious possession. And I want to ruin you as he ruined me."

"Michael did nothing to you! You're supposed to be on his side!" I shrieked at him, finally finding my voice, fueled by hatred for this man. He hadn't assaulted me, but he may as well have. He allowed those men into his club, not caring what they did to women who were unlucky enough to fall into their grasp.

"He kept you sheltered if you believe that, little Liv." He smirked and smoothed down his already impeccably unwrinkled tie. "I'm a little wounded that you never answered my text."

By this point, my heart was threatening to pound out of my chest. "That was you?"

"Aren't you curious to know who killed your

parents?"

"I know Carmine killed them," I said confidently, before realizing something. Why was he bringing that up now? Had Dante not told me the whole story?

Augustine leaned down, bringing his face level with mine. "That's how I made it look. Honestly, it was nothing personal. I just needed to get rid of the competition." He gave me a saccharine smile as if confessing to my parents' murders were nothing but a tick on his laundry list.

"I'll just fill you in since you're already sitting down. Angelo was a pussy. He wanted to leave all this, and yet he was still in line to become don before me, and he was more respected. I had Carmine watching him, and he let me know that he was packing up the family to run away. Now, I couldn't have that." When he reached down to stroke my cheek, I nearly threw myself back in the chair to escape his touch.

I knew he wouldn't hesitate to kill me. I needed to bide my time, with no choice but to sit there and listen to him talk shit about my family and tell me every detail of his efforts to destroy my uncle. "Do not touch me," I hissed.

Flashing me an infuriating smirk, he moved his hand to a lock of my hair and stroked it. "Do you know what I did next?"

I closed my eyes. "You cut the brakes," I answered in a shaky voice, already knowing the answer.

He lightly slapped my cheek. "Smart girl. So, Angelo was out, and then I let Carmine take the fall for the hit. Now there's just one more obstacle in my way," he finished with a self-satisfied smile on his face. When he flashed me his teeth, they looked almost too white against his tanned olive skin.

I wanted to be grateful that Dante hadn't lied to me, but at the moment, all I felt was pain. The version of the story that made Augustine look like a hero was nothing but a lie, and now I knew the truth. Augustine was a traitor.

I narrowed my eyes. "Then why am I here? Grow some balls and confront Michael yourself. You won't survive it, but at least you won't be a goddamned coward."

He raised his brow. "You've got a real mouth on you, little girl. Somehow, I remember you quite differently."

My temper was rising to a dangerous level. "And how is that? You don't even know me."

"I'm very glad you asked." Augustine looked like he was deep in thought for a minute, before reaching into his pocket and taking out his phone. "More like your performance a while back. You might not remember. I enjoyed it so much that I kept the footage. Want to see it?"

I felt my blood run cold. "No!"

I hated myself for being weak, but just the reminder of the worst night of my life sent me into a complete state of panic. The picture formed in my head, like a bird's eye view, watching myself get naked for a bunch of sick freaks. I prayed he was bluffing.

He sauntered uncomfortably closer to me. "Why not? I'm almost glad that I failed in killing you all those years ago. You have quite a nice figure. If you weren't such a snooty princess, I would have loved to have you as a *cumare*."

I couldn't stop myself from physically recoiling at

the idea of having sex with him. "I'm no whore," I spat out angrily. "And even if I were, I'd die before I would have sex with you."

Augustine's smile faded, replaced with anger. "That can be arranged." Then he reached out, grasping my chin in his fist to the point of pain, and directing it to his phone. He leaned in close to growl, "Close your eyes, and I'll let my guys come in so we can reenact it instead."

I froze in place, unable to hide my terror. This man really was unhinged, and I knew that I had no choice but to relive it one way or another. I dragged my gaze to the screen of his phone, letting my tears fall freely. He wanted to break me, and he had succeeded. I tried to focus on a part of the video that I wasn't visible in, and I let my eyes go blurry as I thought about the only thing that I could to make me feel better—Dante.

He was the only one I trusted enough to know about my past. Not even Eric knew, and I thanked God for that now. Dante was reliable. I trusted him with my life, and he'd never done anything to make me regret it. He loved me, even after finally knowing my darkest secrets. If it was possible, he seemed to love me even more because of it. It was resilience, a thing we both shared in common. I took deep breaths and tried to channel him for strength.

When the video finally ended, Augustine didn't seem pleased with my expressionless face. He got some sick pleasure from watching me cry, and I wasn't going to let myself fall apart again. I needed to get out and get back to Dante.

## Chapter Twenty-Seven

*Dante*

All I could do was sit on the couch and thumb the photo I held in my hands. I told Michael my suspicions about Augustine, and then we went into a frenzy, trying to get anyone to tell us where he was. Either Lombardi was keeping this under wraps from everyone, or everyone had turned against Michael.

I had a fleeting thought that we could be wrong, but my gut told me I had always known Augustine was behind this. I didn't want to believe we had a traitor at the head of the family. Ever since Livia told me about her experience at Augustine's club, it only made me loathe him more. There was no way he didn't know what happened to Livia in his own establishment.

I didn't want to scare her more, but I knew Augustine was a twisted freak. He would watch the security tapes catching people fucking and he got off on it. I should have known then that he was behind it all. How long had he been trying to screw with Michael? Or was it about her specifically?

My mind reeled. I didn't even want to think about him laying a single finger on Livia. I had to take deep breaths to calm down as the idea filled me with a deep possessive fury I had never felt before. What was he doing to her while we sat around and waited? We had sent out a bunch of our guys to look for him, but we weren't sure that would pan out. If they were loyal to Augustine, they'd simply lie and say they hadn't found anything. Every moment that passed, I just hoped that she wasn't in pain. I could bear many things, but not that.

I started when Michael finally broke the silence, groaning as he rubbed his tired eyes. "I can't believe this is happening. There's no one I can trust anymore."

This was a man I had always looked up to as a father or an older brother. He rarely showed emotion with me, and yet here he was, broken. I would have been lying if I said it was easy for me to see him like this. I hoped he wasn't including me in his statement, but the wayward look he shot me said otherwise.

"You can still trust me. I would never hurt Liv. I love her." I lifted my head from my hands and let him see the pain on my face. "Do you honestly think that I let this happen willingly? I fought my feelings with every ounce of my being. I can barely think straight, Michael. That's how fucking scared I am of losing her. I've never felt so weak in my life."

Admitting that anything rendered me helpless was difficult, but I couldn't think of how else to show him what I did wasn't a betrayal. I didn't feel guilty anymore about falling for Livia. I hadn't wanted it to happen, but it did. And she loved me too. Something that felt as right as having her by my side couldn't be wrong. Michael just needed time to see that.

It appeared like I was getting through to him as he stared off into space, deep in thought. Then he shrugged, turning stoic again. "None of it will matter if we don't find her."

At least he hadn't torn into me again. Maybe he

didn't have the energy, or the shock of it was wearing off. I selfishly hoped it was the latter. Rather than continue the line of conversation, we began to list places that we thought Augustine might go to bring an unwilling guest. It seemed too obvious to only check his warehouses and businesses, but then again…the thought occurred to me that he might have expected us to come for her. If that was true, then all of this would be over soon, one way or another. And then we sped off to begin the search ourselves. I knew by now our men weren't going to follow through, and we were done waiting around for answers.

It was four-thirty in the morning and neither of us had slept. We were running on pure adrenaline as we went from one stockroom to the next, then to each of his garages, and found absolutely nothing. Eventually, something would have to give. Either the place was abandoned, or there were a couple of people there who claimed to know nothing about Augustine's whereabouts, or even who he was. *Too fishy.*

"We're running out of places to check. Where the fuck else could he have taken her?" Michael hissed as I sped around a corner without slowing. "Shit!"

"I don't know. Not his apartment? That would be too obvious," I answered as I stopped in front of a laundromat. It wasn't a legitimate business but a front. We went inside to ask questions and of course no one spoke English. Or they pretended not to. Frustrated and defeated, we left after we checked the back rooms.

Michael followed me back outside, huffing. "I should have made her come home with me."

I whipped around to face him. His niece was missing, and still, all he could think about was how bad

I was for her? My fists clenched at my sides, and I refused to hold my tongue about his repeated jabs at me.

"Are you suggesting that I don't know how to take care of *my* woman? You are the one who never saw what a limp dick Lombardi was! Maybe if you had dealt with it back then, none of this would have happened! Did you think of that at all? I told you! I told you so many times that he was going to be a problem, but you didn't trust me then, and you don't trust me now. Nothing has fucking changed."

I had definitely stood my ground with him in the past, but I had never come at him like this before. Clearly, he hadn't seen the explosion coming. "You let her go off by herself, and then she was gone! How else am I supposed to see it? I can't let her marry someone who lost her after one day in the city."

"She's a grown woman. She can take care of herself, but I want to be there for her anyway. I can't keep her in a cage to keep her safe. I just need to eliminate the threat instead so she can be free," I finished, knowing that he would pick up the hints I was dropping, mirroring Livia's words from earlier.

Finally, my words seemed to hit home with him, and he sagged his shoulders in defeat, or relief—I wasn't sure which.

We had one more place we could check, but neither of us was hopeful about the outcome. We hadn't found anything at any of the other locations, and I was starting to suspect that he was thinking ten steps ahead of us. Maybe he had gotten another location no one knew about, knowing he would eventually need it. How long had this man been scheming to kidnap Livia?

Michael followed me back to the car and was quiet

for a long time as we headed to the last location on the list. The tension in the car was palpable as he sat stoically beside me, wringing his hands. I had never seen him so anxious before.

I remembered at the beginning thinking about how stupid it was to let yourself care for someone as deeply as he did for Livia. I poked fate, and fate in turn laughed in my face. I considered my lesson learned because now I knew what it was like to really love someone, and to cope with the constant fear of losing them.

I had seen it as a weakness before, and maybe it was—but it was worth it. The fulfillment I felt living with Livia, kissing her, making love to her, or just talking, was unmatched. As much as I hated this feeling, if it meant I got to spend the rest of my life loving her, I'd bear anything. Even leaving all this behind. Move her to the house upstate, and maybe have a kid or two. A sibling for Nero. Even in my fear, I found myself calming down just at the mere thought of these things I had never known I wanted before.

"Are you thinking about her right now?" Michael asked quietly.

I snapped back to reality and glanced at him. "Of course I am. Why?"

"Because you were smiling. You haven't looked like that since you were a kid."

I expelled a heavy sigh. "I haven't been happy since then. Not until her. Aside from music, she's the only thing that's ever made me feel truly happy."

"Promise me something, Dante."

"What is it?"

He let out a deep breath, as if bracing himself, and I immediately tensed up. I would do almost anything for

Michael, but the one thing I wasn't going to do was leave her. Ever. He cleared his throat. "Do whatever it takes to keep her safe. However you can. If you make her happy, then I won't object. But if I ever find out that you hurt her—it's over for you."

I nodded gravely. "I know that. I promise."

He didn't say another word as we pulled up to the warehouse and parked behind a dumpster to avoid being spotted. We both exited the car and quickly drew our guns, then dashed to the warehouse fifty feet away. We flattened ourselves to either side of the door frame of the side entrance. I pressed my ear against the wall to see if I could hear anything. I thought I heard a male voice coming from inside, but identifying it would have been impossible—the sound was too muffled.

There weren't any men outside guarding the side door. Would he be so brazen as to keep her here when he didn't have any backup? I scanned the parking lot for any recognizable cars, and I saw a few in the distance that could have belonged to some of his men. *Then why isn't anyone stopping us?* I leaned in close to him to whisper, "It's too quiet…Should we just walk in?"

"Yeah. If she's in there, I don't want to leave her alone a second longer than we have to." Michael turned the knob as quietly as he could manage, leading gun-first as he walked inside. I followed behind a few steps off to his left. As we ducked behind shelves, the voice became clearer. *Wait. Voices. Male and female.*

"I bet you could put on an even better performance now, baby. You're not a shy little virgin anymore, are you?"

Clenching my jaw when I heard Augustine's voice, I couldn't stop myself from getting a look at what was happening. I popped my head out from behind the shelf to see him leaning over Livia, getting in her face. *She's alive.*

My relief was short-lived when I heard her shaky voice. "How do you know that?"

Augustine laughed, twisting that puny rat tail of his through his fingers. "Oh please. Castellano fucks anything that walks. It was just a matter of time before you spread your legs for him. I'm just curious to know if you're ready to start giving it up without a fight now. Maybe you'll do it to save your uncle."

He reached out to touch her face. I let out a growl before I charged forward, but Michael gripped my shoulders. "Don't. Wait until we have an opening."

I hissed back at him as I wrenched myself from his grip. "I can't let this happen to her again. I'm going to fucking kill him right now. I'm only doing what I promised you five minutes ago!"

Michael cursed and followed behind me in defeat. *You asked for it, you got it.*

I aimed at the hand that had touched Livia, took a breath and fired. Augustine roared as Livia twisted in her seat. Augustine pressed his bloody, mangled hand to his chest, pointing his gun at me with the other. "Come any closer, and I'll shoot her right in the heart."

He spun the chair around to face us, and Livia's face went ashen when she looked up at me in disbelief. "Dante?"

Did she really think I wasn't coming for her? Her eyelids drooped heavily, like she was high. She was filthy; her clothes were torn. I had to fight the urge to run to her. At the moment, the only thing I wanted more than to hold her was to tear Augustine to pieces.

"Touch her, and you die."

Augustine pointed his gun at her chest, using the barrel to pull down the neckline of her shirt. "Would be a shame to destroy such a nice rack. But she won't give in to me, so fuck it."

I kept my gun pointed at him, wanting so badly to fire, but couldn't risk that he wouldn't pull the trigger as soon as I did. I couldn't risk Liv's life just to end Lombardi. "What do you want, Augustine?"

"He killed my parents! I don't want to—" she started, but Augustine interrupted as he lifted his pistol from her chest and smacked her in the back of the head with the butt. Livia's head lolled forward.

"Did I say you can talk, you little slut? I wanted to be the one to tell them." He smirked at us, with not an ounce of remorse. "I want what should have been mine since the beginning. Now I'm going to take what's yours and you can watch."

"You piece of shit!" Michael charged forward the moment Augustine's gun was a safe distance away from Livia, but the man bolted out of the way. The snarl that came from Michael scared even me.

"No!" I shouted when I saw Augustine raise his gun again, this time directly at Michael's face.

"Please, don't!" Livia shrieked, thrashing in her chair.

Augustine fired. All I heard was Livia's screams as I emptied my clip into his chest.

## Chapter Twenty-Eight

*Livia*

Colors flashed behind my closed eyelids. I was too terrified to open them and find everyone I loved was dead. The longer I kept myself in the dark, the longer I could postpone the inevitable. When the ringing in my ears subsided, I heard the piercing noise of someone screaming. It took several moments before I realized they were my screams. If they had shot me, I didn't feel it.

A heavy hand landed on my shoulder, and I flinched—then heard Dante's voice in my ear. The soothing tone penetrated my frantic state. "Livia, it's me. Shh...it's okay. Just keep your eyes closed, baby."

His words confirmed my worst fears; I forced my eyes open. The moment I did, I let out an anguished wail that came out like a dying animal. "Oh my God! Uncle Michael, no! Please!"

The doors of the warehouse crashed open, and five men filed in, machine guns pointed at us. Dante immediately stepped in front of me protectively as the men drew closer, quieting once they took in the bloody scene. My uncle lay beside me on the floor, his face unrecognizable.

The armed men had the nerve to look almost contrite. One of them cursed, then dragged his fingers through his hair, as if to say he didn't sign up for this. I wanted to scream, but my throat was too sore to make a sound.

A loud groan rang out. Everyone looked down to see Augustine still hung on. As Dante stalked over to him, Augustine made a weak attempt to scramble backward, blood gushing from his chest. Even though I hated him, I had to turn my head away from the sight.

Dante didn't look like himself. He wasn't in a rage, which was what I had expected. I saw that something had shifted inside him. The man who just uttered soothing words to me was the same one standing before me now. I could only describe it as a quiet storm as he smiled at Augustine with a cruel tilt to his lips.

Dante slowly lifted his boot, then lowered it onto his throat. Augustine tried to say something, but only wet coughing sounds came out of his mouth. Dante kept his boot on his neck as he addressed his men in an even tone. "Do you want to ally yourselves with a dirty fucking rat? Because you're welcome to join him. If not, then put down your guns and I won't kill you all right now." He brought a second clip out of his pocket and reloaded his gun. "Well?"

I expected them to put up a fight, but the menace on Dante's face left little room for argument. As each of them dropped their guns, one of the men spoke up. "We want nothing to do with this. We had no choice."

Dante gave a tight nod. "One of you untie Livia while I finish this," he stated in a calmer voice than I could have mustered at the moment. He turned away to address Augustine on the floor. "I've always known you were a joke, but betraying your own people? You're pathetic. And to top it off, you kidnap my woman. Bad move, Augustine. Really bad move." He raised his voice louder for everyone to hear, his booming voice echoing through the warehouse. "Livia is mine. If you fuck with her, you're fucking with me."

I stayed silent even when I heard a distinct crack that I knew to be Augustine's neck under Dante's boot. I should have been horrified, but I couldn't summon enough sympathy to feel anything but relief. Staring straight ahead, I felt the ropes loosen from my wrists and ankles, then reached down to rub the feeling back into my legs.

I had no idea how long I had been here. It could have been days, and I'd still be unable to wrap my head around the reality of the situation. I didn't trust my legs to hold me, so I stayed glued to my chair as if I'd still been tied there.

Dante ordered the men to dispose of Augustine and spread the word that he was dead. "Let everyone know that a move against Michael Rossi's allies is punishable by death. This shit ends now."

Almost in unison, the men answered him, "Yes, Don Castellano."

*What?*

As I jolted up from the chair, the blood rushed to my head. Dante appeared at my side, but I couldn't hear a word he said. I saw his face come into view, but it blurred as I teetered on my numb legs. His mask slipped, and I saw the panic on his face as he tried to ground me. I felt like my head was inside of a fishbowl as his words muffled and echoed around me. The room spun and everything went black.

\*\*\*\*

When I woke, I was in Dante's bed, surrounded by

his comforting scent. I stretched out and let out a heavy yawn. It wasn't until I caught sight of Nero at the foot of the bed that I started to piece the events of the night together. Even though I was relieved to see him, it brought everything else flooding back. "No!"

I heard Dante's rushed footfall into the bedroom, and took me into his arms. He stroked my hair gently as he absorbed my heaving sobs into his chest. "I'm here. You're safe now."

"Please tell me it isn't real."

"I'm sorry, Livia. I'm so sorry."

"Where is he? The…where is…" I couldn't make myself say the words. *Where is his body?*

Dante squeezed me tighter before he let me go and met my watery gaze. He looked unsure of what to do, which scared me. "I took care of it. We'll have the funeral as soon as you're ready."

Dante had loved my uncle like a father. A slight twinge of guilt twisted in my stomach when I thought about him dealing with everything for my sake, even though he was grieving, too. I didn't understand how he could find the strength to keep everything together.

"I'm sorry you had to deal with this alone. I know you loved him, too." I brought my hands to his face to stroke his bearded cheek. "And he loved you."

As much as I was hurting, I still wanted to comfort him. He had no one now, just like me. I wanted to make him see that it was okay to break down sometimes and just feel the pain. As if he knew exactly what I was thinking, he let out the heaviest sigh before he choked up. "Thank you for saying that. I just…I hate that you had to witness it. I hate that your last memories of your uncle are tainted. I feel guilty."

I cocked my head at him in confusion. "Why? None of this is your fault."

"I feel guilty because I had a talk with Michael..." He trailed off and gave me a wary look. "You've been through a lot today, and you've been out for hours. Maybe we should do this later."

I shook my head. "No, Dante! Please tell me. I want you to feel like you can talk to me."

I urged him to continue, and he frowned at me. "When I heard Nero barking, I rushed downstairs because I just knew something was wrong. He was there at the door, and you were gone. I freaked out and called Michael right away."

"Oh...God, he must have been so worried..."

Dante nodded and covered my hand with this, stroking it. "We argued for a while before we put our heads together to find you. I think it made him see how far I would go to protect you."

His gentle touches calmed me a little. "What did he say?"

"He made me promise to make you happy." He flashed me a sad smile, before pulling me against his chest again as if knowing I would need the contact. Or maybe he needed it, because I felt his shoulders shaking against me and his short, quick inhales. *Dante...*

I buried my face in his neck and let the tears flow. "We've got no family left."

He shook his head fervently and leaned in to press his forehead to mine. "Another thing we have in common. But we can change that, *tesoro*."

I pulled back slightly to meet his tearful gaze. It took some effort to hide my shock at seeing him cry. "What do you mean?"

He cupped my face in his hands and whispered his response into my lips. "Marry me."

"Dante, are you actually asking me to marry you? I think you're just overwhelmed right now. Maybe we should talk about this—"

He scooted closer to me and took my left hand in his, hushing me. "Liv, when you disappeared, I was terrified that I would never see you again. I don't want to leave this planet without knowing you're truly mine." He brought my hand to his face and pressed his lips into my palm. "And I'm not asking. Do you think anyone could love you as much as me? Tell me honestly. Could anyone else make you feel this way?"

Reaching up, I swiped my thumbs gently under his eyes to wipe away his tears. "Never…You own my heart. I've been yours since the moment I heard your music. It had this longing to it, and I knew you were missing something that I had this powerful urge to fulfill. I couldn't explain it."

"I was just waiting for you to be ready for me." Dante only broke our gaze to lean in and kiss me softly. His lips brushed against mine, and I cupped the back of his neck to hold him to me while he twined his fingers into my hair. "I need you so badly. You make everything hurt less, Liv. My salvation…"

I sighed softly into his kisses, keeping my arms around his neck as I coaxed him to lie down with me. "Let us put each other back together, *caro mio*."

He spoke passionately against my neck as he reached down to pull my panties off. "I'm going to spend the rest of my life loving you, Livia. All you have to do is say yes, and I'll move the Earth for you. I'll burn Manhattan to the ground to keep you safe. Tell me you love me, *tesoro*."

All I wore were my panties and one of his T-shirts. He broke his desperate kisses against my neck only to pull off the shirt, leaving me naked before him. His fingers traced over the small scar on my stomach as he stared into my eyes, waiting for my answer.

It came out in a broken cry. "Dante, I love you so much. Yes. Yes. Yes."

I repeated the words over and over and his face finally broke out in a smile as he hovered over me, claiming my lips in a passionate kiss. I helped him out of his clothes blindly as our lips stayed glued together, sharing heated breaths. When he was naked above me, my eyes fell to his wrapped torso. "What about your wound?"

"It doesn't hurt. Please. Let me love you." His hardened shaft bobbed against my stomach, the tip moistened from his need for me.

My face heated with desire stronger than I had ever felt before. This wasn't just about our strong attraction to each other. It was about appreciating and cherishing something that could so easily be lost. His act at the warehouse had taken a toll on him—that I was sure of. The things he had to do haunted him, and I saw it on the lines of exhaustion on his dear face.

I didn't wait. I reached down and grasped him in my hand, leading him to my entrance until the head slipped inside with no resistance. We both gasped when I arched my back, pushing him fully inside me with one buck of my hips. "Take me. All I want is this. Us. Make me forget."

He pulled his hips back, then slowly powered forward until he was sheathed deeply inside me again.

On a guttural groan, he dipped his head down to take a nipple into his mouth. He muttered against my tingling skin as he lavished my breasts with his lips and tongue. "*Tesoro, tesoro*…never letting you go. You feel so good…"

I wrapped my legs around his back, and he pried my hands from behind his neck, pushing them into the mattress above my head. His penetrating, glowing eyes held me in thrall as he intertwined our fingers together. He pushed forward again, and I felt completely possessed, surrounded, and filled by him. "Don't ever leave me," I cried out when he ground deeply into me. "Promise me."

He squeezed my hands tighter in his grip. "I promise, baby. Nothing could tear me away. You're my life. My everything."

I met his measured drives, slow and deep. Every thrust electrified all my nerve endings, and my skin tingled everywhere that his body touched mine. His eyes stayed focused on mine, but when he circled his hips against me, I tipped my head back and let out a desperate moan of ecstasy. "*Caro*…oh…"

Dante repeated the move again, and again. "I love it when you call me that—look at me. I want to see those molten chocolate eyes when you come for me." He bent his head down to kiss away my tears. "I'll protect you. You'll never hurt because of me. Let go, give me your pleasure, baby."

He swiveled his hips again and drove even deeper, causing my legs to tremble around him. My eyes fluttered open to meet his hooded gaze. I squeezed my thighs tighter around him, his motions pushing me closer to the edge. "Who will protect you?"

"Knowing you need me is all the incentive in the world. I'll be careful to make sure I come back to you every day." I knew he was telling me something with his statement, but I was too afraid to ask, and my core was tightening with his every stroke. My fears were blinded by the pleasure he could bring to my body, and I quivered under him, panting in desperation. "I feel you…you're close."

"Yes! Harder, Dante. I need to come for you. Make me yours."

His eyes flashed with a possessive fire coming from deep inside. "*You are mine, Livia.* No one else will ever touch this silky skin. Those beautiful eyes lost to the pleasure only I can give you. I'm the only one who will swallow your soft gasps as I fill you completely."

He pumped forward with more power, sending a shockwave through my body as he leaned down again and devoured my lips.

I was completely lost in him. My only awareness at that moment was of his damp skin touching mine, his lips hungrily sucking on mine as if he would starve without me. His hips shooting forward to fill me, his cock twitching and thickening inside me. He was close. My nipples grazed against his chest with his every movement, and I felt like my entire body was on fire for him. "*Caro mio!*"

Dante let out an anguished moan as he slammed deep inside me, almost scalding me from his powerful climax. "Only yours…"

He collapsed on top of me, both of us spent from the fervent lovemaking. I had no desire to move, feeling safer than I could ever imagine with his heaving, sweaty body covering mine. I spent what felt like hours tracing small circles on his back with my fingers, while he let out the occasional low, contented moan against my neck.

"You smell so good. I could get drunk on it. Never need a drop of liquor again," he muttered into my hair as he inhaled deeply.

I smiled to myself as I brought my hand up to brush my fingers through his dark hair. As he continued to inhale me like oxygen, the gears in my head started to turn, and a quick flash of the earlier events played through my mind. Once, twice, and a third time.

They had called him "Don Castellano".

The reality hit me like a ton of bricks.

## Chapter Twenty-Nine

*Dante*

Livia slept peacefully for a few hours. After leaving the warehouse, I was in no fit state to comfort her. I needed to get my head on straight first. I managed to take out some of my fury on Augustine's thick neck, but it wasn't enough. The only man I ever looked up to was dead. And I had no one to blame but myself. Had I insisted on going downstairs with Livia to walk Nero, had I not called Michael, we wouldn't have been here now, mourning and burying our sorrows in each other. The sound of Livia's wails of torment would be burned in my memory for the rest of my life. I wanted to scream right along with her, but instead I turned to the only thing that would be constructive in the moment—brutality. Anger was the best mask for pain, but she didn't need to see me like that now.

She needed tenderness from me, but I couldn't wind down after exacting my punishment on Augustine. It wasn't as if it were the cruelest way I had killed someone—it wasn't. Not by a long shot. What disturbed me most was that I had exposed Livia to it. Michael had done everything in his power to hide this part of our world from her, and now the veil had been violently ripped away. Not only had she seen her uncle shot at point-blank range, killing him instantly—she had seen me flip my switch, turning into a ruthless, vengeance-seeking murderer. Even in his figurative grave, I was disappointing him.

*She deserves better, but I just can't let go.*

I spent the few hours that Livia slept pacing through the apartment, trying to get myself calmed down so that I could be there for her when she woke up. I reached for my violin, but I didn't want to wake her, so I sat there trying to rosin my bow without snapping the thing in half as my hands shook. Defeated, I put it away where it would be safe from the outburst of nervous, angry energy that threatened to destroy anything I touched. I had to get myself under control and fast.

I paced into the kitchen, throwing open the freezer for the bottle of vodka that I had been meaning to throw away. I pulled it out and stretched my hand, pressing my palm against the cold smoothness of the glass bottle. *Just one?*

Before I could think about it, I unscrewed the cap and caught a whiff of the vodka, the harshness burning my nose hairs. The smell alone caused me to close my eyes and relish in it.

*What the fuck are you doing, Castellano?*

When I heard Livia stir from the bedroom, I felt the sudden panicky impulse to hide the bottle. It was all I needed to break the spell. The last thing she needed was to wake up and meet Dante the Drunk, on top of everything else. I would never let her see me that way. Everything I was known for in the underworld was only amplified when I was shitfaced, and I would never forgive myself if I were ever purposely cruel to her.

Just the idea made my stomach turn because it reminded me of my father. All it took was tragedy and loss of willpower to turn me into a nasty fucker like him. That was the real reason I hated him—because I knew that we were two sides of the same coin. I needed a purpose, a reason to hang on to keep myself from flipping. Livia was that reason.

I tipped the bottle over and poured the contents down the sink, before going downstairs to discard the bottle in the trashcan at the curb. I was embarrassed that I felt it was necessary, but she knew I was an alcoholic. Even though she had better things to worry about, I didn't want to add to that by having to explain an empty bottle of vodka in the trash.

When I went back upstairs, I peeked in the bedroom to check on her. She lay on her side, and Nero had curled up in front of her protectively, his head and leg bandaged. It overjoyed him to see her again. The whole time I had been with Michael at the apartment, Nero had been limping and whining, looking for her. I wanted to be mad that he hadn't bitten the motherfucker that grabbed Liv, but I couldn't blame him for being kicked around. He tried his best. I swore he was more human than beast, because I could almost see the guilt in his eyes. I knew Nero would be watching Livia like a hawk from now on.

Watching her sleeping so soundly made me fearful about the eventual conversation we needed to have. It had been hard enough to get her to accept the idea of living in the city again, and I couldn't even blame her for her trepidation. We had been back in the state for barely a month. And in that time, I had been shot and Livia lost the last member of her family. There were more implications than I wanted to think about at the moment. Whatever they expected of me, it would have to wait.

\*\*\*\*

After we made love, I felt Livia slowly putting the pieces of my heart back together again. I didn't know how a person could bring me more comfort than I could bring myself, but she did. I was weak for her, and she didn't judge me. She only stroked me softly as we lay in silence together, and I let myself bask in her glow.

Even though I had my face buried in her neck, I could tell she was thinking really hard about something when her fingers stilled in my hair. "What's on your mind, Liv?"

She sighed lightly and resumed her gentle touches. I had been so worried about being intact to take care of her, and yet, here she was caring for me and holding me like a baby. "I'm just trying to keep myself together. I'm overwhelmed."

There hadn't been time to ask her what she'd been through, and I wasn't sure right now was the time to ask, but maybe she needed to talk about it. "Do you want to tell me what happened tonight? Before we came for you, I mean."

When she didn't respond right away, alarm bells went off in my head and I peeled myself off her to lie beside her. She appeared to mourn the loss of contact. "I haven't even had time to think about it. What happened after was so much worse that I don't even know if it's worth talking about...I don't know."

Why was she trying to avoid this? "Of course, it's worth talking about...Did he try something with you?"

"No. Not really. He alluded to it, but no. He mostly...told me things," she said cautiously in a way that told me that I wasn't going to like what I was about to hear. She shot me a wary glance. "If I tell you, will you promise me that you'll let it go?"

What was she talking about? Anything that Augustine had done was moot at this point. I couldn't revive him and kill him again, even if I wanted to. I raised a suspicious brow but hesitantly agreed. "I promise."

She let out a breath of relief. "Okay...well he told me something when I woke up...I didn't want to believe it at first, but as I'm thinking about it now, everything makes sense. Those guys you said were stalking me at campus...they weren't there for me."

I froze in place. "What are you saying?"

Her eyes darted between the bridge of my nose and my eyes, agonizing over her next words. "They came to see Eric. He didn't tell me how they got him to agree to take that photo, but I'm assuming they threatened him."

She was trying to gauge my reaction to see if I was about to go berserk. And she was right. I was. That spineless little prick had betrayed his best friend and violated her privacy, then had the balls to swoop in like the hero and make a move on her?

I bolted upright immediately. "He stole my fucking key! He's a dead man."

"You promised! I know you hate him, and I kind of do, too. But I don't think he got any pleasure out of what he did."

*Yeah, right.* "Somehow, I doubt that. You are completely oblivious to your effect on men, Liv. The way he looked at you made my skin crawl. I wouldn't be surprised if he jerked it to that photo before he handed it over."

"Dante!" She screwed up her face in disgust and slapped my arm. "It doesn't matter anymore. I'm not

Rose Thorgaard

going back to California. I'm done with him. He has to live with what he did and know that he's lost me for good. That's punishment enough…"

I took a few calming breaths to get myself under control again. "Fine. But I don't like this. He shouldn't get away with it."

She scooted closer to me and grasped my hands in hers. "I know, but…what you had to do back there…it had to take a toll on you. I don't want you killing every man that looks my way. It's not worth it."

I snorted with derision. Of course it was. I silently cursed myself for promising before I knew what she was going to say and vowed not to fall for that one again. "Worth what?"

Her eyes glistened with a seemingly unending pool of compassion. "Your humanity."

*How is it possible that she exists? So pure…*

I couldn't ignore the relief I felt hearing her describe my merciless treatment of Augustine as something I *had* to do. As she recounted her experience as his prisoner, it took everything in me to hold in my rage. I wanted to bring him back to life and kill him again, but mostly I wished I hadn't needed to do it in front of her.

She didn't see me as a complete monster yet, and I could barely hide my shock at the revelation. Livia was so pure, yet she made allowances for me. I didn't know whether I wanted to kiss her or tell her to run for the damn hills, because my skewed morality threatened to taint her at every turn. It would only get worse from here. How long would she continue to look at me with those reverent eyes? At what point would I cross the line and become unsalvageable? I didn't think I could hold on without her to anchor me.

What remained of my humanity was reserved for her.

\*\*\*\*

We took a week off from the real world, spending that time burying ourselves in each other. It was as if we were afraid that if we separated, one of us would disappear. We didn't need to voice it. Every kiss and every touch we shared that week had a longing undertone to it. A deep, visceral need to be in constant contact. I knew Livia felt it too because we were both drowning as we tried to keep each other afloat. If we both fell apart, who would be left to pick up the pieces? We had no one but each other now.

She was either in denial, or she was trying to be strong for me. Either way, I didn't push her. I only brought up the subject of Michael once to ask about funeral arrangements, since she was the next of kin. I couldn't bear to make her deal with the preparations. Given the way that Michael died, a wake with an open casket was out of the question, and I didn't breathe a word about it to her. I only consulted her to choose a date for the funeral. She was his only blood relative, but unfortunately, this would involve more family than just blood. A certain amount of fanfare was expected; Michael was the boss, after all. I knew she wouldn't be happy about that, especially with that lingering question that hung in the air that neither of us would speak about.

On the day of the funeral, I found Livia in the bedroom in her bra and panties, staring into the closet blankly.

"Let me help you, baby," I whispered as I gently guided her toward the bed to sit. I quickly flicked through her side of the closet until I found a plain black dress, then held it up for her approval. I looked down at her as she shrugged with a completely blank expression on her face. I hated to see her this way. *Once this is over, it'll get better.*

"I can't seem to focus on anything." Livia stood and took the dress from me before she slipped it on. Without a word, she turned around, and I zipped it up for her. "Thank you. I don't know what I would do if I didn't have you...I can't even think straight. Is this real?"

I circled around her to rest my hands on her shoulders. Gazing into her watery eyes, I felt a stab in my chest at seeing her so lost. "I wish I could tell you it isn't. But remember, I'll be there by your side the whole time. We can say our goodbyes and then let him be at peace, knowing that you're safe and cared for. That's all he ever wanted."

She gave me a slow nod before she leaned in to rest her forehead on my chest. "I wish I could be stronger for you, *caro mio*. I know you're hurting too."

I took a step back and cupped her face in my hands, waiting for her gaze to fly up to meet mine. When it did, I gave her a sad smile. "You are so much stronger than you know. You've been kept in the dark for so long, and everything came crashing down on you these past two months. Somehow, you took it all in stride with your head held high. I'm more in awe of you every day, Livia."

She gave me a look that told me she didn't believe me. "I feel like I'm spiraling."

I pulled her into my arms, crushing her against my chest. I poured all of my need, my strength, and my love into her. "You have to permit yourself to grieve. I know you've been trying to keep it all in for my sake, but you don't have to. I'm devastated, yes. But I still have you. If we're together, everything will fall into place, *tesoro*."

She sniffled into my chest, and then I felt the heat of her palms seeping through my suit jacket and my shirt, straight to my skin. Her touch told me that she needed me just as much as I needed her. "How do you know that?"

I stroked her hair as I whispered into her ear, "Because you make me feel like the tragedy of my life hasn't all been for nothing. You shine a blinding light on a part of me I thought was dead and gone. You make me feel...honored."

Thank you for purchasing
this publication of The Wild Rose Press, Inc.

For questions or more information
contact us at
info@thewildrosepress.com.

The Wild Rose Press, Inc.
www.thewildrosepress.com

www.ingramcontent.com/pod-product-compliance
Lightning Source LLC
Chambersburg PA
CBHW070101030726
47506CB00002B/553